DREAM OF ME

DREAMS AREN'T ALWAYS WHAT THEY SEEM

ST. JOHN'S SECRETS
BOOK 1

SELENA COLLINS

ENDLESS

ENDLESS ROMANCE PUBLISHING

Published by Endless Romance Publishing

Second Edition June 2025

ISBN 978-1-963671-02-5 (paperback)

ISBN 978-1-963671-03-2 (ebook)

SelenaCollins.com

CONTENTS

To my mom, who thought she was giving a young girl a romance book but instead gave her a world of strong women creating their own happily ever afters.

1

———

*H*e came to her again that night, as he did nearly every night, and it was as unwelcome now as it was the first time.

She heard his haunting cries before she saw him standing eerily still in the dim hallway. The little boy shuffled toward her slowly, and each time she blinked the hallway shrank, bringing him closer and closer until he stood at the edge of her bed. She wouldn't have guessed he was dead but for the bloodless pallor of his skin and the fact that he was haunting her dreams night after night. He was small and so sad, only two or three years old, with fair skin and dirty blonde hair that shone red wherever the light touched it. He wore fleece footed pajamas covered in tiny black and white pandas drifting peacefully on fluffy white clouds. Somehow, those pajamas made it all the more heartbreaking. His lips and chin quivered, and his cries continued on. One tiny fist knuckled his eye while the other held fast to a faded yellow blanket that dragged on the ground.

Mia watched him warily, pushing herself up in the bed and gripping the covers as if they would protect her. The romantic flower print clashed with the dark ambiance of the dream. The boy sniffled and stared at her, but he didn't say a word. He never did.

Suddenly his eyes widened, and his pupils dilated, becoming endless wells of blackness. His mouth opened and opened and opened, reveal more black so deep it threatened to drag her in.

"No, momma!"

Mia jolted awake, the sound of his voice ringing in her ears. It was the first time he'd ever spoken, a jarring experience, to say the least. Her heart and head pounded in time, and she could feel the sweat pooling on her chest, neck, and lower back as if cold, damp washcloths pressed against her. Her breathing was fast and labored, her pulse racing. She stared at the white ceiling and dusky green walls, willing herself back to reality. Yellow light from the hall spilled into her bedroom through the cracked door. Thankfully, there was no little boy standing in it.

The dreams had become a constant in her life, and they were nearly always the same. She saw the little boy so often, she should be used to it by now, but the dream was as terrifying now as it was the first time. Once, Mia tried to work out why she was having these dreams or what they meant, but there were always more questions than answers. Maybe one day she could figure some of them out. Until then, she was resigned to regular visits from a little dead boy and the heart pounding terror he brought.

She glanced at the clock on her nightstand, its

numbers glowing a pale blue in the darkness. It was barely eight, too early to have gone to bed for the night, but late enough that all she wanted to do now was curl up and fall back asleep. The setting sun filtered through curtains she'd drawn to shut out the world. Willing herself calm, she took deep breaths until her heartbeat slowed. Apparently, even her naps were being disturbed by the nightmares now.

Her ears perked up at the sound of a knock on her door, and she considered rolling over and ignoring whoever was on the other side. The knock echoed through the apartment again, this time more insistently. With a groan, she swung her legs over the side of the bed and sat up. She pushed aside the mass of dark brown hair and looked down to make sure she was at least wearing pants. Then she padded across her apartment, slid open the bolt lock, and cracked the door. The woman on the other side took one look at her pale face, complete with bloodshot eyes and dark circles, and said, "Lookin' rough, honey."

"What in the world are you doing here?" The last thing Mia wanted at the moment was to socialize with anyone, even if that person was her best friend.

"Movie night.. Wine... Maybe some nice man-butt on television. Any of this ringing a bell?"

Mia vaguely remembered plans being soft balled to her but was fuzzy on the details.

"It's alright if you completely forgot about your bestie. My feelings aren't hurt at all," Alexis said. "But you could at least invite me in out of the cold."

"It's June," Mia said flatly, but she stepped aside enough for Alexis to squeeze in.

"What crawled up your butt?" Alexis breezed in, her arms loaded with grocery bags that rustled against her legs as she walked.

"Nothing. It was just a long day." Mia pinched her fingers on the bridge of her nose. She followed Alexis into the kitchen and grabbed a bottle of aspirin from the oak cabinet above the oven. It made a soft thump when she closed it. She popped open the top of the little white bottle and tossed the pills into the back of her mouth. Swallowing, she turned to see her friend staring at her thoughtfully.

"What?" Mia asked, trying (and failing) not to sound cranky and defensive.

"Something's up." Alexis pulled boxes of crackers, packs of deli meats, and blocks of cheese out of the bags, setting them on the counter next to the island that divided it from the living and dining rooms.

"No, it's not." Mia moved to get a plate for the snacks. She slid behind Alexis and opened a cabinet on the wall to her right. She grabbed hold of the edge of a large square platter and pulled it from the shelf, but the weight of it was more than she expected, and it dipped dramatically and slipped out of her hand. The plate smashed at her feet and sent ceramic shards spraying across the linoleum floor. Mia closed her eyes and breathed so deeply through her nose that her nostrils flared. Splotches of red dotted her cheeks, and her mouth pulled into a tight, thin line. "Don't say a word."

"Not a sound," Alexis said, her hands up and lips

clamped tight. She watched Mia as she bent down and tossed a few of the bigger shards into the trash. "Okay, I lied. I—"

"Not a word."

"You know what you need, hun?" Alexis said, unbothered.

"A good night's sleep?" Mia tiptoed barefoot across the floor to grab the broom from its hook on the wall. She unclipped the dustpan from the broom handle and began sweeping the shards into it.

"You need a change of scenery."

"I do not."

"Come on, Mia. You've been holed up in this apartment since..." her voice trailed off, and she busied her hands with a new plate. They both knew how long it had been. Since the funeral. Since the day Mia buried her husband. "Well, a long time. I know it's hard, but it's time to get out, Mia. You know you need it. Take a vacation. Meet a stranger. Have wild and crazy sex. Something other than going from work to a crappy apartment and back again."

"My apartment is not crappy," Mia said.

"Right. It only has about the same amount of personality as a grain of white rice, and the fact that you painted and decorated the bedroom doesn't negate the rest." Alexis gestured to the bare off-white walls around them. "Now, about getting out."

Mia dumped the last of the shattered plate in the trash and hung the broom up. "I get out," she grumbled.

"If you say so." Alexis thought for a moment, tapping her finger on her chin, and turned to face Mia. "Hey!

We're all going to The Railway for karaoke night in a couple weeks. You should come. Maybe you'll meet someone mysterious. Preferably someone tall, dark, and handsome."

Mia shook her head. "I have no intention of meeting anyone. If you haven't noticed, dating tends to lead to marriage, and marriage and I don't have an impressive track record."

"Who said anything about dating?" Alexis asked. She popped an olive from the plate into her mouth and wiggled her brows with a grin.

Mia rolled her eyes and laughed despite herself. She couldn't deny that a good bout of steamy sex would be an interesting way to unwind, but sex was rarely uncomplicated, and she wasn't interested in complications. Alexis' push to get back out there wasn't the first to come her way. Far from it. Her mother still brought it up during every conversation, but the "put yourself back out there" talks really started in earnest the year before, a year after Ewan died. Apparently, one year was the prescribed amount of time to mourn before shoving that grief aside and pursuing a husband and babies like a good little woman, regardless of how she actually felt. At least it was according to her mother, and maybe the rest of society.

The truth was... more complicated. Mia wore her grief around her like a cloak, and she didn't have any motivation to remove it. That she felt stuck in place, trudging through the mud of life without ever really getting anywhere, was a moot point. In fact, it was an incentive. If she never faced her grief, she'd never have to face moving forward alone. It didn't have to be real. She didn't have to stop thinking of her and Ewan as a unit. They'd grown up together, and there was never any doubt that they would always be a part of each other's lives. That is until he died. So much of her identity was tied up with a man who was no longer there, a man who would never be there again. How could she walk through life alone when she'd always envisioned her future with him? Fate cruelly ripped him from her life. How could anything so much as a future be normal again?

"Why are you thinking about dating? Aren't you still seeing the guy from that conference?" Mia asked.

"Chad? No. Too many red flags," Alexis said. She tossed a cube of cheese in her mouth and poured herself wine from the deep red bottle. Taking a slow sip, she watched Mia from over the rim of the glass. She felt for her friend, but she admitted that her patience was running thin. As much as she wanted to be steadfast and supportive, she missed the Mia from before, the friend who asked about her day as often as Mia complained about her own, the one who didn't forget about girls' nights. But those thoughts were for another day. Mia's grief had (understandably) locked her away for far too long. Today, she needed a push.

Putting a bright smile on her face, Alexis poured Mia a glass of wine and asked, "So, will you come out with us?"

"I don't know." Mia shrugged, grabbing the glass Alexis offered and taking a sip. She already felt bad about forgetting their night in today. The last thing she wanted to do was agree to another outing under pressure and disappoint Alexis again.

"Well, you've got to do something," Alexis said, her

tone matter-of-fact. She carried their snacks into the living room. "Until then, we watch men beg. Coming?"

Mia followed Alexis out of the kitchen and folded herself onto the couch beside her. Alexis set the tray of snacks on the stiff rectangular ottoman and grabbed the remote to turn on their show. It was a familiar ritual of food, wine, and conversation, and it gave Mia time to think about Alexis' words. Not about the sex, though she admitted to missing that, but about her needing to do something. Anything. She hated to admit it, but it was like Ewan's death had hit the pause button on her life, and she'd never hit play again.

Later that evening, with her mind buzzing from the alcohol, she burrowed down into the soft covers on her bed. Mia looked around the room with a sigh. It was the same room she'd shared with Ewan, the same bed, the same apartment. She even had the same photos on the walls. As sparse as Alexis complained it was, there were touches of Ewan and Mia everywhere. Everything was Mia and Ewan. The unit again. The broom in her kitchen hung from a hook Ewan screwed in after months of Mia's complaining. The dish and bath towels, even the rug on her kitchen floor, were wedding gifts. The hobbies they'd shared, they shared, and there was very little Mia remembered doing that Ewan didn't also enjoy. She wasn't even really sure she had any hobbies at all that weren't a together kind of deal. Honestly, there wasn't much in her home or her life that represented her and her alone.

Maybe that was the problem. She was so young when they'd married, and while she didn't regret it, she didn't really know the woman she'd grown into. Who was she?

The woman with the dead husband who dreams about a little ghost every night? The editor who works long hours and eats dinner alone? She was more than that, and Alexis was right, but it was time for more than a change of scenery.

It was time she figured who Mia was again.

2

―――――

The next morning, Mia called in sick for the first time in months. She felt a touch of guilt—the pile of unread emails and manuscripts was only going to get bigger—but this was something she needed to do. For herself. Her life was essentially a reel of reruns, an endless cycle of wash, rinse, repeat, and she was ready to stop the cycle.

Where had the vivacious, fun loving, daredevil gone? Where was the woman who'd gone cliff jumping with her friends in college and shark diving on her honeymoon? The strong and confident woman who worked her ass off in college and applied to publishing houses relentlessly until she'd found her dream editing job. Where was that woman? Her husband may have died, but Mia was still very much alive. It was time she started acting like it.

Maybe she needed a vacation complete with a hot beach and an even hotter whirlwind romance, the kind that came with no strings and no promises. That was what

Alexis had in mind, and it didn't sound like a bad idea. She couldn't remember the last time she went on a proper vacation, certainly never alone. Grabbing her purse, Mia drove to the local travel agency. It felt a little old-fashioned, but the idea of trying to plan a vacation for herself right now was overwhelming. When you needed expert level intervention, you found expert help!

She parked on the street, took a deep breath, and walked down the covered walk, pushing open the door. A bell tinkled above her head, and the cardboard open sign clicked softly against the glass door behind her. She stood just inside as a young woman sitting in a desk off to the right held up a finger with a smile and talked into a headset. Directly in front of her there was a small sitting area with a sofa and end table. On the table was a vase of blue and white hydrangeas, and Mia couldn't help but smile at the happy blooms, a smile that died as soon as she saw her reflection in the mirror behind the vase.

Alexis was right. She looked rough. Her dark hair, usually wavy and smooth, frizzed at the roots, and her eyes appeared puffy and tired. Staring at herself, Mia pushed a hand through her hair and tugged the hem of her shirt straight.

"Sorry about that," said the woman at the desk. She tapped the side of the headset with a manicured fingernail painted race car red and smiled, then gestured to the two chairs on the other side of her desk. "How can I help you?"

"I think I need a vacation, but I have no idea where to start," Mia said.

"That's what I'm here for. I'm Stacy, by the way."

"It's nice to meet you, Stacy. I'm Mia Clark."

"Clark? I know a few Clarks. Any relation to Martha and Dean Clark?" Stacy asked.

"In-laws," Mia said with a polite nod. "They were my late husband's parents."

"Oh, now I'm sorry to hear that. I forgot Ewan passed away a while back," Stacy said.

"It's alright, and thank you." She found that people often expected to be thanked when they told you how sorry they were to hear about your loved one's passing. It seemed a strange thing to need to be thankful for, though.

"Well, Mia, can you tell me a little about where you might like to go or what you like to do?" Stacy asked, positioning her hands over the keyboard of her computer.

Mia's chest rose sharply, and she fidgeted in her seat. What did she want to do? She hadn't actually given it much thought. There were a great many things she loved to do. Reading and writing were two of those. That seemed like a good place to start. She also considered herself somewhat outdoorsy. Perhaps that would be useful. "I love to read, and I paint and draw a little. I've been hiking and camping with friends and enjoyed myself. To be honest, I'm terrified of underwater caves, but I've tried snorkeling and bungee jumping. Does any of that help?"

"That's perfect," Stacy laughed. "What about where you'd like to go? Do you see yourself on a beach reading a sexy book or having drinks at a mountain retreat? Maybe hiking somewhere exotic?"

"Maybe? I've grown up on the beach, so I know that's not really a vacation for me, but a retreat in the mountains might be nice. Going alone may not be much fun. Peaceful, though. Hiking might be nice, I guess. I don't know. I honestly didn't expect it to be so hard to decide. What do people do when they're alone?"

"Some like those mixer type events. Would you be interested in a cruise for singles?"

"No!" Mia said, her fingers clenching on the arms of her chair. Was the entire world hellbent on getting her paired up with someone? Her heart clenched painfully, and she pushed aside the wave of grief that rolled over her. Even after all this time, it still left her feeling raw.

"Alright, hold your horses. We'll get you all fixed up. Hmm..." Stacy tapped away at her keyboard. "What about a trip abroad? Rome or Barcelona? I've got a fantastic connection at a bed-and-breakfast in Spain that people rave about. "

Mia thought about how exotic both options sounded, but the thought of long flights and jet lag had her shaking her head. She shot down more ideas, always finding a seemingly legitimate reason why they weren't a good fit for her. She explained that a time zone change would complicate matters, and she didn't have a wardrobe appropriate for cold weather. Mia spent another half hour with Stacy before she finally raised the white flag. "I'm sorry. I know I'm being a pain." She pushed her hair out of her face and blew a breath out through her lips. "I think I just need to think about things first."

"That's alright, sugar," Stacy said. "You take all the time you need. I'll be right here when you're ready."

"Thank you."

Not really knowing what else to do, Mia drove back to

her apartment and, once there, threw herself back on the couch in defeat. So, no vacation away from this place. How was she supposed to go on an epic adventure of self-discovery without a destination? The idea of a vacation tempted her, of course. Surely she could settle on an adequate place and, by the time she departed, work up to being excited about it. But the idea wasn't as appealing once she got her teeth into it. What if she ended up hating her impulsive choice? Or regretting the trip? That would be almost like taking a step backwards.

"Change of scenery. Change of scenery," she said to herself, almost like a chant. She sat forward and leaned over her knees, scrubbing her hands over her face. "What am I going to do for a change of scenery?"

She blamed her friend for her current crisis. If Alexis hadn't brought this whole thing up, Mia could have continued to exist in her comfortable bubble of sameness. No matter that she knew deep down that Alexis was right. Or that the numbness and grief were taking over her life. The devil she knew was always less scary than the devil she didn't. The problem was she knew that devil, too, and her friend's words were like the siren's song calling her to the shore. Only she wasn't sure if it was toward a safe dock or to be run aground on the rocks.

Instead of a vacation, maybe the change she needed was in her job. That was the next logical place to look, right? There weren't any promotions she was interested in or even remotely qualified for at the moment, but she could look outside of the company. Maybe she could become a freelance editor. It wasn't like she didn't have enough experience. It even sounded romantic—she would work with independent authors helping them polish up their books and breathe life into them—but it also sounded stressful. The market had to be saturated, and she wondered how to even get connected enough to make a decent living. Before she gave herself more than a few minutes to think it over, Mia was already talking herself out of the idea completely.

No, searching for a job wasn't what she needed after all.

"Ugh," she groaned out loud, her shoulders slumped in defeat. "I've apparently got to get out of this apartment, but I have no idea how I'm supposed to do that."

As the words left her lips, Mia had a thought. It was a brilliant and crazy and impulsive thought. She looked around her tiny apartment as the idea took hold. She thought of every project she'd ever wanted to do in her home, only to realize that as a renter, she couldn't do it. No color on the walls (she'd cheated and painted her bedroom anyway) or DIY projects. No quaint little garden out front or white picket fence. But if she *owned* a house, she could do all of that and more. True, it would be more responsibility—there would no longer be a landlord to call for repairs, for example—but she would also make a place of her own.

You couldn't get more change of scenery than that, really, and the thought of making a home for herself was appealing. It would be a home just for her. Mia's home. It would be a novel experience for sure, a way to step outside of her comfort zone and start figuring out who she was again. Wasn't that what she was really trying to do?

She got up off the couch and sat at the desk, snugged

into the corner of the room. She opened her laptop, bringing up a website that listed local homes for sale. Fear hovered around the edges of her mind, but she pushed back against it. Somewhere inside her was the fearless woman she'd been, and she was determined to find her again. *How to figure out who you are... in 6 months or less.* Why 6 months? Who knew... but it seemed as good a deadline as any. Surely there was a self-help book somewhere bearing that very title. She filtered out house results by neighborhood, size, and price, imagining the book in her head.

Step 1: Call out to the universe and claim something (anything, really).

Step 2: Chase the dopamine and impulsively buy a house.

Ha! And what would the next step be?

She scrolled down the page, thinking about self-help books and houses. There were several that boasted four bedrooms, fenced yards, and spacious bonus rooms in finished basements. As beautiful as they were, they weren't for her. She wasn't looking for a new husband, two and a half kids, and a dog. Scrolling further, she stumbled across a smaller bungalow style home. She clicked the listing and smiled. It was adorable and close to move-in ready, though it was light on the curb appeal. The bones of it looked good, though, and the listing photos showed a floor plan that was spacious without being overwhelming. Overwhelming as in: *here's a house ready for you to grow your family in. Look at the great schools right around the corner, and wouldn't this smaller room make the perfect nursery?* No, she was not looking for a family-friendly home. In fact, if she'd met the minimum age requirement, she'd be looking in retirement communities instead. She imagined that was as far as she could get from the matchmaking busy bodies of her small town. Still, retirement communities aside, this house was promising. Even if the wallpaper on the bathroom walls made her wonder if it had been someone's retirement home themselves.

On impulse, Mia picked up her phone and dialed the number of an old high school friend, Savannah Abernathy. If she remembered correctly, Savannah was a real estate agent who still lived and worked in the area. Less than 30 minutes later, Mia was standing outside the bungalow just a couple of streets away from St. John's downtown square. The house was a little rougher than in the listing photos. Patches of dirt showed through the lawn, and the paint on the porch was peeling. The mailbox sagged a little, as did the porch stairs, but the roof was brand new and the foundation recently inspected, so the real estate agent said.

"Are you ready to go inside?" Savannah asked, her hands folded in front of the pressed lines of her practical burgundy pant suit.

Mia nodded and followed the agent through the interior. She noted the light cosmetic updates that were made inside. The floors, original to the home, were sanded and refinished, and it smelled of wood and fresh paint. The previous owners had updated the kitchen here and there, and new light fixtures were in every room. Mia listened as Savannah continued to list other improvements, facts about the neighborhood, and local amenities, but she was only partly paying attention. The house pulled at her already. Each room felt good, like there was no shortage of laughter and smiles and memories imprinted on these walls. It was a cheerful house, and it helped her believe she could create a life like that of her own, of new happy memories. It wasn't what she originally envisioned for her life, but she knew better than anyone that you didn't always get a say in how your life unfolded.

It didn't escape her observation that this house was likely one Ewan would've hated. It was close to downtown St. John's for one, meaning that when the tourists came to explore historic coastal Georgia, there was sure to be more foot traffic than usual. That would've never suited Ewan. It was also old-fashioned, but Mia found it charming. She craved the comfort of people and neighbors and closeness, how this home called out to her with its potential. While it would certainly be an extensive project, she could make it whatever she wanted.

"I'd like to put an offer in," she said, realizing she'd cut Savannah off mid-sentence. Mia gave her a lopsided, apologetic smile. "How soon can we close?"

They spent the next few minutes negotiating terms and talking through the logistics. Savannah gave her a quick hug, her mouth stretched into a wide smile, before locking up behind them and walking back to her car. Mia stepped out from under the shade of the porch and into the sunshine, her legs wobbly beneath her. She gripped the railing for support, then had herself a good ol' panic attack.

"Deep breaths," she said to herself, all the while smiling and waving Savannah off as her heart raced in her chest. When Savannah was out of sight, she lowered herself onto the step and dropped her head to her knees.

Breathe in.

And out.

Repeat.

Bent over, hands on the back of her neck, Mia coached herself down until her heart no longer felt like it was about to beat right out of her chest. People bought houses all the time. And didn't the agent tell her over and over how this was such a good time to invest in this neighborhood? It was totally normal that her first step to rediscovering herself would be to vault into home ownership. It wasn't as if that was dramatic or impulsive or anything. No, it was not impulsive, she corrected herself. It was decisive. It was taking the bull by the horns, as the saying went. She was taking the first step into the rest of her life. Looking back at the house, she smiled at the thought that they actually suited each other well. Both she and the house had good bones. True, the paint was peeling, the decor inside was outdated, and the yard had seen better days, but one could say the same about her. She stood and looked down at her body, plucking at the hem of her pants.

Mia walked down the stairs and looked back at the house, lifting a hand to shade her eyes from the sun. With a little love, some hard work, and a bit of luck, they could bloom together.

3

"I'm glad you agreed to come out tonight," Alexis said as they walked through the doors of The Railway, a bar that got its name from the abandoned railroad tracks behind it. The sounds of music and conversation and laughter washed over them as they entered, as did the smell of fevered bodies, perfume, and frothy beer.

Mia looked at her friend, and the corner of her mouth turned up in a small smile. Karaoke at her favorite neighborhood bar sounded like something that could be fun, but more than that, it was the kind of thing she should be doing. It kept with the whole "find yourself" and "you just bought a freaking house" vibe. *That* type of woman would say yes to a night of karaoke with her friends. Mia found herself thinking about the person she was years ago. Of course, she would've agreed to go out without a second thought. Even though getting out again now after so long shutting the world away felt uncomfortable, she reassured herself it was the right thing to do. Every step, no matter how small, was important.

"Just remember the deal, Lex. No meddling."

"Scout's honor. No matchmaking of any kind. Cross my heart."

A promise never sounded so ominous, Mia thought.

Alexis raised her voice above the music. "Come on, relax. You just bought a house."

She and Mia walked over to the bar where they ordered drinks and turned to survey the room. Mia rested her back against the rounded edge of the lacquered bar top, letting herself slide into the catchy song playing over the speakers. No one stood on the stage just yet, but it was early still, and the drinks had only started flowing. The stage was to the far right, with tables in front and bars on either side. People milled around those bars, propped themselves on stools, or sat at the tables. Others gathered in packs around the flashy modern jukebox lit with long bulbs of neon along its sides, giggling as they chose their karaoke songs.

One by one, these people would go up and make asses of themselves in front of friends and strangers alike, though every now and again you'd hear someone with unexpected talent. It was a somewhat silly ritual when she thought about it, but Mia enjoyed the self-deprecating fun despite herself. Really, if you couldn't laugh at yourself...

Alexis walked away from the bar to say hello to a few friends. She turned back and waved Mia over, but Mia simply shook her head with a smile. This outing was more like dipping a toe back into the social pool, but she was not quite ready to jump into the deep end. Not to mention, there was a tiny petty part of her that felt betrayed by those who were happy to wave to her now but had been M.I.A. when Ewan died. Where were they when she'd needed them most? Never mind that she'd successfully pushed nearly everyone away. She sent up a silent prayer of thanks for Alexis and the few others in her life like her, the ones who treated her like a wounded animal lashing out instead of a leper to be avoided.

Taking a deep breath, Mia shook herself out of that dark place. Those thoughts would not serve her tonight. She grabbed the drinks from the bartender and squared her shoulders. Tonight was to be enjoyed. She was going to dance and drink and maybe even get up on that stage and make an ass out of herself, too. She weaved her way over to the table where Alexis stood, and Alexis looked up at Mia and grinned.

"Come and sit," Alexis said. "I don't think you've met Brad's wife before. This is Sarah. Sarah, this is Mia Clark."

Mia smiled at the blond with the picture perfect smile and shook her outstretched hand as Alexis scooted onto a chair between them. "It's nice to meet you. How are you enjoying married life?" she asked. She wasn't sure when Brad remarried, but it seemed the polite thing to say.

"Still in that honeymoon phase even after more than a year and a half, so I'd say that's a good sign for us," Sarah said, that bright white smile never leaving her face.

"I'd have to agree," Mia said. She turned to Brad then. "How have you been?"

"Can't complain," he said simply, leaning back in his chair and taking a sip from a glass of beer. "I heard you're buying a house downtown."

Mia turned an accusing gaze on Alexis, who immediately threw up her hands in front of her. "I didn't say a thing!"

"Your agent, Savannah, is my cousin," Brad explained. He gestured to someone behind her, and Mia turned to see Savannah wave at them from the bar. "She said it's a nice place. Close to the square they've been restoring. You'll want to check that out, too. They've done good work."

"Don't listen to him! His company's the one the city hired to do the restorations." Sarah nudged her shoulders against his playfully.

"I'll have to walk down one day." The conversation continued around her, and Mia was surprised to find herself enjoying the evening more than she expected. Other friends and acquaintances stopped by their table to a background of terrible singing. Some just dropped in for a quick hello. Others pulled up chairs, ordered drinks, and stayed longer. It was nice, comfortable even, and it made her feel like the widows in her favorite historical romance novels who finally shed their mourning clothes—their widow's weeds as they were often called—and ventured back into society. Though there was one key difference between her life and that of her fictional world, because she was most assuredly not shedding her widow's weeds in pursuit of a husband.

Amid the cross-talk, she learned Sarah worked at the hair salon minutes from the downtown square and had invited Alexis in for a visit soon. There were apparently several scandalous affairs between other couples Mia knew, resulting in one separation and one divorce. Sarah also filled her in on babies born recently and various neighborhood feuds. The woman seemed to know everything about everyone, and Mia told her so.

"Well, honey, I'm a therapist as much as a hair stylist. You'd be surprised what people will say once those foils go on," she said with a laugh that turned into a squeal when Brad suddenly grabbed her hand and hoisted her out of her seat. A lively country tune played over the speakers, and Mia watched as he twirled her out onto the small dance floor between the tables and the stage.

Alexis leaned over. "You know, for being the town gossip, she conveniently leaves out the fact that she was the center of it when she and Brad got hitched."

Mia propped her chin on her hand and leaned in toward Alexis, enjoying the conspiratorial atmosphere. "Why's that?"

"Because it was not even six months after his wife died," Alexis said, taking a sip of her drink and raising her brows at Mia.

Mia's gaze moved back to Sarah and Brad, smiling at one another as they moved in time with the twangy guitar. "They seem happy enough now," Mia said. She remembered little about Brad's first wife apart from occasionally seeing her around school as teenagers, and she certainly didn't remember her death.

"They do now, yes, but you know what they say. Once a cheater, always a cheater."

"Brad?"

Alexis made a noise of agreement and nodded dramatically. "Rumor was he and Sarah were quietly a thing when he was still married."

"How did I miss that?" Mia asked.

"I think it was around the time you lost Ewan. Maybe a little while after. I'm sorry. I shouldn't have brought it up," Alexis said with a grimace. She laid a hand over Mia's.

"It's alright." Mia turned her hand over and squeezed gently. "You don't have to apologize for talking about him."

Alexis gave her a small smile, and they lapsed into comfortable silence. Mia watched the dancers give way to another round of karaoke singers. Brad and Sarah rejoined their table, and when the buzz of alcohol threatened to turn into something stronger, Mia decided to end her night out. Her capacity for socializing now matching her capacity for drinks, Mia said to Alexis, "I'm going to close out my tab and head home."

Alexis nodded and leaned over for a quick hug, whispering something about being glad she'd come out. Either that or something about hitting the gym when the sun was out. She couldn't quite hear over the noise, but she assumed the former, knowing her friend.

"Oh, you can't leave yet," Sarah said when Mia stood.

Mia shook her head. "I'm exhausted. Not sleeping too well at the moment, I'm afraid."

"More ghost dreams?" Alexis asked. Mia gave her friend the look, a stiff smile on her face, and nodded.

"Ghosts?! How exciting! You have to tell me all about it before you go," Sarah said. "I talked to my psychic once about this dream I kept having. A lady kept coming into the salon for a manicure, and every single time I'd just file her nails right off. I don't even do nails! So, she (my psychic) gave me this book about dreams—I'll have to give it to you—and I've just made myself an amateur expert on the subject."

She wanted to brush her off, but she actually liked the bubbly woman. So Mia sat back down and indulged her. "I don't know for sure that it's a ghost, but it seems to make sense, I guess. The dream is always the same. Scary vibes meet crying kid, the haunting, scared kind of crying. He's only a little thing, and he has the sweetest pajamas on with all these sleeping pandas all over it. It would make you cry if it wasn't so terrifying," Mia said.

"I can imagine. Oh, Brad, didn't David have some sweet little pajamas like that?" Sarah asked, turning to her husband.

Brad went from relaxed, as if he'd only been half-listening, to stone-faced in an instant. "Yes," he said. He stood abruptly and walked away.

"Darn. I've really put my foot in it now," Sarah said apologetically. "Excuse me."

Mia watched Sarah trot through a sea of people to get to Brad, saw him grab her somewhat forcefully by the upper arm and lead her out, and decided she officially had enough of adults who'd overindulged in their drinks for the night. She turned to Alexis. "I think that's my cue," she said. "I'll see you at work."

Mia headed back to the bar to close out her tab. She leaned forward on the slick bar and signaled to the bartender. The music around her was too loud, the smells of sweat and perfume and people overwhelming. Tapping her fingers on the bar top, she willed the bartender to hurry with her receipt and credit card. Struggling to calm her sudden anxiety, she felt as much as saw a man lean into the bar next to her. His bicep brushed against hers, and she shuffled to the side to accommodate him.

She turned with every intention of saying, "Excuse me," but the words stuck in her throat, and all her powers of speech deserted her. Right out of a bad dream, Nicholas Robinson stood before her. Big as life, with a few strands of gray streaking through the dark brown hair at his temples, he was still as devilishly handsome as ever. If anyone in her life could be considered a nemesis, it was him.

"Mia," he said, his tone surprised. He angled himself toward her and propped an elbow on the bar. He smiled stiffly in a way that reminded her how you smiled at someone you were secretly hoping to avoid completely. "How are you?" he asked.

Mia didn't want his smile or his forced politeness. She wanted to curse him, scream, punch him in the nose. Anything that would give her a way to channel this fountain of rage that was bubbling up inside of her. "What in the hell are you doing here?" she asked instead. "Aren't you supposed to be in New York... or hell?"

"Come on, Mia. Don't be like that."

"Don't be like what, Nick? Like you dropped me like a bad habit? 'Hey Mia, sorry your husband is dead. I know he was my best friend and all, but I gotta run.' Fuck you."

It wasn't exactly eloquent, she thought as she scrawled her signature on the receipt, but it felt good. She grabbed her credit card, shoved it in her pocket instead of her purse, and stormed out without a backward glance.

4

Moving day, and Mia should be excited. On some level, she was. Truly. She was also good ol' fashioned terrified, with a healthy dose of incredibly sad. The walls of her apartment were her home, had been her home for years. She'd gotten engaged here, married, landed her dream job, started building a life. She certainly never planned to stay in this apartment forever, but it always felt like a comfortable holding place. It was where she'd dreamed all those fantastical dreams about her future life, as you do with the one you plan to spend the rest of it with. To keep the tears at bay, she busied herself with last-minute packing and coordinating with the movers who quickly transported furniture and boxes from her apartment to the new house. That was the easy part and what kept her attention on the tasks at hand rather than how she felt about it all. She needed to decide on things like...

Where should that couch go?

Did she want the bed against the window or the wall?

Should the shelves go over here or there?

More than before, she was thankful for the ability to close on the house quickly. Paying cash and avoiding the lengthy bank loan process (thanks to the forethought and financial planning of her late husband), greased the wheels, and the speed of it all kept her from overthinking and backing out last minute. Now, though, as she stood by the front door holding a bag of odds and ends, she cradled a lonely fake succulent and looked around as the apartment was slowly emptied room by room. The plant was a present Ewan had given her after she'd successfully killed nearly a dozen others in that many months, and a few tears threatened to fall when she looked down at it. She dashed them away dramatically.

"Not today, Mia," she said to the empty living room. She would not cry, and she'd be damned if she'd continue to live like Miss Havisham in this apartment. Yes, it was filled with memories of a life she'd lived—a beautiful life—with the love and dreams of a man who'd been her world. It was at that stove that she'd accidentally set a dishtowel on fire. They'd made love on that living room floor, shared intimate showers in the bathroom down the hall. He'd nursed her through the flu in that bedroom, and they'd sat outside on that porch more times than she could count watching the stars and making the kind of big, impossible plans of arrogant young couples in love, so sure of themselves and their place in the world.

But that life was gone.

It was sudden and tragic and awful, and it was gone. Nothing she did would bring it back. With one last look around, Mia took a deep breath and stepped out of the apartment for the last time, out of her old life and into the new. The sinking feeling in her stomach didn't dissipate until she was in the narrow driveway of her new home. It was still a little surreal that it was actually hers. Looking up at the wood and bricks, she realized she was more grateful for the improvements and updates it needed than she realized. It was here that she would make her mark. She started making a mental list of the various projects she wanted to get started on first. She'd never been a homeowner, after all, and she desperately wanted to be good at it. What a funny thought.

Getting out of the car required a bit of juggling between the plant and the other books and bags she carried. Most of her furniture was already set up in its final resting place, so Mia spent the next few hours adjusting it slightly here and there, arranging book-shelves, and unpacking her toiletries and clothing. She tried to put the kitchen to rights in an effort to avoid ordering takeout… and then gave up and ordered anyway. While she really had accumulated little over the years, the kitchen was a completely different story. Mia believed that no matter how minimally you lived, your kitchen would always be full of things. It would likely take her several days to get it all unpacked and organized the way she liked it.

Next were the bathrooms and bedrooms. The house contained two bathrooms and two bedrooms; one bath-room was attached to the master bedroom, and a smaller spare room was situated next to a half-bathroom across the hallway. She focused on just the master bedroom and its adjoining bathroom, leaving the spare bedroom and guest bath alone for now. It wasn't like she planned on having company over anytime soon. In the bathroom, she hung soft gray towels and set out a cluster of pillar candles in all different heights in the corner of the large garden tub. On the counter, she arranged a handful of pretty crystals in a shallow white bowl tipped with silver around its edge. She didn't know what half of the rocks signified, but if having pretty little rocks all around her made her feel just a little better about her life, then she firmly believed they were worth having.

Walking out of the bathroom, Mia spied a small grouping of boxes set in the far corner of the bedroom under the tall window. All the windows in this house were tall like this, with windowsills so low they were all the way down at her shin. She sat down cross-legged and pulled a box to her. She might as well dig into it now and get as much unpacked as possible today. Her neck ached, and her back had a spot mid-way up that was on fire, but she knew she'd feel better with everything in its place.

Pulling open the top, Mia immediately realized Ewan's things filled the unlabeled boxes. She remembered packing them away the year before, intending to donate them, but she had never been able to go through with it. Instead, she'd promptly shoved them to the back of the closet and forgotten about them until now. Reaching in, Mia drew out a sweater from the top and found it wrapped around a picture of Ewan, Nick, and her hiking in the Appalachians. She rubbed her thumb over the soft fabric and dropped it in her lap, setting the photo to the side. Just below it was a black pouch, all zipped up. She knew what was inside, and her hands shook when she unzipped it. The smell hit her like a physical blow to the face. She smelled his cologne and deodorant, the shaving cream he kept. Instantly, her chest felt tight and her throat closed up. She was overwhelmed with memories, with the sights and sounds of her life before.

She cried out, and her body crumpled around the fabric. The keening sound of grief was as real and raw now as it had been the day he died. Her breathing became rapid and shallow as sobs ripped through her body without mercy, tears pouring down her face in hot rivers.

"Why did you take him?" she cried out angrily to the room and again with more desperation, her voice breaking, "Why?!" She curled onto the floor in a ball, gripping the soft sweater tight to her chest as if it was a life preserver. She buried her face in it and let the waves of grief crash over her again and again. Her body shook with the force of her sobs, and she stayed curled among all that was left of her dead husband until her tears finally ran dry.

When the sun dipped down and the house became noticeably darker, Mia stayed curled on the floor for many minutes more, still and quiet and emotionally spent. Finally, and moving so slowly, she placed the boxes of Ewan's things in the back of her closet and closed the door with a dull clink, her hands lingering on the wood as if she was saying goodbye. She floated from room to room, flipping on lamps and refocusing her thoughts on the accomplishments of the day. Anything to take her mind off her bruised heart. Other than pictures and wall decor, little was left to unpack. As physically and mentally exhausted as she was, she doubted sleep would come easily. She walked into the living room and chose a book to read, something dark and tragic that would match her mood.

She pulled one from her "to be read" pile and settled into the chair she'd found years ago at a thrift store and bought specifically to designate as her reading chair. It was a faded blue somewhere between an aqua and teal and was as soft as sin. The previous owners of the house had left the curtains, and the orange light of the sun filtered through the lace to cast a golden-white glow on everything in the room. Though it wasn't her initial plan, the lace added a vintage charm to the room, and she decided in that moment she would keep them after all. Mia snuggled deeper into the chair and tucked her feet beneath her.

As she read page after page, her eyes became heavy, her body finally relaxed, and Mia slowly slipped into sleep with the book still open on her lap. She drifted gently into dreams where the world seemed softer, the light going from golden to gray, all hazy and warm.

In her dream, she was walking down a wide corridor, a nightgown floating out from her legs with every step. She smiled as her husband caught her around the waist and pressed her seductively against the wall. He leaned down to kiss her. She ran her hands up his arms and gripped his neck, pouring herself into the kiss. "Where did you go? I've missed you so much," she sighed into him. His mouth moved to her jaw, then slid up her neck to nuzzle her ear.

"Momma," he whispered in a voice that wasn't his own. The breath she thought would be hot was instead icy cold. Mia

lurched back in shock. The face was his, Ewan's, a face she knew as well as her own, but the voice that came out of his mouth was not. "No, momma!" he cried.

His face disappeared, and she was tumbling backward onto a cold, hard bed. A baby mobile of animals and clouds circled above her head. Shadows from the animals bounced off the walls, their shapes morphing and becoming misshapen as they danced around and around. Their colors bled together and apart again. From the corner of the room, Mia heard the familiar crying of the little boy, but she couldn't turn her head to look at him. Her body was too heavy, every thought sluggish. Movement from the doorway caught her eye, and she heard the scream again. "No, momma!"

Suddenly, something soft and wide covered her face, and she couldn't breathe. She tried to struggle, to push against the thing across her nose and mouth, but the weight of it smothered her. Her lungs burned, and in that moment, she knew she was going to die.

With a gasp, Mia jerked awake. Her lungs heaved as she looked around the room with wide eyes. The sun had set, leaving the room dark except for the lamplight, the chorus of cicadas, crickets, and frogs outside a soundtrack to the night. Just a dream, Mia reminded herself. She took a deep breath and stood. Clearly, she was processing a lot of emotions at the moment, and her subconscious was going haywire. Of course, that was it. She grabbed her book and headed into the bedroom to get what sleep she could.

And when she did finally sleep, it was with all the lights on.

5

Mia let herself sleep late into the morning before willing herself out of bed. It had not been a pleasant night's sleep. In fact, now that she was thinking about it, it was odd that the dream was so different from the norm. Usually the stories were variations of the same theme, but this one was darker, more sinister. No longer was it just a little boy crying but a melding of her reality and the ghostly nightmare, as if he was trying to show her something important. She shook her head at the thought.

"You need more sleep, my girl," she murmured to herself. Ghosts weren't controlling her dreams, and no one was trying to tell her anything. It was the excitement of the move, nothing more. Thinking about how quickly she'd bought the house, and so impulsively, started her pulse racing. She worried that this was all a mistake. The dreams could be her subconscious warning her to slow down. Why they were all variations of a sad child's night-mare? She didn't know, but it was a possibility. *Right?!*

She pulled out her phone and quickly sent a message to Alexis. If anyone could help her not lose her mind right now, it was the most impulsive person she knew. They met shortly after the text exchange at the local bookstore. A national franchise, it was large and obnoxious for her taste, but the staff was lovely, the bakery was delicious, and the book selection decent.

Mia sat at a table and was grateful when Alexis was only minutes behind her. Walking quickly from the door to the table, Mia admired Alexis' confident stride, the way she held her shoulders back and dared the world to get in her way. Her hair was down today, the highlights of gold and caramel running through the brown curls and making her hazel eyes seem brighter and her brown skin warmer.

"You must have rushed out of there!" she said, refer-ring to the office where both she and Alexis worked.

"Oh, no. I was already cutting out for lunch." Alexis said. "So, what's up? Why the emergency meeting?"

"I moved into the house," Mia blurted.

"What?! How? When did you close?" Alexis demanded, her jaw dropping open in shock.

"It was a cash offer, so we closed really quickly, and I didn't see any point in waiting. So, I moved in," Mia said.

"I was imagining you'd take a vacation or something, but set up a new house?" Alexis said. She hesitated, and Mia worried she didn't support the rash decision. "That's so much better."

Mia let out the breath she didn't know she was holding. "I don't know how to feel about it yet," Mia said. "I'm excited, of course, and I'm already thinking of all the projects I want to do, but I'm also terrified. It's hard figuring out what I'm supposed to be doing when I never thought I'd be doing this alone."

"You will, and you're not alone. Not completely at least," Alexis said. "Something led you to that house. It's a sign."

"I don't know about all that."

"You're going to make good things happen. You'll see."

"You're only saying that because you love all that woo-woo stuff."

"You have no idea," Alexis said cryptically.

Mia scrunched her brows at that and wondered what it meant, but in the interest of not putting her friend on the spot, she put the thought aside. "Nope, and I'm glad of it. I believe in what I can see and hear and touch."

"So says the woman who dreams about a dead kid every other night."

"Touché," Mia said, taking a sip from her coffee mug.

"Well, spill the beans, hun. You can finally tell me about this new house."

Mia caught herself sighing with a smile. "It's adorable, a little bungalow style one-story," she said. "It doesn't have much of a backyard, and what's there needs serious TLC, but it has the cutest front yard. It's a little rough around the edges inside, too, but most everything it needs is cosmetic."

"You said it's close to the square, right?"

"Only a few minutes' walk, less than that if you drive downtown. You know that little neighborhood toward the beach right off the roundabout?" Mia asked. "It's down that way."

"Oh, I know where that is! Those houses are so cute. Aren't they from the 1950s or something?"

"The '30s actually. It's pretty cool."

"It's definitely not something I would expect you to be panicking about, but I know that it's a huge step, so it's understandable that you are. I'm really happy for you," Alexis said.

"Thanks. I'm trying to work toward happy again, too," Mia said. It was the first time she admitted she was unhappy, and Alexis reached out and covered Mia's hand with hers.

"I know. There's a time to laugh, a time to weep, a time to mourn... and a time to dance."

Mia laughed. "Did you just rip off a bible quote from Flashdance?"

"A classic, obviously, and appropriate for you," Alexis said, flicking her tight curls over her shoulder dramatically.

"You watch way too many old movies."

"I watch just enough, thank you!"

Mia shook her head and smiled. They sipped coffee and slipped into comfortable silence. Well, almost silence.

"Seems noisier here than when we were in last, doesn't it? Maybe it's kids being out of school?" Alexis suddenly asked.

Mia nodded. "I was thinking about that when I came in today. I wonder if there's a smaller bookshop downtown. It'd be nice to support the businesses I'll be closer to now, and I wouldn't mind someplace a little quieter."

Alexis shook her head. "There isn't anything book-wise anymore. There used to be that discount place down on Nash Street by the music store. What was the name?"

"Oh, I think I remember the one. It had those horrible orange shelves in the back and the glass case with all the antique books by the front door. Errol's, I think?" Mia guessed.

"Yes, Errol's!" Alexis said. "It closed down about a year ago, but it wasn't really a book nook type place. More of a thrift store for paper, really. Still sad, though."

"It's always sad when those little shops close," Mia said. She wasn't sure what else to say. The more steps she took down this path of reawakening, the more she realized she'd missed over the last two years. It was a strange feeling, living your life and yet not really taking in any of the events that happened in it.

"Maybe you should open a little bookstore instead. Wouldn't that be fun?" Alexis said. "You could have a little cafe inside it and host monthly book club meetings."

"No, thanks." Mia sipped her coffee and set the cup back down with a click of finality.

"Seriously, hear me out!" Alexis said. "This place has no charm. It's noisy, there's no good place to snuggle in with a book, and they don't even do author events. The closest ones are always in Atlanta, which means we almost always miss them. You could fix that! Give 'em a run for their money."

Mia considered it briefly before pushing the thought out of her mind. While having a quaint little place to go sounded lovely, being the one to actually own it? That was completely out of the question. There was no way she could start up a bookstore out of nowhere. Just to open the doors, you'd need to have a location, books to sell. Surely you'd need connections with agents and publishers beyond what she did now. Moreover, she was sure she'd need knowledge of how to actually run a business. None of which she had.

Sure, she knew good books thanks to her job as an editor, but knowing how to shine up a good book did not make her qualified to sell an entire store of them. And that job, she reminded herself, was her dream job. She was paid to read for a living, a childhood dream made real. Never mind the workaholic hours and near complete lack of a social life. It's not like she was that much of a social butterfly.

"Absolutely not."

"You're right. It's probably one of those things that's more fun in theory," Alexis sighed.

Mia nodded in agreement, her eyes casually scanning the room. Buying a home and relearning who she was were big enough steps for the time being. As she mulled over exactly what her next step might be, she watched booksellers restock shelves and help customers while children begged over the toy display. She turned back to Alexis, ignoring the pang at the sight of a mother snuggling an infant close. For a moment, she wondered if that would've been her by now. Would she have been the type of mother who took her child to story time at the library and shopped for books in the children's section of the bookstore? Would Ewan have bundled a baby fresh from the bath into soft pajamas and settled down with them to read a book before bedtime? Shaking her head, she pushed the thoughts from her mind. Dwelling on what might have happened wouldn't bring him back, wouldn't bring that life back. The only way to go now was forward.

"Mia, what's the matter?" Alexis asked. Her brows drew together, and she looked concerned.

Mia wondered guiltily how long she'd been trapped inside her head. She gave Alexis a quick smile and said, "Nothing, I—" Just then something, or rather someone, caught her eye, and she zeroed in on Nick as he turned and met her gaze. "What is he doing here?"

Alexis turned and followed Mia's gaze. "Who? Oh."

Well aware of Mia's feelings for Nick and her reasons for them, Alexis snapped her mouth shut. It would surely be a balance interacting with the two of them. Loyalty commanded her to support her closest friend, meaning there was little room for friendly conversation with him. But southern manners and her nostalgic friendship with him made her feel obligated to at least make polite conversation. She watched as he excused himself from the store clerk he was speaking with and walked over to them.

"Hey, Alexis," he said. "Mia."

"Hey, Nick. I'm surprised to see you in town. Are you visiting?" Alexis asked. Mia glared at her, and she returned the expression with one that clearly said, well, what did you want me to say?

"Actually, no. I moved back a few months ago, but between the move and work, I'm just coming up for air. How have you been?" Nick asked.

Before Alexis could answer, Mia said, "Lovely to have you back. Now, go away, Nick."

His smile disappeared, and his eyes moved from

Alexis to Mia. "I don't know if I should. You and I need to talk."

"I have absolutely nothing else to say to you," Mia said. She removed her hands from the speckled top of the table and folded them primly in her lap. Out of the corner of her eye, she saw Alexis look at her with a confused expression.

Nick shifted his weight to his back leg and crossed his arms over his chest. The gray cotton stretched over the muscles of his chest and arms. He took a deep breath, the kind you take when you're trying not to murder the person in front of you. "Then you can listen because there are things I need to say to you."

"I'm not interested in hearing them. I don't have time for your excuses or your stories," she said, crossing her arms in return.

"Some stories need to be rewritten."

"And some need to end."

Nick looked at her, his eyes intense and narrowed. The muscle in his square jaw tightened like a pulse. "Some do... I guess it just depends on who's writing it," he said. He stared at Mia a moment longer and then turned to Alexis. "Later, Lex."

Alexis watched him walk away with a speculative air and then turned to Mia with her brows raised. She took a pointed sip from the straw in her iced coffee. "Well, that was interesting."

Mia sniffed and flipped her hair over her shoulder. "Annoying is more like."

"So when did you talk to Nick?" Alexis' eyes held

something in them she couldn't quite place. Accusation? Curiosity? Both?

"I ran into him that night at The Railway. It was nothing, really," Mia said with a dismissive wave of her hand.

Alexis made a hmm noise in the back of her throat. "Why do you think he's back?"

"Maybe he got a debilitating case of writer's block, and his movie star wife cheated on him in a public scandal. Then his writing career tanked," Mia fantasized, her voice dripping with sarcasm.

"All in a couple years? Busy boy."

"A girl can dream," Mia said. She took a sip of her coffee and found it was cold. Frowning at it, she refused to allow herself to wonder why Nicholas Robinson was back in St. John's. Plain and simple, he was back, and that was that. This town may be small, but it was big enough to avoid him until he ran away again. Adult life was messy and complicated and hard, so it was bound to happen one way or another. She could be patient.

Maybe next time he'd run to another country.

6

The next morning, Mia rose, feeling less than well rested but determined, nonetheless. In her kitchen, she smothered cream cheese on a bagel and set the teakettle to heat. While the water came to a boil, Mia dug a pad and pen out of a box. Today, she decided, was a day for planning. Not that she really thought she could plan the rest of her life—she wasn't unrealistic—but to her mind, every great life started with a plan. It might be the kind of plan you made and then threw out the window when spontaneity hit, but it would be a plan all the same.

It seemed silly to write "Mia's Life Plan" across the top of the paper, so she settled for labeling it "GOALS." That felt less in the realm of school assignment and more adult-like. Tapping the pen on the pad, she wondered what her goals should be. Some of the easy ones that came to mind were those she'd already accomplished. Education, buying a home, getting a fulfilling job, those were all things she'd already done successfully, and wasn't this an exercise to help her take the next step? First, she needed to figure out what that was.

The kettle whistled, and Mia walked over and grabbed it off the stove. She poured the hot water in a mug and dunked a tea bag in. She pulled the tea bag in and out of the water, watching as it bobbed up and down on the surface, wisps of tea stained water whipping off the bag with every movement. Her achievements so far seemed like pretty big milestones in the traditional sense, but they didn't really define her as a person. She wasn't her job or her location. She was so much more. But what exactly? Outside of reading, there wasn't anything she was really passionate about. Even the extra-curricular activities she'd done in the past were more because Ewan enjoyed them. Not that she hadn't, too, but her desires weren't the driving force.

"Okay," she said and wrote, *Find something you're passionate about.* That was good! Boosted by the success of it, she continued writing, and more goals followed.

Read a book (not for work).

Learn something new.

Eat out alone.

Make a home.

Looking around the room, she considered what her ultimate goal might be. What was the one thing she wanted above all else? With a smile, she put pen to paper.

Find yourself, she wrote.

Satisfied, she looked over the list. It was good to get it out of her head. The lost feeling was still there, lingering around the edges, but it was like a shadow was being chased out by the light. Grabbing her mug and discarding the tea bag in the trash, Mia walked out onto her front porch. For now, she'd placed a dining room chair out front, but soon she'd choose a couple of rocking chairs. She imagined they'd be white wicker with a potted plant set on a little white table between them.

Find something you're passionate about. That was item number one of her list of goals. What did she want to be passionate about? There were a great many things she liked. Gardening was one, she thought as she surveyed the front lawn and made a few mental notes for a trip to the garden center. She also enjoyed making things, little crafts and soaps and candles and the like. She had a decent hand at art, she supposed, but none of those things really lit her up. Reading did, she thought.

It was part of why she'd chosen the career path she had, but copy editing wasn't exactly reading for fun. All around, it was work she loved, but there was far more emailing and meetings and not as much pleasure reading in publishing as one might think. Sitting down with a manuscript remained her favorite part of the job, though. Of course, there were times when reading a manuscript was more like trudging through a bog, but more often than not, it was enjoyable. It was her dream job, she reassured herself again.

She supposed it was a lot like owning a bookstore. She didn't imagine you could only stock the shelves with books you loved personally. Surely there were books you carried and probably hated, but your customers loved them, so you stocked them all the same. Her mind jumping from passion to passion, she leaned out over the porch railing to check the state of the lattice and nearly spat out her tea when she saw out of the corner of her eye Nick step through her neighbor's doorway. She gawked at him, wondering why the universe was cursing her with his presence everywhere she went! She couldn't hear exactly what was said, but his casual manner and lopsided grin could only mean one thing.

Before she could make an escape, Nick turned, and his eyes caught hers. His smile was hesitant, and he walked down the porch steps and across the grass toward her. The closeness of the homes had seemed a cute little detail when Mia first toured the home. Now it seemed the greatest inconvenience.

"This your place?" he asked, pulling up just short of the corner of her porch and looking up at her.

Mia wondered if it was too late to dash into the house. She didn't really want to talk to anyone just then. She was busy figuring out the rest of her life, thank you very much. With a bracing breath through gritted teeth, she decided she wouldn't run. She was a woman with spine and grit, and she wouldn't hide like a scared rabbit every time she had to encounter Nick. "It is."

"It's nice. How long have you been here?" he asked.

"A few days. Excuse me, but is there something you need? Because I have better things to do than have a pointless conversation with you."

"Actually, yes," he said, "And I wouldn't call it pointless."

Mia gave him a bland look and sipped her tea. There was something a little dramatic about the act, and she couldn't help but revel in that.

"You want to explain the outburst at the bar? And the bookstore?" he asked.

"I have nothing to explain to you."

He took a step back and scoffed. "Really. So, you get to just hurl accusations at me, tell me to fuck off, and expect me to bow down and say, 'Thank you, ma'am?'"

"Yes," she said, raising her brow and looking down at him as if he was gum stuck to the bottom of her shoe. "That's exactly what I get to do. Now go away and leave me alone."

For a moment, he looked as if he meant to jump the porch rail and strangle her. His jaw muscle flexed, and he took a deep breath, his chest rising sharply. It was clear as crystal that he was used to getting his way, the arrogant ass. He half-turned, as if to walk away, but he paused and looked back at her. Mia steeled herself for an argument, preparing to unleash two years of anger on him, but the look he gave her was so deep and so heartbreaking that it simply stopped her breath.

"You weren't the only one hurting, Mia."

But Mia didn't want to hear it. His betrayal, his desertion, cut so deep she couldn't possibly put the depth of her hurt into words. When he said nothing more, she morbidly indulged her curiosity. "Why did you come back? New York not doing it for you anymore?"

Nick shrugged and looked down at his feet. He glanced up at her from under dark brows, his eyes filled with regret. He looked as if he'd say something and then changed his mind. "I missed home... and maybe I was tired of running."

His answer was cryptic, but Mia was in no mood to

decipher the puzzle. She didn't care to hear any excuses about why he'd run or how sorry he was now. "I can't talk to you right now," she said.

Nick nodded, his jaw still tight. He started to leave, and again he took a few steps before turning back to her abruptly. "Ida says she'll be stopping by with a cake to welcome you to the neighborhood," he said, in the same way someone asks their spouse to pick up a gallon of milk on the way home.

"Ah, alright." Her brows drew together, and she wondered exactly how she was meant to respond.

"She likes chamomile and green tea if you keep those on hand," he added.

"Okay," she said slowly. She wondered how long he and the mysterious Ida had been together and, if he was going to be virtually at her front door, how often she'd have to avoid him.

"Alright then." And as if called by magic, the door of the neighboring house swung open, and a woman somewhere nearing seventy stepped out onto the porch. She held something out in her hands and hailed Nick.

"Your sunglasses," the woman said.

"Thanks, Ida! What would I do without you?" His voice betrayed nothing of the stony visage of a moment before. Nick trotted over to grab them, gave her a quick peck on the check, and turned to Mia. "I guess I'll see you around then."

Realizing that he probably wasn't dating the old woman, Mia felt a strange combination of relief and regret, but that didn't mean she wanted to see any more of him. His recent appearances were more than enough. "I wouldn't count on it."

"Sure you can. I'm just two doors down."

With that, he turned and walked away, leaving her slack jawed and feeling like she'd just been sucker punched.

7

———

Mia walked back inside before any other neighbors decided to casually swing by and ruin her day. Dropping onto the couch, she wondered at his words. What did he mean he was tired of running? Running from her? It wasn't as if what had happened was a small slight or a minor insult. She'd been grieving the loss of her husband, something she was wholly unprepared for, and a person who had been so central to their lives up and disappeared. No conversation or notice at all. Just a cameo at the funeral and a string of unanswered messages and calls. The most painful part of it all had been just how alone she'd felt. Nick and Ewan practically grew up together. Both without siblings, they'd formed their own kind of brotherhood. No one but Nick loved Ewan like she did, and his abandonment was like another death in her life, an empty hole no one could fill.

Looking back now, she understood he was hurting, too. Perhaps he'd been hurting more than she realized.

She wondered if it was even a little selfish to have expected him to manage his grief and hers, as well. Certainly, he shouldn't have just walked out of her life. There was no doubt about that. But could it be that she expected too much of him? Maybe it was unfair of her to hold such a grudge. Though her pride pricked at that. She wasn't ready to forgive him, but maybe she owed him some sort of apology for cursing at him in public... twice.

As a sort of penance and a way to work through some of her thoughts, Mia dove into physical labor. She made a list of items she needed to give her front yard a proper face lift. The garden center would likely have everything she'd need, but she also wanted to explore the downtown shops and get a better feel for the neighborhood, so she detoured on the way and drove down the narrow streets.

Most of the buildings were red brick, some faded and some obviously newer, except for the white marble courthouse. She could see where Brad Williams' company was hard at work on the restorations. It was beautiful work to be sure! The landscaping was clearly being updated, bricks pressure washed and sometimes painted, and some of the business signs were new to match the updates to the building and the surrounding greenery. The blend of old and newly restored buildings felt vibrant, as if a sleepy downtown square was coming back to life. She'd never spent much time downtown to know much about what it looked like before, but she appreciated the improvements all the same. She and Ewan had lived closer to the larger metropolitan area to the south and spent more time commuting into the city for their entertainment.

She turned down a street off to the right, intent on

heading to the plant nursery, and she immediately spotted a flower shop. Or perhaps it was more than that. Blooming planters hung from a rack outside, and there was a table set with watering cans and tools. Several medium-sized bushes growing out of plain black containers flanked the doors. The effect was charming and useful, and Mia appreciated the balance.

She pulled her car into an open parking space on the other side of the road and jogged across the street. Mia wasn't a plant expert by any means, but the hanging baskets looked to be heavy with begonias, and she knew the bushes were azaleas and hydrangeas. She loved their pink and blue blooms, and she didn't stop herself when the urge took hold to cup them and sniff each in turn.

As Mia looked at the azaleas next to the hanging baskets, she wondered if her yard had the right amount of sun or shade for them. She considered being patient, noting the patterns of sunlight in her yard and the type of soil in her beds, and then threw out the notion. She refused to overthink a plant and risk talking herself out of it, so it was only a few minutes later that she was hauling her prizes back to her car—along with a few other items she thought walked the line between essential and indulgence. Like her new hat, for instance. It was wide brimmed and straw colored and adorable, but as sweet as it was, it would also keep the hot sun out of her face. Lord knew Georgia could put on a scorching summer.

She piled what she could into her trunk, sat the watering can and hat onto her backseat alongside the azalea, and was skirting the front of her car when she glanced over at the row of shops again. Call it fate or coincidence, but her eyes immediately narrowed on the empty window to the immediate right of the garden shop. The *For Lease* sign jumped out at her.

This is *crazy*, she told herself, but it would make an adorable spot for a little bookshop, and there was no doubt it got a lot of foot traffic being on the square as it was. She wasn't sure why, but something about that little shop pulled at her, and Mia found her feet moving toward the wide, empty window. Holding her hands up to the glass, she peered inside. The space wasn't large, but it was well kept. Impulse had her pulling out her phone and saving the number written on the sign. Saving it didn't mean she had to call it.

"Find something you're passionate about," she whispered.

Books. She was passionate about books. Was the universe sending her another sign? Or was she having an early mid-life crisis? Thinking both were possible, Mia dared herself to be brave and called the saved number. She had no idea what she was going to do or say when she talked with whoever answered the phone, and her stomach twisted itself into knots as the phone rang in her ear. When someone actually picked up, her brain and mouth switched to autopilot. Before she knew it, Mia had an appointment to tour and discuss the property. Apparently, she was more amenable to entrepreneurship than she thought.

Hurrying back across the street before the heat of the inside of her car killed her new plant babies, Mia slid into the driver's seat and stared at her reflection in the rearview mirror. It was the same face that looked back at her all her life. Thick waves of dark brown hair fell around her face, a little frizzy from the summer humidity, and framed brown eyes the color of dark chocolate. They looked a little too wide today, her olive skin a bit too pale and yellow, but that seemed appropriate considering she'd bought a house and was considering opening a business not long after. Was she seriously considering opening a business right now? What business did she have running an actual business? But it was much like leaping into home ownership and desperately wanting to be good at it (whatever that meant).

It wasn't like she was completely unqualified, she reminded herself. She'd worked in publishing for most of her adult life. She knew the industry, what sold well commercially, what niches you could tap into with your smaller crowds, what the book clubs were reading in her small town, school kid trends, and more. It wasn't a complete leap to move into store ownership, and a perk of the job would be that she would be surrounded by the thing she loved most: books.

The more she mulled it over on the short drive home, the more exciting of an idea it became. She imagined spinning circles between stacks of stories, and the vision was tantalizing. Slow down, she ordered herself as she pulled into her driveway. Even if she was going to jump headfirst into this thing, she had to have some semblance of a plan. Plans were essential. For one, banks would most certainly require a formal business plan before dispersing any loans. And two, well, she needed one!

Mia used her gardening time to think things through. As if she hadn't already done that to exhaustion, she chuckled to herself. She didn't have to decide anything right now. Once she tucked her plants into their beds, she promised to spend at least two hours at her computer later that evening typing up her little book shop ideas and mapping out whether this was even viable. Satisfied she was on the right track, Mia dove into a day of planting and home improvements. It was sweaty, manual work, but it was the perfect way to channel her anxiety. So much was happening all at once, and although she was leading the charge, she wasn't quite sure how to handle all the changes. She'd always thought she was the type of person to go for whatever she set her mind to, but then Ewan died, and her entire world crashed around her.

Standing and dusting her hands off, Mia walked to the side of the house and dragged a bright green garden hose out from under the porch. Sun bleaching faded it so that the green was more yellow in places, and cobwebs clumped with dry bug carcasses, leaves, and pine straw covered its length. She stifled a squeal before rolling her eyes at herself and slapping the debris away. With a barely contained shiver, she tried not to imagine all the bugs that surely crawled on the hose like it was their personal highway. Then she loosened the knob that opened the flow of water to the hose. She babied her new plants with a gentle stream of water, twisting the ancient rusted nozzle on the tip of the hose so that it sprinkled rather than sprayed.

How sweet the azaleas looked dancing under the droplets of water, and when she was done, they looked perky and refreshed. Wiping the sweat from her brow, Mia decided she needed similar refreshment.

"Looks good."

Mia turned abruptly to see Nick walking toward her. He held two glasses filled with iced water, already shimmering with condensation. When he was closer, he offered one to her. Her initial instinct, albeit petty and mean, was to push it away, turn on her heel, and go inside without a word. However, she was in self-improvement mode, she reminded herself, so she accepted the glass and took an appreciative sip. Still, appreciation couldn't quite keep the acid from her tone. "Two visits in one day. Aren't I the lucky girl?"

"You know better than to be out here this long in this heat," he said.

"I haven't been out long," she said defensively. "And I don't have to answer to you."

"Just a friend trying to help."

"Debatable."

"That I'm trying to help?"

"That you're a friend."

He frowned at her. "Have you ever messed up so bad that you didn't know how to go about fixing it?" he asked, squinting his face and using a hand to shield his eyes from the sun.

"I've never hurt someone on purpose."

"I didn't—" He stopped. "You're not going to make this easy, are you?"

"And why should I?"

Nick was silent for a long moment. He looked past her, past the garden and the bushes and the house. He looked toward the ocean behind them, and Mia wondered what he was thinking. Turning back to her, he lowered his head and his shoulders, so broad and strong, sagged. He angled his head at her. She could barely see unshed tears, but they made his hazel eyes shimmer in the sunlight.

"I miss him." His voice cracked.

Tears trickled down his cheeks. It turned out he was a quiet crier. His chest puffed up and became tight as he struggled to prevent the sharp ragged breaths from shaking his torso. As more tears streamed down his face, all of Mia's defenses broke, and her cheeks flushed with shame. Her righteous anger dissipated, and she covered her mouth to contain her own emotions. How could it still be so painful? How could it still feel as if the worst moment of her life had happened only yesterday? And then lay the blame for her own grief at Nick's feet?

Tears rolled down her cheeks, and before she knew quite what was happening, Nick's arms came around her. He drew her close, pressing his face into her neck, and she wrapped herself around him in turn. She couldn't help it. She clung to his shoulders with fingers that went white at the tips. A breeze stirred the hot air around them, and the smell of freshly dampened earth and leaves filled her nostrils. She felt his body shake as the wave of grief took them both under, and it was many moments before either of them could breathe or speak normally again.

"Come on," he said. His voice like gravel, his tone clipped. "Let's talk inside before the neighbors think we're crazy."

Mia nodded and led the way.

~

"Well," Mia said, clearing her throat and wiping her eyes. She sat on the couch in her living room with her back ramrod straight. Her eyes flitted around the room, still littered here and there with a few remaining moving boxes, and she clamped her hands together in an attempt not to fidget.

"Aren't you the one always saying sometimes a good cry is necessary?" Nick asked, taking a seat beside her.

"You know, being an arrogant know-it-all isn't an attractive quality."

"You used to say it was kind of cute."

"I used to say a lot of things. Clearly, I said that one to be nice."

"You were never nice," he said, one strong brow arched.

Mia ground her teeth together. "Of course, I'm nice," she said hotly. "Are you here to apologize or piss me off?"

Nick's eyes, still slightly puffy from crying, danced. "You are many things, Mia, but nice has never been one of them."

Mia's mouth dropped open, and she jerked her neck back. "What am I then?"

"Smart, clever, too capable for your own good, hot-tempered, and never nice. But as loyal a friend as one could hope to have." He paused, and his voice became quieter. "And one of the most beautiful women that I've ever known."

His eyes locked on hers in a way that made her breath catch, and she wondered why he would say such a thing. Perhaps it was a brotherly compliment. Surely it had to be as innocent as that, but despite her denial and her hollow self assurances, neither of them seemed able to move. She cleared her throat, finding it suddenly hot and tight. The noise dispelled some of the tension that thickened the air, and Nick finally jerked from his frozen state and shifted uncomfortably in his seat.

"If you think I can be all that, then clearly you're just like every other idiot man of your species thinking women are far more complicated than they are," she said lightly, though she wasn't sure if she was trying to convince him or herself.

"So, am I forgiven for being an idiot man, then?"

"I don't know, Nick. You hurt me." She wasn't sure if she could forgive him or if she even wanted to.

"I know," he said sadly. "Would it make any difference if I told you I thought I had good reasons?" Mia shrugged but didn't respond. Nick watched her for a moment and then gave himself a small nod.

Looking around the room, he asked, "Will you be painting in here soon?"

"I might," Mia admitted. "I'm a little nervous in that department."

"Give me a holler when you decide, and I'll lend a hand. Then you can come pretty up my flower beds in exchange."

"Maybe," she said. It was clear he was extending an olive branch of a sort, but she found her grasp on it was tenuous at best.

Still, he looked relieved and smiled at her with that crooked smile of his. It never failed to remind her of all his boyish antics as a child, and her heart did a little flip in her chest. How long could she stay mad at him when he was smiling at her that way?

"Now that the woman has made me cry my eyes out, I think I'll get going then," he said. "Later, Mia."

He kissed her on the cheek in much the same way he'd done to their elderly neighbor and moved to gather up his plastic cups. He shot her another lopsided grin as he stepped out the door and left, unaware of the hot flush Mia felt where his lips touched her cheek. She didn't imagine his kiss affected the old woman as it was affecting her now, and surely that was something to think about.

8

The next few days passed quickly. Between work and the remaining unpacking, Mia wasn't left with much time to rest or even think for that matter. To be fair, she didn't view that as a negative, but as she made the drive home from work and grew closer to her street, she couldn't help how her thoughts turned to her unexpected neighbor. Her reunion with Nick stirred up emotions she wasn't ready to face, emotions that she buried a long time ago. There was the obvious grief resurfacing, of course, but there was something else skirting just below the surface, something that left a knot in her throat and an uncomfortable fluttering in her stomach. The way he looked at her was unnerving. It was piercing, heated even.

Shaking her head, she told herself there was no way there was anything remotely sexual about the way Nick looked at her. She was simply a typical woman currently deprived of a certain physical type of satisfaction with a man for far too long, and that, she was finally willing to admit, was not exactly because of grief. Of course, after Ewan's death the last thing she'd wanted to do was hop into bed with someone, but staying celibate for so long was a more emotional choice than a desire to avoid physical relationships. In fact, it was a survival tactic. It was impossible to feel that depth of sadness again if she never let anyone get close enough to become attached. As physically satisfying as sex would be, it was the perfect way through the wall she'd carefully built around her heart, a hidden door to the secret garden, so to speak. Sex led to attachment, which led to relationships, which led to commitment, and Mia had absolutely no intention of sharing her life or her heart with someone else. She wouldn't survive it.

Mia glanced out of her car window and saw that thick clouds of gray, purple, and blue were quickly rolling in from the east. Fat drops of water fell onto her windshield as she pulled into her driveway, and gusts of wind sent her pink azaleas dancing. Throwing open the car door, Mia yanked her reading bag over her shoulder, the one she carried manuscripts from work and reading books alike in, and dashed through the rain to the cover of her porch. She pushed her key into the lock, cursing slightly when it stuck for not the first time, and made a mental note to replace it soon. She was only inside a few moments before someone knocked on the door. Startled, Mia turned and peered through the peephole, her hand reflexively ready to turn the deadbolt in a pinch if the person on the other side turned out to be a serial killer. Because obviously that was a completely valid concern to have on a random, rainy afternoon.

Standing on the other side of the door, though, shaking droplets of water off a newspaper was her neighbor, and lord love a duck, she was carrying a generously iced bundt cake. Mia opened the door and smiled politely, not because she was particularly desiring company but because the woman looked so adorable with her damp paper and cake.

"You must be Ida," she said, gesturing for the woman to come inside.

"Yes, and you must be Mia. Nick said he'd warned you I'd be coming along. Welcome to our little street."

Ida pushed the cake into Mia's arms and shuffled her way through the living room to the kitchen. She turned back with a bright smile as she walked. "I hope you don't mind if I make myself at home. Old habits are hard to break at my age, or so I tell myself every time I want to make excuses for whatever it is I want to do."

Mia chuckled at that and followed her through the room. "Not at all. I take it you were friends with the previous owners."

"Oh, yes. Nancy and Eugene lived here even longer than I did, back when this road was nothing but dirt and gravel. Raised two beautiful boys here, too," Ida said.

"Do they still live close by?" Mia asked.

"No, no, no." Ida pulled out a chair at the little kitchen table for Mia and then sat in one herself. "Eugene passed some years ago, and Nancy went to live with one of her boys. That's the way of it sometimes."

"It is," Mia said noncommittally. "Here, let me cut this

cake and brew us up some tea. Nick mentioned you like chamomile?"

"That would be lovely. How are you settling in?"

"Pretty good, actually. It's nice to have more room than I had in my old apartment, that's for sure. I almost don't know what to do with the extra space."

"It looks like you've done most of your unpacking, too."

"I blame my neat-freak mother," Mia joked.

"Mine was just the same. Are you close?"

Mia shook her head as she brought small plates and mugs of steaming tea to the table. How did one talk politely about strained relationships with their parents? She cut two fat slices of the chocolate cake and pushed a plate in front of Ida, setting a fork on the rim.

"No," she said, taking a seat and a cautious sip of tea. "She prefers her life as it is, and I prefer mine separate from hers. We catch up every now and again. But what about you? Does your family live close?"

Ida knew an evasion when she saw one, but she let that sleeping dog lie for now. "Not as close as I'd like. My husband—Johnny, rest his soul—passed away, oh, thirty years ago now, and my daughter lives about two hours south of here with her wife and their three kids. Teenagers now. They bring them all to see me every few weeks."

"It must be hard living so far away from them."

"Nick drops in and checks on me every few days," Ida said, as if that made it easier to bear being so alone.

Mia couldn't claim surprise, though. It was already clear that Ida and Nick were close, but she wasn't quite sure how to feel about it. In her mind, he was still the villain of her story. Deep down, Mia always knew that Ewan's death had torn Nick up just as much as it had her, but it wasn't something she'd ever been willing to admit to herself. Because to admit that meant that maybe he wasn't the monster she wanted him to be. He might not be the ultimate betrayer, and there was something comforting about giving him that label. If she was angry at Nick, then she wouldn't have to deal with the fact that she felt empty and lost and vulnerable. She could focus on that anger, and that's something she was quite good at.

"Outside of Nick's visits, it really depends. Some days I'm happy enough left alone to putter around my flowers or stretch out for an afternoon nap. Other days, I find myself missing a house full of grandkids or my Johnny, and those days are harder."

"I had a husband," Mia blurted out. She wasn't sure why she'd said it. It wasn't like she really wanted to talk about such a sensitive topic with a virtual stranger, but the woman had an aura about her. It was hard to describe. She felt warm and safe, as a mother or grandmother should, Mia supposed.

"Did you now?" Ida asked.

Mia nodded and took a careful bite of the cake. "His name was Ewan, and he had magic in his eyes. They always looked like they were twinkling with mischief, like he was up to something."

"My mother used to say that when a man loves you, deep down in the gut loves you, his eyes can't help but tell you all the time."

"I like that."

"What happened to him?" Ida asked, bringing the cup of tea to her lips.

"He died two years ago. Carjacking gone wrong," Mia said, surprised she could describe it so simply and without the threat of tears. That was progress.

"I'm sorry to hear that, dear," Ida said. "You loved him very much."

It wasn't a question. Ida said it so matter-of-factly that Mia couldn't help but smile. There were so many happy memories they'd made together, so much joy. Sometimes it was nice to be reminded of that, to be reminded of just how much they'd truly loved each other.

"How did your husband die? If you don't mind my asking," Mia said.

"The usual way, I suppose," Ida said. "He had a heart attack one afternoon after work. He came home early not feeling well, laid down to take a nap, and never woke up. I miss him every day, but I'm sure you know what that's like."

"I do," Mia said with a slow nod.

"Grief is a funny thing. It never really goes away. We just get better at carrying it along with us."

"So I'm learning."

They polished off the cake and tea, and Ida listened to Mia's plans for the rest of the landscaping and some of the cosmetic changes she planned to do inside. Ida listened intently as she laid out her grand plans. "Nancy would be pleased to see you making this place into your home," Ida said.

Mia smiled bashfully. "It's on my list. To make a home, that is. I have a list," she confessed.

"A list?" Ida asked.

Mia leaned from her seat at the table to the kitchen bar where her notepad still sat, her goals scrawled down on it. "See?" She set it on the table in front of Ida. "I've been feeling a little lost lately. Well, to be honest, I've been feeling a lot lost for a long time. I thought a list might help me find myself again."

"Makes sense." Ida pulled the reading glasses that hung from a chain around her neck up to her eyes. She didn't put them on, just held them all folded up in front of her eyes and scanned each row of words. "Now, I see you've got yourself and your home on here, but I'm not seeing anything at all about love. Call me a romantic old fool, but a young girl like you should be making some room in your life for it."

"No," Mia said with a laugh. "I am absolutely unequivocally not getting into that kind of mess right now."

"And since when is that 'kind of mess' a bad thing I'd like to know?" Ida asked, raising her brows at Mia.

"Did you ever consider getting remarried after your husband died?" Mia countered, her brows lifting in kind.

"Ah, now, that's different, honey," Ida said. "My baby was grown, my life already half lived. Sure, I welcomed the quiet most days, and I saw men here and there, but no one ever really stuck like my Johnny. It wouldn't have been fair to any of them for me to settle."

Mia was silent as she considered that. She wondered how she'd feel in a year, five, even ten. Would she enjoy the comfort of solitude? Would she still be wrapped up in her grief? Would she want something more?

"You've got a whole life left to live, my dear. That's a lot of time to spend alone. I should know," Ida said and patted Mia's hand gently.

"I suppose."

"Now you wipe off that frown right now," Ida said. "You're a brave girl, braver than you realize, I reckon."

Mia thought of her upcoming meeting with the storefront's landlord and wasn't as certain, but she sure was going to find out.

MIA'S MOTHER, for all her flaws and shortcomings, taught her one thing well. When you were going to make a powerful decision, you cloaked yourself in power, and Mia was glad she'd listened. She dressed in a black one piece jumpsuit that floated around her legs, hugged her curves, and dipped into a v at the cleavage. It perfectly balanced casual femininity and professionalism, and damn, did she feel powerful strolling into the empty storefront that morning.

Familiar anxiety and self-doubt hovered around the edges of her consciousness, but her shield, a power outfit and a slick of red lipstick, held strong as she met with the landlord. An hour later, Mia tossed her hair over her shoulder and fairly floated out of the shop she'd decided was officially hers. It didn't even feel real yet, as if it was a completely out-of-body experience. The woman who'd months ago sat in her apartment, hiding from the world, was not the same woman who stood on the sidewalk holding the keys to her soon-to-be bookshop in her hand.

Mia thought back to her life years before, so young

and naïve and trusting that the world was good and fair. It could be, yes, but it could also be cruel for no reason other than its own fickle love for humanity. It was hard to recall that innocence as she rounded thirty-ish years old now, but she supposed it wasn't something you were really meant to hang onto. She opened the door to her car and leaned across the seat for her bag. Pulling out a notebook, she clamped a pen between her teeth, shut the door, and walked to a bench directly across the street from her shop. *Her* shop.

The location was ideal, and she jotted down notes for window displays, signage, and outdoor displays that could lure customers in when the weather was nice. She would host monthly book clubs, morning story time for preschoolers, and coordinate with the local schools to keep their assigned books in stock. Looking down the strip, Mia noted other local businesses. There was the flower and garden shop on one side, of course, an antique shop on the other, and even a bakery on the corner a few hundred feet away. She noted ideas for potential partnerships. Hanging planters would add an inviting, whimsical touch to the outside, and antique furniture and lighting could turn a cold bookstore into a homey book nook just as she envisioned. She could even offer cookies and muffins and the like from the bakery, alongside complimentary coffee and tea, of course. Mia made a note to check if she'd need a special license to serve food and drinks inside. Inside the book shop (where she'd already taken measurements of the space), Mia planned to carry a wide selection of fiction books for all ages, focusing specially on local and indie authors along with those who prioritized inclusivity and diversity. She could hit the internet later to see if there were any local writers' groups.

Satisfied that her ideas were sufficiently fleshed out, Mia got back in her car and started on the second part of the day's adventure. It was more terrifying quitting your dream job than leaping into entrepreneurship, but it was a step that needed to be taken. She considered taking a sabbatical instead of putting in her notice at work, but it seemed cowardly. She didn't want to keep making decisions (or avoiding them) out of fear. *Find something you're passionate about*, she reminded herself. Really, though, that was only part of the goal. Find something you're passionate about, and *do it!*

She felt like the proverbial frog who leaped before it looked. She only hoped that the leap would end up with her landing on solid ground rather than splashing into the water. Though it was some comfort that even if she did land smack dab into the water...

Frogs could swim.

9

The house was dark around her, so dark that the shadows filled the room with undulating ribbons of blackness. They twisted and writhed over and under each other, across the floor and up the walls. The air was heavy with silence. If despair had a feeling, this was it.

A sliver of light from a cracked door across the room was the only relief from the unending black. Cautiously, Mia sat up in her bed as familiar cries drifted hauntingly into the room. She braced herself for the emotions she knew were coming—sadness and terror in an epic tug-of-war with her the victim destined to be torn apart no matter which won. She watched as the door was pushed open by some invisible hand, and the little boy, so recognizable now, stood before her. One hand clutched a blanket dragging on the floor, and a tiny, round hand knuckled tears away from his eyes.

Amidst his tiny whimpers, Mia heard an unfamiliar voice echo from somewhere far off.

"David!" It was a man's voice. Over and over he yelled,

growing more frantic until it was his screams that pierced the air. "David! David!"

But the little boy didn't move. He stared at her, impossibly small, his tiny sobs like the consistent drum beat of a song. The man's voice grew to an almost deafening volume. Over and over he said the boy's name until she heard his voice crack, and a heart wrenching cry tore the air. And the boy didn't move.

His sobs stopped—or maybe the man's wailing simply muffled them—and he said in a voice that was impossibly small, "I don't wanna go."

Then in a rush, the little boy's face contorted, his body crouched low on the ground, and he rushed at her with an unnatural scampering gait. Mia's body jerked. She pushed herself back into the bed and opened her mouth to scream.

Instead, Mia shot up in bed, and the scream escaped her throat as a strangled gasp. Her chest heaved as the visions of the nightmare blurred into reality in that gray area between awake and asleep. She frantically pushed waves of hair from her face and scrubbed a hand over her eyes, willing her brain to wake up completely. She fought to remember every moment of the dream, trying to make some sense of it. Maybe if she could figure out what it all meant, she could figure out a way to make them stop.

As the fog inside her mind dissipated, the jumble of thoughts and images and memories came together like the pieces of a puzzle slowly snapping into place until they revealed the entire picture. The main commonality in all the dreams was the little boy, always crying, dressed in the same pajamas, and carrying an obviously well loved and well worn, faded yellow blanket. In her most recent dreams, he'd called out for his mom. Or rather, he told her no. It was strange that in this one, the little boy hadn't initially spoken at all. Instead, there had been a man, one who she'd never really seen, and he'd called the boy David. Did that mean something? That she'd heard a man's voice but not seen any sign of one? That now the little boy had a name?

So many unanswered questions... and the ridiculousness of it all. Here she was trying to solve a mystery created because her subconscious mind refused to process Ewan's death in any sane way. No one could convince her otherwise—the nightmares hadn't begun until after he died. No psychologist would contradict her, she was sure. Deciding that a tea and a happily ever after was the only way she would get back to sleep, she slid her legs over the side of the bed and threw the covers off her body. Mia was about to stand up when a movement caught her eye.

The door to her bedroom slowly swung open, and there the little boy from her nightmares stood. This time she did scream, grabbing the discarded blanket as if it would offer any sort of protection, but before she could blink, the figure faded into nothing.

"Oh my god," Mia said in a rush of breath. She pressed a hand to her chest, and a shiver rolled over her body in a cold, prickly wave from her scalp to her toes. She willed her breathing to return to normal, but her heart still pounded a hard and fast rhythm under her breast.

Because now the little dead boy from her dreams had very much stepped into her real life, and she didn't know what in the hell to do about it.

She hadn't been able to fall back asleep, but Mia thought she was feeling alright the next day, all things considered. It certainly wasn't every day that the ghost of your dreams walked into your bedroom, and she'd spent the better part of the morning trying to convince herself she'd still been dreaming. As morning slipped into afternoon and she puttered about her house, taking care of little chores here and there—the dishes, laundry, dusting—she knew she was lying to herself. The picture of the boy standing in front of her was simply too real, and unlike her nightmares, he'd been bereft of the soft haze that always surrounded him in dreams. Rather, his skin looked waxy and dead, his eyes hollow and sad and not quite alive either. Grabbing a pile of newly folded clothes from her bed, she walked to her dresser, determined to push the image from her mind and move forward with her day. It was time to take proactive steps to get rid of these nightmares, but today was not for the ghosts. Today was for her.

Satisfied that the inside of her home sparkled, Mia turned her thoughts to her To-Do list around the rest of the house. She wanted to finish decorating her porch and, if time allowed, spruce up her mailbox. Later, she would start on more of the indoor updates she had in mind, like painting or her garden. There were also projects she wanted to get to work on at the bookshop, but those needed more planning before she could tackle them, and she wanted to wait until her vision was more defined before investing time or money there. For now, her day would likely end with furniture assembly and planting.

Mia pulled on a pair of gray cloth shorts and an old

black t-shirt with more than a few paint and bleach stains. She lovingly thought of this outfit as her "get it done" outfit, but it was just as good for comfy reading on the couch and mid-day naps, two activities she promised herself she would indulge in soon.

Heading outside, Mia decided painting her mailbox was the first order of business. It was a fairly quick process, and if it needed a second coat, she could work on the porch while the first coat dried. First, she took a sanding block to the existing mailbox post. Its original white paint was badly peeling like the paint on the porch, and she was grateful that it made the job easier. Satisfied, Mia popped open the quart size container of white paint with a screwdriver and gave it a good stir with the long wooden stick from the hardware store. She dipped the brush in and began working on the mailbox post in long, even strokes, starting at the top and working her way down. It only took a few minutes, but the results were exponential. Instead of run down, the mailbox now looked inviting, as if to say, "Yes, please stop in and grab a drink."

Putting away the paint supplies, Mia reminded herself not to forget to wash out the brush. She glanced at the sky and estimated she had a few hours before the storm clouds rolled in. That was enough time to sort out the porch situation, she thought. On the porch, Mia laid down a towel, dragged three recently delivered boxes from beside the front door over to the roomier side of the porch, and prepared to assemble her new furniture.

"Hey there," Nick called from the sidewalk.

Mia lifted her head and searched left and right before

her eyes focused on Nick. "Hey yourself," she said back. She was careful to keep her voice casual, but she couldn't (and didn't want to) hide the caution in her tone. As much as she was excited to have a more welcoming front yard, playing the gracious hostess to this man wasn't exactly how she'd envisioned it working out.

Nick walked up the drive and along the curving path to her porch steps, his hands tucked into the front pockets of his shorts. Despite herself, she watched him take every single step. He wore a plain white tee and a pair of cargo shorts whose hem had long ago frayed. Like her, he'd opted for simple flip-flops.

"What are you doing out? Shouldn't you be buried in your next book or cursing your editor?" Mia asked.

Nick shrugged and propped an elbow on the railing post. "I thought I'd get a bit of air."

Mia raised a brow. "In this heat?"

"Mmhmm. What are you putting together?"

"Just a few pieces of furniture. I'm hoping that box over there contains a table that requires little to no assembly, because I'm pretty sure these rocking chairs will be the death of me."

Nick scratched his chin, and Mia noticed he hadn't shaved. The look suited him, she decided. It made his nose and cheekbones appear sharper, more defined than they already were, which worked well for him, as did the weight and muscle that maturity and likely time at the gym had put on him over the years.

"Want some help?" he offered.

"Why would you want to?"

He shrugged again. "I like fixing things."

"Assembly doesn't count as fixing," she said with a skeptical look aimed at him beneath raised brows.

He looked at her meaningfully then, his eyes filled with regret. "Sometimes things need to be built or rebuilt to fix them."

She wanted to tell him to go away—a voice inside her warned her to—but there didn't seem to be a valid reason to listen to it. Not if she was being a mature adult, at least. Clearly, he was trying to mend their friendship, and it seemed petty not to at least let him try. Though she assured herself that a bonus for her would be nagging him at every turn, and she could imagine finding a great deal of pleasure in that brand of retribution. Besides, while decorating the porch sounded fun, assembling furniture did not, and she was not too proud to turn down his help.

"Fine, but you get to do the chairs," she said with a smirk.

He took the stairs two at a time. "Alright. Shoo, shoo," he played.

"Don't have to tell me twice." Mia darted into the house, set on hunting up everything she deemed essential to turning her front porch into a personal oasis. After all, if he was helping, she wasn't above taking full advantage of it.

10

———

For the next hour, they worked in tandem. Nick screwed together pieces of wood and dark rattan, a material woven like wicker but more like thick plastic with a rough texture, and Mia transformed the neglected space into a charming reflection of her eclectic personality. She hung a fairy and crystal wind chime at the corner of the porch furthest from the front door. In the garden just below him, she placed stone gnomes of various sizes and styles. She'd collected them from different places over many years, and now finally they would rest around azalea bushes bursting with bright pink trumpets.

She moved around him as she tacked up lengths of lights around the perimeter of the ceiling. Every time she moved past him, sweet wafts of her scent filled his nose and set his senses on fire. She smelled of fresh soap, laundry, sweat, and a touch of lemon. He didn't know such a combination could be so intoxicating, and he had to remind himself that this woman—this one, particular woman—not only hated him, but she was also the wife of his friend. Firmly off limits to his debauched thoughts. Mia finished stringing up her lights, each tiny bulb positioned inside a small globe of crackled glass, and he wondered what they would look like when they shone out into the night. As he was tightening the last of the bolts on the chair, she dropped a thick, rough welcome mat in front of the door with a final splat and a murmur of approval in her throat.

"You're all done?" Nick asked, banging the palms of his hands together in a force of habit even though there was no dirt or wood dust on them. He adjusted the assembled chairs, set the small table between them, and balled up the sheets of foam padding and packaging that littered the porch. Mia bent to help, catching his eye with a reluctant smile on her face, and thanked him.

Nick's breath hitched at the sight of that smile. It was a strange sensation, that jolt. He'd seen her smile at him hundreds of times before. Yet this one made his stomach clench and took his breath away. Perhaps it was because he was finally breaking through that wall of ice she'd so successfully built around herself. That had to be it. Ewan's death was the first genuine tragedy of his life, and it wasn't as if anything really prepared someone for something like that. He admitted he'd acted like a selfish ass through and through, but he was hoping Mia would allow him to make it up to her now. It was the least he could do, and it seemed to his way of thinking like he owed it to Ewan, too. When you loved a guy like a brother, and you truly loved his wife as an extension of him, you made it your duty to take care of them both, no matter what happened.

It was funny that over the years, he'd often encountered a new situation and wondered what Ewan would do or say. Not that Ewan was this incredibly wise or omnipotent being, but he'd had a calmness about him. He was grounded. Nick wondered if that contributed to the way his death affected him... and Mia, for that matter. Ewan was their rock, their sense of stability. Without him, it was like they'd been tossed adrift in a violent sea, thrown around in a hurricane without a boat or even a life jacket.

"Come out with me tonight," he snapped. At her sharp look, he softened and clarified, "Not a date. Just a night out to celebrate and catch up."

"Celebrate what?" she asked slowly, her vowels, already lengthened simply by way of being a born and bred southerner, drawn out even more.

"The porch," he said simply, gesturing at the surrounding space. He could add that they'd also be celebrating a tentative bridge in their relationship, but since that would only push her away, he kept that part to himself.

Mia followed his gaze and took a moment to appreciate what they'd accomplished together in such a short period. He watched her face settle into happily contented lines as she took in the lights and the wind chime and the seating area, her breath sighing out of her softly. She looked back at him, and he was disappointed to watch her face slip behind that careful mask. She wanted to say no. He could see it in her eyes, but he held his breath. He wasn't sure why he wanted her to come out with him, but he wasn't a man who questioned his gut, and he was arrogant enough to believe she'd cave to his request. Mia Clark needed some fixing of her own. She just didn't know it yet.

"I don't know," she hedged, shuffling her feet against the rough, peeling paint of the wood below their feet. The afternoon sun shone over her, and his fingers itched to touch her hair where the light laid golden over the deep brown.

"Come on," he said. "It'll be fun. We'll grab some dinner and go walk the beach."

"Nick, it's going to rain soon," she laughed and lifted a hand at an approaching storm cloud. As if on cue, a strong wind plunged its fingers through her hair, much like he wanted to do, and warned of the storm to come.

"And suddenly you're afraid of the rain?"

"I don't want it soaking me through when I'll have to drive home in wet clothes, no."

"Fussy woman."

"Practical woman."

She was looking at him with an arched brow as if he'd grown a third head, though he admitted that given their most recent interactions, it seemed strange that he'd be so insistent. Still, she needed someone. Him. And didn't he deserve to assuage his own guilt, too? Nick looked up at the sky, raising a hand to shield his eyes from the bright sun. He knew her well, and if an easy excuse would get her out of something she didn't want to do, she'd latch onto it like a sucker-fish to a shark. He needed to make sure the weather was not that excuse.

"Doesn't look like it's going to rain until tonight. Come on. Say yes, Mia," he teased.

It was an old phrase he and Ewan used on her (often and successfully) any time she wasn't immediately on board with whatever crazy plan they'd cooked up. "Say yes, Mia," they'd crow until she finally gave in. Granted, they'd been young and dumb, hellbent on breaking the rules just for the sake of breaking them. Still, somehow getting Mia's endorsement made it more acceptable. When she didn't reply right away, he worried if using that phrase might backfire on him. If it made her sad instead of nostalgic, he could've just set back his efforts.

"Fine, yes," Mia relented, and Nick smiled to himself. It seemed the time spent building furniture on her porch was paying off. "But I need to change first. Meet me back here in about thirty minutes. And you're driving."

"Done. Be thinking about what you want to eat." He loaded up his arms with the packaging they'd collected and stopped by her trash can to dump it off. "And don't say you don't care."

He waved and started the short walk down the sidewalk that separated their houses.

"Hey, Nick!" Mia called, putting her hand to the side of her mouth. He turned to look at her. "I don't care what we eat."

He chuckled all the way home.

MIA WASN'T sure what to make of Nick or anything that was happening as she watched him walk away. She noted

—in an educational, non-personal sort of way, of course—
that his butt looked quite nice in those shorts. Not that it
mattered, but she wondered if he was seeing someone.
She hoped not. Platonic or not, outwardly she knew this
outing would look like a date, no matter what Nick said.
The last thing she wanted was to be on some other
woman's bad side—that's why she was so concerned with
his current relationship status, of course.

Giving it another moment of thought, she decided he
probably wasn't seeing anyone. No one had dropped by
that she'd noticed. At the bar, he wasn't with anyone as far
as she knew. Nor had he brought anyone up in any conversation. If he were seeing someone, she was sure he would
have mentioned them by now. Nick may be a lot of things,
but he wasn't a liar or a cheater. Flawed, irritating, arrogant, and evasive, sure, but he wasn't selfish or (his
behavior two years ago aside) intentionally cruel. Despite
that, she was curious enough about his motives and this
sudden desire for reconciliation that she was willing to
entertain his company for the time being.

Mia took her time showering and getting ready, not
because it was some important date (it wasn't), but
because she wanted to. And wasn't that reason enough?
She chose a simple black cotton dress with thin shoulder
straps that fell in loose waves from the deep neckline to
her toes. It was a suitable choice for a casual evening out
with a friend, or at least someone who used to be.

Thinking about the summer heat they'd be walking in
even with the breeze coming off the water, she opted to
skip most of her cosmetics, choosing only to smudge a

line of dark eyeliner along her lids and pull waterproof mascara through her lashes. She wove her damp hair into a loose French braid to keep it off her neck and out of her face, letting the thick braid drape over her shoulder. Looking at herself in the mirror, she chastised herself for going through even this much effort.

"You're overthinking all of this. It's only Nick you're seeing," she muttered.

When the doorbell rang, she padded barefoot down the hall and through the living room and opened the door.

"You look gorgeous, Mia," Nick said with a smile of appreciation. She'd always known he found her beautiful, platonically, of course, and she was pleased he still felt the same.

He stepped inside, wearing the same shoes but swapping out the worn cargo shorts for a pair of black denim ones. His shirt, a simple dark polo, stretched comfortably across his broad shoulders, shoulders that were well muscled. She remembered from their building exploits earlier.

"Thank you," she said. "Let me grab my sandals, and then we can go."

"No rush."

He turned slightly to shut the door behind him, presumably to keep the hot air out and the cold in. Mia slid her feet into her shoes beside him. Then something strange happened between them. A meeting of moments in time converged so effortlessly.

Mia looked up and stepped forward at the moment

Nick swung the door closed and turned to face her. Suddenly, they were but a breath apart, so close that their lips nearly touched. His eyes heated and bore into hers. Their breathing quickened in unison, and her gaze darted to his lips. He didn't miss the movement, nor did she miss his swift intake of breath. The air crackled with electricity.

Mia took a hurried step back, and Nick fumbled for the door handle he'd only just let go of. He pulled it open and hurried to the car, putting much needed distance between them. Mia waited until he was a few feet ahead of her before following him through the door. She deliberately stayed several paces behind as they marched to the car.

Nick cleared his throat a few times before opening the car door for Mia. He skirted the car quickly to take his seat on the driver's side. By the time they'd both settled into the drive, they'd each convinced themselves the electric moment was nothing more than proximity. Opting for simplicity, they agreed to stop at a small food truck and grabbed an order of street tacos before continuing down to the beach. The breeze off the ocean was strong, but the approaching storm made it cooler than normal. Mia felt flushed all over and was grateful for it.

"Ida said she enjoyed her visit with you," Nick said. He took a bite of his taco.

"She's a doll," Mia said. It was as safe a topic as any. She chewed her food thoughtfully and swallowed. "I can't believe she's lived there since the roads were dirt."

"It's crazy, right? I don't think I've stayed anywhere more than one or two years since I was twenty."

"You always rented locally, though, so that's kind of staying in place. At least until…" Her voice trailed off, and they both knew what she was avoiding. She didn't want to mention his desertion. It was the only time he'd been away from their small town in any meaningful way.

"We always rented, too," Mia said to break the tense silence. She cleared her throat gently. "Did you buy that house you're in now?"

Nick swallowed the last bite of his food and balled up the wrappings. Without thinking, Mia handed him hers, an old habit she overlooked, but he did not. He tossed them both into a nearby trash can. "No, I wasn't sure if I was back for good."

"Are you?"

He looked at her out of the corner of his eye. "I am now."

"Hmm. It makes sense to figure that out first, I suppose. I wasn't sure I'd want to stay or put down roots, but I'm finding I really love the idea of making a space my own. I never have to check the lease or ask a landlord to approve paint colors," she said with a little laugh.

She bent down to remove sandals that had filled with soft dry sand and hooked her fingers through the straps to carry them. She relaxed into the conversation, watching him in her periphery. His posture was casual enough, but she could tell from the tightness in his jaw that his thoughts were less relaxed.

"Have you decided to paint, then?" Nick asked.

"I'm thinking of doing the living room walls green and stripping this horrid rose wallpaper that's in the bathroom at some point. No offense to the previous owners, of course. But I've been a little distracted by the shop."

"Shop? Your shop?" he asked, looking at her with brows raised.

"Yup. The one right off the square by the antique shop," she said almost reluctantly, already regretting letting it slip out. She didn't know if she was ready to share this part of her journey yet. What if she hated it? What if she failed?

"Congratulations, Mia. That's…" He cleared his throat and brought the pitch of his voice back down to a reasonable level. "That's really great. I'll have to bring you muffins or something from the bakery one morning to celebrate. Have you been there yet?"

"No, and we're celebrating something right now, remember? You don't have to keep coming up with reasons to smooth my feathers, Nick." She wasn't sure what she wanted him to do instead, but the long stoked anger within her was cooling.

"Consider it my penance, then," he joked. He shoved his hands in his pockets and then immediately pulled them out again, slapping them mindlessly at his sides. The gesture was so awkward it was endearing.

She sighed. "Against the advice of my baser instincts, I think I've already decided to forgive you. Even without your muffin tithe."

"Why?" he asked. He turned to her, and surprise slowed his gait. A little line formed between his brows, and he cocked his head to the side.

She took a deep breath and stopped walking. She

turned and met his gaze. This was important to say to his face.

"Because you helped me make an old front porch like home. For no reason other than to be nice to me. Because maybe you're not the villain I've made you out to be in my mind. Because maybe I was too hard on a boy who'd lost someone, too. I guess I thought it was easier to be mad at you than to be sad. I'm better at mad than sad," she said and began walking again.

"Yes, you are," he agreed, matching her pace, and she shoved him for it with a laugh.

Her hand lingered on the crook of his arm, and he covered it with his own and smiled at her. Call it a moment of weakness, but she desperately wanted to lean into him and rest her head against his shoulder, to feel comforted by a friend who understood what it was to lose someone. Despite that, or perhaps because of it, Mia pulled her arm from his and drew back into herself. Nick eyed her for a moment, but he said nothing.

They walked together in silence, the whooshing waves and the rough sound of their heels digging into the sand a soundtrack to their thoughts. Mia wondered if he came here often with other women. While she certainly wasn't thinking romantic thoughts, she would be blind and delusional if she didn't admit that Nick was a virile, attractive man, and this scene set the stage for some serious romance.

"Do you believe in ghosts?" Mia asked abruptly.

"Of course, I do. Why?"

"What do you mean, of course you do?"

"I write about things that go bump in the night for a

living. Of course, I'm a sucker for a ghost story. Isn't that a given?" he said.

"Maybe, but that's beside the point."

"What is the point?" he asked, turning to her with amused curiosity.

"I don't know," she said, her voice somewhere between misery and mild frustration.

"What's the matter, Mia? Seen a ghost lately?"

"Yes," she admitted. It was the first time she'd told anyone outside of Alexis, and she wasn't sure why she'd shared it with Nick.

He stopped walking and looked at her hard. "You're serious," he said, baffled, and Mia nodded. "Really? When? What happened?"

So Mia told him of the little dead boy she saw again and again. She told him of the first one and the last, of seeing the little boy cry, hearing his name for the first time, and seeing him standing in front of her when she awoke.

"Interesting," he said at last.

"Not for me, it isn't. It's quite terrifying, actually. If Ewan were alive, he'd probably laugh it off and tell me I'm being dramatic, which I can be. In fact, he—"

Mia stopped herself and glanced at Nick. Their truce seemed so tenuous, and she wasn't sure where any of the boundaries were anymore. Was he at the point where she could casually bring up his dead friend in conversation? Was she even there? He felt like the same person she'd known forever, and yet somehow things were completely different between them.

His eyes went soft, and he said quietly, "It's okay, Mia. I miss him, too."

Nick watched her nod and blink back tears. They took a few more steps together, and he grasped her hand in his. He rubbed his thumb back and forth, a comforting gesture, but she felt more than comfort. There was a heat between them, and it terrified her.

11

It was a long, albeit productive, day at the bookshop, but it was all worth it to bring this new chapter to life. Unfortunately, more than just the long hours caused Mia's exhaustion. Every night that week, David had visited. Sometimes in her dreams, yes, but he'd also taken to standing at the foot of her bed, his tear-streaked face barely visible above the edge. His small size did nothing to diminish the terror of waking in the middle of the night to the stares of something not alive.

Some nights, she doubted her sanity, and more than once, Mia considered giving the local psychiatrist a call. Though it was almost too humiliating to admit out loud. Like something out of an old horror film. The whole "I see dead people" kind of thing, and wasn't that so tired and overdone?!

Taking matters into her own hands as she drove home, Mia stopped off at a new age store just a few blocks from her shop. The place nestled into the end of a dark hallway in the back of a brick building. She assumed it to be one of those repurposed old factories, probably an old paper mill now partitioned off into individual offices and stores. Inside, she perused the stacks of books and diligently read the signs on every table. There had to be something here that would help. It certainly couldn't hurt.

She gathered black candles to ward off negativity and bundles of herbs with labels tied on that promised to cleanse evil when burned. She chose crystals like amethyst for serenity and black tourmaline for protection. Mia wasn't sure exactly what any of this was supposed to do or if it would even work, but it seemed as good a bet as a ghost hunter or a priest.

A couple, a man and a woman who looked far more normal than she expected, checked her out. They made small talk with her, sharing facts about her choices. To her relief, they didn't ask any prying questions and wished her well as they handed her everything all wrapped up and packaged into a neat brown paper bag.

Once home, she emptied the contents of the bag onto her bed. The candles and crystals she placed around her home, though she concentrated most of them in her bedroom. She lit the smudge stick, blew out the flame, and walked through the house as instructed. She moved so that the smoke filled every corner and visualized it banishing negative energy from each room. Satisfied she'd done her amateur best, Mia went back to her bedroom and settled into bed with her evening book. She wasn't sure how confident she was that any of it would make a difference, but she was desperate enough for sleep to be hopeful. The night wore on, and she snuggled deeper into her bed, letting her mind slip into the story as her eyes moved across the page.

The summer sun finally set, and the songs of crickets and frogs and cicadas filled the night air. Occasionally, she heard the sounds of a car driving down the street or a dog barking. It wasn't long before her vision blurred and her eyes became heavy. She wanted to pull the chain on the bedside lamp and submerge the room into blessed darkness, but the last thing she wanted if she had another nightmare was to wake up in pitch black. With the lamplight glowing, Mia marked her page, set the closed book next to her on the bed, and let herself drift into sleep. At first, she didn't dream at all. Or rather, it was a dream that wasn't yet a dream.

She floated weightless in the darkness for what seemed like hours. She likened herself to Alice falling down the rabbit hole, though unlike Alice there were no cupboards or bookshelves to keep her company. Only miles and miles of nothingness all around her. She closed her eyes against it and drifted.

The cold, hard surface touched her feet before she saw it, and when she opened her eyes, the drifting feeling was fading. The weight returning to her body made her feel overly heavy and sluggish, like weights were tied to every joint on her body. Instead of darkness, she stood on an icy tile floor facing a bright room too hazy to make out clearly. Arched doorways surrounded her, and through them she could make out tall windows that sunlight shone through, furniture, and the toys and trinkets that filled a typical family's home.

No matter how hard she squinted or where she looked, though, nothing came into focus. From somewhere nearby, she heard a child throwing a tantrum and a frazzled mother muttering. A shadow brushed past her, and the smell of rose perfume and baby powder filled her nostrils. Mia turned in place, searching for anything familiar. The rose scented shadow brushed past her again, only this time it whispered, "Kill it. Kill it. Kill it."

Behind her, another voice screamed. Mia jerked around to follow the sound into another room, and the hazy white film around her vision turned sharp and black as if a curtain suddenly surrounded her. The smell of death, heavy and acrid, burned the inside of her nose and throat as she inhaled. It turned her stomach upside down and made her gag.

On the floor before her, a woman was lying on her back, surrounded by moss and a foul-smelling mud. The woman thrashed wildly against something, her hands clawing at her neck, the heels of her feet kicking the ground over and over again. Mia could hear harsh choking sounds, smell the rot and the roses and the baby powder. The woman's bloodshot eyes bulged as her body twisted beneath whatever weight held her down, and then she went slack. Mia inched closer to the woman, the cold mud squishing between her bare toes. The woman on the ground was pale, her eyes closed, lips blue. She wore a plain shirt and pants, and one sock was missing. From behind her, Mia heard the cries that had become a kind of morbid lullaby. Out of the corner of her eye, she saw David standing with his blanket. He stared at her with tears running down his cheeks, but she couldn't tear her eyes away from the woman.

Then the woman's eyes opened, and her head twisted sharply. Her eyes bored into Mia's, flooding her with feelings of despair and rage and sadness. It filled her to bursting and then rushed out of her, leaving her hollow and empty.

"Find my words," the woman croaked, her last word stretching out into an otherworldly groan. Her mouth opened impossibly wide, the teeth inside caked in brown and black sludge. Black ooze rolled out of the corner of her lips, and the croaking sound grew until it was deafening. Mia covered her ears and fell to the ground, burying her head in her knees and rocking as she prayed for morning.

~

When Mia woke, it was daylight, and the echoes of her dream played like reruns in her head.

"So much for you," she said bitterly to the candles and crystals scattered around her.

The room still smelled of sage and rosemary and pine, so she briskly stripped the linens from the bed and threw them into the washing machine with at least double the amount of detergent and a good dash of fabric softener. The last thing she wanted to smell was the thing she blamed for the worst nightmare yet.

In the bathroom, Mia took time to shower, ready herself for the day, and consider the most recent dream. They had to mean something. They had to be telling her something, anything. She was just missing it. Why else would the dreams come so often or change so dramatically if not to impart some piece of information? Was she meant to learn the truth of what happened to these people? Was she supposed to know where to look next?

As silly as it seemed, Mia thought back to all the ghost movies and books she'd ever seen and read. When the ghosts were at the door, what did the main characters always do? *Find my words*, the woman said. Based on her limited personal experience and the vivid imaginations of Hollywood, she considered that a clue. Next, she thought back on all the dreams she'd had so far—it would have been so smart to have kept a journal of this, but it was too late now—and tried to pull out any other clues.

Obviously, there was a crying little boy, and his name was David. There were other adults in the most recent dreams. It was probably safe to assume they were his mother and father. She supposed it was just as possible they were other close relatives, but Occam's Razor and all that. She was going to call them his parents. He always wore the same pajamas and carried the same blanket. Had he died in those? Did ghosts always look in death as they had passed away in life? Hollywood said yes, and it made sense. She didn't have any evidence to say otherwise. Why would a ghost change clothes? Especially a child ghost who probably couldn't dress himself in real life.

Wait. Didn't Sarah mention something about Brad's son, David, wearing similar pajamas? Mia frowned and pulled on a pair of sweatpants. Was that a coincidence? Maybe it was a clue she was meant to follow. The timing of trends in toddler sleepwear must ebb and flow with other fashion trends. Perhaps it could point to when he died.

It's not like she had any other leads or even an idea of where to start. Likely, all of this was simply a tragic news story, melding with bits and pieces of local gossip in her mind. Or maybe Brad's David and the little ghost boy had the same pajamas. Thinking about the small size of the baby section in her local store, it wasn't so outside the realm of possibility. The fact was, she knew little about Brad's life. He was married once before Sarah—she'd gone to their wedding but couldn't remember his first wife's name—and she remembered that they'd had a baby, but he'd drifted to the periphery of their circle of friends after that.

Mia moved to her bed and smoothed the comforter down. Her mind was stuck on the possibility that her ghost and Brad's son were the same. She couldn't explain it, but her mind wouldn't let it go. To pad her back, she stacked pillows against the headboard and then wiggled into a sitting position on the bed. She drew her legs up and pulled her computer onto her lap. Pushing it open, she started with a basic internet search for "dead boy" that unsurprisingly yielded nothing, so she switched tactics and pulled up the local newspaper's website.

"David" and "child death" turned up too many search results to sift through, which seemed unfortunate and unbearably sad if she thought about it. Next, Mia entered "Brad Williams" into the search box. There was an article highlighting his efforts on the historic restoration, a few unrelated articles about what she assumed was someone else with the same name, and then she hit on something...

An older article about the death of a toddler and his mother.

Her stomach sank, and she leaned closer to the screen. She read about an apparent murder-suicide where a mother had smothered her son and hanged herself. The father, identified as Bradley Williams of St. John's, Georgia, was reported to have discovered the bodies after returning home late from work. A photo at the end of the article showed Brad leaving the home, police tape already strung across the front lawn. Local officers escorted him from the property, clutching a worn blanket Mia instantly recognized from her dreams. She sat back from her computer and took a shaky breath. This was David. She was sure of it. There were too many coincidences. But what was she to do now? She had some answers, but there were still so many questions, including why she was seeing their ghosts.

Glancing at the clock, she put a pause in the day's research. As much as solving ghost mysteries appealed to her, especially as those ghosts were currently disrupting her sleep. Every night. She had a new business to get off the ground. The mystery would simply have to wait.

12

Getting out the door took longer than she expected, and Mia barely made it to the shop in time to sign for the mountain of deliveries arriving on her doorstep. Turning her thoughts from the morning to the task at hand, she parked her car across from the shop as had become her habit and ran across the busy street. Waving her hands like a lunatic (albeit an excited one), she hailed the delivery truck driver. With a sigh of impatience, he hopped down from his truck and presented her with a thick tablet. She signed on the tiny screen. He punched a few buttons across the tablet, and it beeped loudly. With that, he tossed the device back onto his seat and unloaded boxes from the back of the truck.

When they were stacked on the sidewalk, Mia watched the truck pull away and spent the next twenty minutes using a rickety dolly to wheel the heavy boxes inside, cursing colorfully each time the wheels stuck on the threshold. Who knew that owning a bookshop would be so good for her upper body strength? After at least four trips, Mia could finally unpack the treasure trove of books inside. She leaned down and carefully sliced into each box with a box cutter. The smell of new books wafted up with every box she opened. Butterflies danced in her stomach as she arranged the books into piles on a long folding table set up as a temporary sorting area. She pulled out a pad of sticky notes and labeled each pile with its respective genre, watching with barely contained glee as the piles grew larger.

After she sorted the books and littered her floor with empty shipping boxes and reams of thick brown packing paper, Mia turned her attention to the shelves she had assembled in the days prior. A framed rectangle adorned the top of each shelf, waiting for their cream-colored cards to be filled out. It would be an easy way to display the genre of books on the shelves below with a handmade touch. What made these shelves special, though, was that a different fantastical character accented each framed rectangle. Small and delicate and carved right into the wood. There were wyverns and faeries, gnomes and barbarians, aliens and wizards. It lent a touch of whimsy and charm to the space and echoed the tone she wanted to set for the entire shop.

Grabbing her sticky note pad again, Mia set about labeling each shelf with the genre it would hold. Later, she'd spend the time handwriting on each card with care, but for now this would do. Wading through packing paper, Mia decided she'd better clear out some floor space before attempting to walk across it with armloads of books. Dutifully, she broke down all but one cardboard box and bundled the packing paper into it. This she set aside and turned her attention to the beautiful piles of books.

Picking up a handful, she thought to herself that there were few things that topped how amazing she felt right now. She was moving closer toward realizing a life so wonderful she'd never even dared dream it up, chipping away at her list of personal goals, and slowly but surely uncovering the bold, fearless woman she'd once been. It surprised her to realize she was happy. For the first time in far too long, she was truly happy.

"*Now, isn't that something?*" she thought.

"Isn't *what* something?" a voice from behind her said.

Her eyes widened when Nick step inside the shop. He looked like he was walking right out of a magazine and through her door with sunlight kissing the high points of his face and body. He had high cheekbones and a strong jaw washed with days of stubble. Against his dark eyes and strong brows, it added a dash of danger. Realizing the direction of her thoughts, Mia scoffed at herself. There was no reason she should dwell on Nick's appearance.

"Oh, nothing. I didn't realize I said anything out loud." Gesturing to the sack he carried, she asked, "What's that you've got?"

"Penance," he said. He handed over a large brown paper bag. The bottom was warm in her hands, and the sweet scent of the blueberry muffins inside wafted out from the top.

"Ahh," she said, remembering their conversation. "They smell heavenly. Thank you."

"There's more outside. Take a break and come look at

your presents." He stepped outside and held the door as Mia followed. He gripped her shoulders gently and turned her around so she could see that positioned on either side of her door were large flower pots, each overflowing with a dazzling assortment of flowers and trailing vines.

"They're beautiful, Nick. You didn't have to do this."

"A handful of flowers seemed a pretty pitiful apology, all things considered, so I upgraded it a little." He moved to sit on the wood and wrought-iron bench in front of the shop window and gestured for her to join him. "Come sit. I'll bet you haven't been off your feet all day."

She was fine, but she sat all the same, even if it was with the sass of a petulant child. "It's still early."

"It's after one," he argued.

"Already? The morning must have gotten away from me."

"And half the afternoon, too. When are you planning to open?"

"I haven't set a firm date, but I'm thinking about next month. That gives me a few weeks to get things set up, do some local marketing, maybe get an exorcism," she said.

"What?" he laughed.

"Nothing," she said with a wave of her head.

"No, really, what?"

As much as she didn't want to say anything to anyone, she was at a loss there. It wasn't like she could drive over to Brad's house and pepper him with questions. Reluctantly, she filled Nick in on what she'd learned.

"Those are some pretty big coincidences," he said.

"I know," Mia said. "But now I don't know what to do

about it. If I'm seeing the same David who died in real life, our friend's kid, what does that mean?"

"I don't know."

"I'm sorry to interrupt, but I couldn't help but over-hear. Are you talking about the Williams boy?" Nick and Mia turned to see an older man standing not three feet away from them. He wore a plaid flat cap over thinning white hair, a button-up shirt, suspenders, and khaki dress pants. He slouched, as if his body had started to bend from the weight of a lifetime of memories, and he shuffled when he walked toward them. Mia hesitated, but she nodded.

"Such a shame what happened to that boy," the man said and shook his head sadly.

"David?" Mia asked.

"And his daddy. I've known Bradley all his life—used to come in with his grandma every Sunday after church. I'd sneak him lollipops, cigarettes when he was older. No parent should have to bury his baby," he said.

Mia nodded. She, of all people, knew what it was like to bury a loved one, but even she couldn't imagine having to bury your own child.

"What happened to the mother?" Nick asked.

"Emily? News said it was a suicide, though I can't say I remember the how of it," the man said.

"Did they ever say why she did it?" Mia asked.

"If they did, I never heard," the man said. "Come to think of it, there was a sister, of the mother, who went off the rails during an interview once. She insisted her sister was innocent and didn't kill herself. Think she was arrested for drugs a few months later. Poor thing."

"Mmm," Mia murmured.

"Seems to be doing better nowadays, though. She has me picking up refinished furniture at that old horse ranch every couple of months."

Mia nodded. It seemed like the polite response, and she wasn't sure what else she should say. It felt odd to sit and gossip about a family's past and present tragedy. There was a pause, and the man abruptly pointed behind them.

"You the new owner here?" he asked.

"Yes, I am. I'm opening a bookstore." Mia worked to keep a confident tone in her voice, though she felt anything but. "I'm Mia, by the way."

The man tipped his head in approval and said, "Nice to meet you, Mia. I'm Alan. You stop by anytime you need a thing. I'll be looking forward to the grand opening." He turned at that and shuffled back inside the antique shop, and the door closed softly behind him, leaving Mia and Nick to exchange amused glances.

"Well, that was interesting," Nick said finally.

"Not exactly the conversation I thought I was coming outside to have," Mia agreed.

"Are you thinking about finding that sister?"

He stood up from the bench and stretched out a hand to her. Mia took it and ignored the zing as her fingers touched his. She allowed him to help her to her feet, but as soon as she was standing, she pulled her hand away and clasped them together in front of her. It all felt like being pulled in too many directions, and she wasn't ready to acknowledge the existence of these feelings, let alone what any of them meant. When she stepped back inside, she sent a prayer of thanks to whoever invented central air conditioning. The heat was already brutal despite it being June, and she expected it would only get worse as summer came into full swing.

"As crazy as it sounds, I think I have to," she said, pushing her feelings aside and focusing instead on her personal mystery.

"I don't think it sounds crazy. Up for a drive?"

"To the ranch? Now?"

"Why not?" he replied, tucking his hands in his pockets.

"Why would you want to go?" She eyed him skeptically. She suspected she was being a jerk, but she really couldn't help herself.

"I told you," he said, his eyes taking on that mischievous glint. "I'm a sucker for a good ghost story."

13

———————

They drove to the ranch where Rachel Lowell lived. Luckily, Nick remembered Emily's maiden name. Not that the ranch she lived on was hard to find without it—it was the only horse ranch within several hours of St. John's—but as they pulled into the dirt driveway, Mia still wondered if they were in the right place. The online listing for the ranch boasted it was an elegant southern bed-and-breakfast where one could enjoy "unforgettable ranch vacations in historic coastal Georgia," but there was nothing that seemed elegant or even enjoyable about it. The dirt road was wildly uneven, with overgrowth, debris, and potholes that shook the car. Long tree limbs hung from above and scraped the roof of the car as they drove beneath them.

No horses nor any other animal stood in any of the pastures she could see to the left or right. Overgrown fields flanked them, and the fences barely holding them at bay crumpled in dozens of places. The house itself sat at the end of a half mile lane and was just as neglected. Beautiful once to be sure, the roof of the house now sagged, shutters either missing or tenuously hanging on by sheer willpower, and the siding looked as if there was a gray filter over it all.

Nick parked the car and killed the ignition. He and Mia stepped out together. She could hear the sounds of rowdy chickens somewhere behind the house, and a bad tempered rooster crowed incessantly. The smell was a curious mix of greenery and forest clashing against a wall of animal feces and damp. As they walked toward the front door, a dog began barking inside, and a woman stepped out onto the porch.

"Y'all looking for someone?" the woman asked.

"I'm hoping to find Rachel Lowell?" Mia said.

"That's me. What can I do for you?" Rachel said.

"I'm sorry to bother you. I know this might sound out of the blue, but I was hoping I might ask you a few questions about your sister and nephew," Mia said.

Rachel dug into her pocket and pulled out a soft pack of cigarettes and a lighter. She plucked one out, clamped it between her lips, and spoke through the cigarette as she lit it. "Why would you want to do that?"

Mia thought about lying. She could probably pull off a fairly convincing excuse about being a writer or a reporter interested in Rachel's story. But in the end, lying didn't feel right. "I've been researching your sister's story, and I'd like to get more information on what happened, on what you think really happened. Could I have just a few moments of your time?"

"No," Rachel said. Without thought or consideration

or explanation. She dropped the cigarette at her feet, smashed it with the tip of her faded boot, and walked back inside. The sound of the screen door slapping closed behind her felt like a slap in the face, and Mia was stunned. She exchanged a look with Nick, and for several moments, they simply stood in place. She didn't even know what to do. What now?

With nothing left for them here, they made their way down the porch stairs and across the lawn, their pace unhurried. Mia dropped into the passenger seat, her whole body on autopilot as she processed what happened. Nick got in next to her and started the engine. Feelings of defeat and confusion must have shown on her face.

"Now what?" Nick asked, turned to look at her as he pressed down on the brake pedal and shifted the car into reverse.

"I don't know," Mia said. "I honestly didn't think she'd say no."

"Well, she doesn't exactly have a lot of reasons to talk to a couple of strangers, especially ones who probably sound like some aspiring private investigators researching a case for their next internet show," Nick said.

"You're right." Mia sighed.

Nick moved his foot from the brake pedal, and the car lurched backward. The sound of dirt and branches shifting and snapping under his tires reverberated up through the car.

Mia suddenly put a hand on his arm. "Wait."

She hadn't meant to touch him, not for more than a moment at least, but again, her fingers felt electric at the touch. Her breath caught, and she couldn't seem to break the connection. She felt his muscles flex beneath her hand. Nick looked at her intently, his brows drawn together, heat flashing in his eyes. She felt the warmth of a flush creeping up her cheeks and cleared her throat to redirect the thoughts that had suddenly turned anything but platonic. Nick put the car back in park, and Mia let her hand drop, trying to steady her racing pulse. She needed to focus.

"Just a moment," she said.

She opened the car door and hurried back up to the porch as if demons from hell were nipping at her heels. Mia took the stairs two at a time. She rang the doorbell, and for good measure, she knocked briskly on the door through the screen. The mesh scratched at her knuckles, and she rubbed at the smarting skin.

While she waited, she tried desperately not to think about the electricity and heat of the moment they'd just shared. Anything to steer her thoughts away from the completely inappropriate fluttering in her stomach. Of course, it was natural to feel that physical pull of attraction for someone who was admittedly very attractive. In fact, he was quite delicious to look at, and beyond that, he had a good heart... even if arrogance and poor judgment historically overshadowed it. Of course, it would be normal to feel that for someone like Nick. Normal, but unwelcome all the same. As sex-deprived as she was at the moment, intimacy simply wasn't in the cards. She wasn't willing to risk it ever becoming something more, especially with someone who had already proven he could run out the second life got complicated.

The opening door snapped Mia out of her thoughts. Rachel bit out a sharp command to the dog barking madly again on the other side, and she leaned into the crack between the door and the frame. She looked Mia up and down cautiously, but there was a curiosity this time, as well. "You still here?"

Change tactics, Mia ordered herself. "I see your sister in my dreams. I've watched her die. Maybe I'm crazy—I sound crazy to myself most days right now—but I've seen her. I see David, too. Almost every night. I can't explain why, but I need to know what really happened to them, and I think you're the only one who believes something else did."

Rachel eyed her, brows drawn together. Then she opened the door wider and asked, "You're not a psychic, are you?"

"No," Mia laughed. She pushed a hand nervously through her hair, wiping the other on the side of her pants. She glanced at Nick as he ambled up the stairs and stood beside her.

"Well, y'all come on out of this heat."

Rachel opened the door completely and spread her arms wide, inviting them inside. Mia pulled open the screen door and gestured for Nick to follow her. She surveyed the front room while they walked through it. The space, which once appeared to be a living room, was now filled with stacks of boxes, grocery bags of trash, piles of dirty clothes, and overflowing ashtrays. Rachel sat on a dark green club chair, and Mia set herself down on a dingy yellow sofa covered in a faded flower print. Years of wear and tear had thinned the sofa, and patches of thread were coming apart to reveal the padding beneath.

"Sorry for the mess. I spend most of my time in my workshop out back. Don't have much company or cause to tidy in here," Rachel said.

Her attitude toward the mess seemed to be somewhere between apathy and embarrassment, and Mia wasn't sure what to say to that. She erred on the side of caution and kept quiet, scooting over to make room for Nick to sit beside her.

"So what do you want to know?" Rachel asked. She reached out to pat the dog settled at her feet.

Mia shifted awkwardly and cleared her throat. "I'm hoping you'll tell me what you think happened to your nephew and your sister. And why?"

"Now, those are a couple of big questions," Rachel said. She lit another cigarette and blew out the smoke. "Emily was one of the sweetest things the good lord ever made. Momma used to say that she got all the sweet, and I got all the salt. The only thing she ever wanted to do was be a mom, a good mom. Not like what we had growing up. Then David was born, and she was amazing, like something out of a sitcom."

"Did something change?" Mia asked.

"Yeah, it did. After David, she was in and out of the hospital for postpartum something or other. She saw a shrink for a little while about it, too. She didn't talk much about it, but I know she was on and off meds for a while."

"That must have been hard on David and Brad," Nick put in.

"On David, sure," Rachel said and took another drag

on her cigarette. "Brad just got mean. Emily told me once that he thought she was just looking for attention."

"What did you think?" Mia asked.

"I believed her. Girl didn't have a lying bone in her body. She was sick, and that son of a bitch treated her like a whiny child." Rachel smashed the cigarette out in the pile of cigarette butts in the ashtray beside her. "Never did like Brad, but David was nothing like him. He was always such a sweet boy. Just like his momma. He didn't talk much, but he was still a little thing then. I don't think Emily was worried about it. Things seemed okay for a while—I didn't hear from Emily much—and then all of a sudden I started getting calls from her almost every day. First, they were about Brad being violent. She said he hit her or held her down or something or other. I tried to help, but I never did see a mark on her, and she wouldn't go to the police. She always said it was nothing, an argument that got out of hand or she lost her temper. Then the calls got worse. She started talking about hurting herself, hurting David. I told Brad he needed to take her somewhere."

"And did he?" Mia asked.

"Nope. Son of a bitch didn't do a goddamn thing. The next thing I know, I'm getting a call from Emily, and she's babbling like a lunatic. Says David can read her mind, that a demon possessed him, and she had to save him. The whole conversation was nuts, but I couldn't get her to calm down. I got in my truck and called Brad. I called him over and over and over, but he never answered." Rachel's voice cracked. She paused and wiped at tears that welled in her eyes, clearing her throat forcefully. "By the time I got to her house, the police were there. I guess you know the rest."

"I'm so sorry about your sister and David," Mia said. Rachel didn't respond, only shrugged a shoulder and propped her foot up on her knee. "The news reported that the police ruled it a murder-suicide, but you said on the news that you didn't believe that. Can you tell me why?"

"I went into the house after, and the story they told didn't add up. I saw the beam they said she used to hang herself, but there was no way she could've gotten up there. There wasn't a thing tall enough anywhere around, anywhere in that house, I suspect. So how would she have gotten up there to hang herself? When you've got a husband like Brad, it doesn't make sense."

"What do you mean, a husband like him?" Mia asked. She twisted her hands together in her lap, trying to remember a time Brad had acted violent.

"Emily was terrified of him," Rachel said.

Mia thought about what little she knew of postpartum depression and psychosis. Admittedly, it wasn't much, and she made a mental note to look it up later. "Could she have been hallucinating any of it? The abuse or anything that would make her hurt David?"

Rachel's tone sharpened with anger. "No! All Emily ever wanted to do was be a good mom, a regular Susie fucking homemaker. She would never hurt David. Never."

Mia and Nick exchanged looks. Mia wondered what could've caused Emily to make such a strange phone call. What had happened in the minutes before... or after? She thought about the dream and what Emily had told her to do. *Find my words.*

"Did she ever write any letters or keep a diary? Her doctor might have recommended it," Mia said, hopeful it would help her put even some pieces together.

Rachel rubbed her chin and said, "Yes, actually. She kept a journal. Some shrink recommended it a few months after David was born, a lot of good it did for her. Let me see if I can find it."

Rachel stood and left the room in no particular hurry, leaving Nick and Mia to stare awkwardly at anything but each other. It was a strange feeling to have shared such an intimate moment right before talking about murder and death with a near stranger. And that's all it was, Mia reminded herself, a tense moment between distant friends who were simply trying to get to know one another again. She heard Rachel's footsteps coming back, and then Rachel was dropping a book in her lap.find my work

"Here," she said simply.

"Oh," Mia said. "Thank you."

"You're welcome to take it. There's a locket in between those pages there." Rachel pointed to a chain threaded between the middle pages. "I'd like that back before you go."

"Thank you, Rachel. Truly."

"I can't say that it's my pleasure, but I don't see as how hanging onto that book is doing me any good around here. It feels off, if you know what I mean," she said. "Now, I don't mean to rush y'all out, but I've got some work to finish up out back."

"Of course," Mia said.

She desperately wanted to open the locket before they

left, but the clasp stuck, and it seemed rude to ask Rachel for anything else, including help opening it. So she handed it back to Rachel and followed Nick outside. Clutching the journal tightly in her hands, she wondered if this would tell her what actually happened to Emily and David or if it was simply another step on a tragic journey littered with more questions than answers.

14

———

The drive home began in silence, only this time it wasn't the comfortable silence of friends but the uncomfortable silence that falls in the wake of tragedy. Because whatever they had learned and whatever positives might come from that information, they were immersed in a real life horror story where at best a boy and his mother had been killed and at worst the mother herself had done it.

Mia sneaked a quick look at Nick and wondered what he thought about all of this. Was he as invested as she was? Did he feel as helpless as she did? Unlike the sister, she wasn't sure Emily hadn't killed her son. She wasn't an expert by any means, but she knew enough that it wasn't a surprising fact that moms could experience postpartum psychosis and do things they'd never typically do. But what about Emily's death? She'd watch Emily strangle to death. Was it some kind of metaphor? Had she really watched Emily hang herself? Mia mulled it over, trying to recall more details from her dream. She remembered watching Emily's body writhe and kick on the ground, her hands clawing at her throat. She wondered what if someone else had been in that room? What if someone else strangled Emily? But then what about David? How did it fit together?

"What will you do next?" Nick asked, snapping her out of her thoughts.

"I don't know. It's not like it's this cold case mystery waiting for a new lead. The case is closed. As far as the living are concerned, it's solved. But maybe they—the ghosts or whatever they are—want someone to know what really happened to them," Mia considered. "That's if you even believe they're real."

"You'd have to believe it to have come this far."

"I suppose."

"It's a shame what happened to her."

"Emily?" Mia asked, looking away from the fields and trees they passed and toward him.

"Yes, but I was thinking more of Rachel," Nick said. "How she ended up, how little resources there are for people like her. The world doesn't look kindly on addicts."

"How do you know she's an addict?"

"The man outside your shop mentioned it, and I got a glimpse of track marks on her arm," he said with a shrug. "She'll struggle, and maybe she'll get out of it alive, but it'd be a hell of a lot easier if people would stop treating addiction like a moral failure."

"I agree," she said slowly.

"You sound surprised," he said, taking his eyes off the road to glance at her.

"Maybe a little. I'm surprised you'd be so understanding. Most wouldn't." She looked back out her window as they drove, oblivious to the way his jaw tightened.

"The woman lost her baby nephew and all but walked in on her sister hanging. That's enough to send a lot of people over the edge. Why wouldn't I be understanding? You know me better than that."

Mia shrugged uncomfortably. "But I don't. Not really. Not anymore. I haven't seen you in two years, Nick. People change."

"People don't change that much."

He sounded so sure of himself it made her blood boil. Hadn't she watched him change? From friend to stranger and now she was supposed to believe he was suddenly the friend again?

"And sometimes they don't change at all," she said pointedly.

"I thought we moved past that." His voice was flat.

"Well, I guess I'm not as past it as I thought," she snapped.

Mia crossed her arms over her chest and angled her body away from him. Being surprised, remarking on it, and then stating a fact—that's all she'd done, and he had no right to criticize her for it, however passively. The fact of the matter was, he had been gone for two years, and people did change. People changed a lot in less time than that. How was she to know what had and hadn't changed? It wasn't as if he had a track record of making decisions that were always in line with a stellar character.

Taking a breath, she relented. That wasn't exactly a

fair judgment against him, but at the moment, she was too angry to care.

FOR THE REST of the drive, the air was as stiff as freshly starched sheets, and Nick could hardly wait to get out of the car. He was being volleyed from one side of the court to the other—from reluctantly reconnecting friends to resentful enemies—and he couldn't catch his breath. It was almost enough to make him throw in the towel and abandon whatever personal mission friending Mia again had become. He could pack his things and get out of this town once and for all. His hands tightened on the steering wheel, the knuckles going white, daring himself to consider it. He'd been fine without her in his life for over a year, two really. He could be fine again.

Except that he couldn't.

Now that he'd walked back into her life, he wasn't sure he could walk away so casually. Not that there had been anything casual about the way he'd left before, but this time things were different. She pulled at him in a way he couldn't quite describe. Just the thought of seeing her had his stomach in knots, and more than once he caught himself coming up with reasons to walk by her house. But this was still Ewan's wife, and while he couldn't bring himself to acknowledge what his growing attraction to her meant, he couldn't separate from her either. He didn't know how he felt about it... or what he was going to do.

He pulled into his driveway, killed the engine, and

turned in his seat to face her. "Do you mind if we get some fresh air? I'll walk you home from here."

Mia stiffened and hesitated. She didn't want his company, that was clear, and he couldn't blame her. He didn't want his own company either. Reluctantly, she nodded. He watched her slide out of the car and nearly slam the door behind her. He could all but feel the anger rolling off her in waves, but their moods were well matched. She'd all but directly accused him of being an uncaring bastard, the kind of man who stomped on those around him for sport. It was absurd, insulting even. Petty enough to want the high ground, he resisted the urge to slam the car door, too, and instead shut it softly with a pointed look at Mia. She rolled her eyes, crossed her arms, and walked around the car.

As she came toward him, a summer breeze whipped up her hair, and she casually flipped it out of her face. It was a thoughtless gesture he'd seen her do countless times, but this time his body tightened in response. His nostrils flared as the scent of her drifted on the breeze. Despite his anger, maybe because of it, all he wanted was to press her against the car and assault her with his hands and mouth. He imagined how her curves would feel beneath his hands, how she would feel as he ground against her, his lips hot at her throat. Hell, if he imagined it any more vividly, he'd soon have a conspicuous problem in his pants.

Nick turned away from her before the heat in his eyes gave him away. Mia was off limits. She was the wife of his boyhood friend, a man who'd been closer to him than any blood relative ever had. No matter how much he desired her—and wasn't that a strange thought—she could never know. To keep his hands busy and, more importantly, off of her, he shoved them into the pockets of his jeans, and they began walking together toward Mia's house. Their shoes scraped against the concrete of the sidewalk with each step, and Nick noticed how Mia adjusted her gait to avoid ending up on any cracks.

"Mia, I—" he said, stopping himself. There was so much he wanted to say, but he couldn't form the words.

"Nick, this was a mistake," she interrupted.

"What was a mistake?" he asked, his words clipped.

Mia groaned and pushed at her hair, turning to walk up her driveway. "All of this. You being here. Whatever this redemption attempt is. I just—" She paused with a breathy sigh. She turned her body toward him, lips pinched together, and inhaled deeply through her nose. How could she explain the vast pit of emotions pulsing through her? How could she make him see how twisted up she was? "I can't do this. I have all these questions and all this confusion and so much rage built up, and I've got nowhere to put it. I'm... I'm so mad at you."

"You know, Mia, you're not the only one who was ripped in two when he died."

"Yes, but I'm the only one who didn't tuck tail and run."

"And there it is!" He threw his hands in the air and announced it with a humorless smile. "What did you expect from me? I couldn't be what you needed."

"And that justifies it?" she yelled. Throwing her hands out, she paced away from him and back again.

"Maybe," he said. He shoved a hand through his hair

and looked up to the sky, pulling down on his neck. He put little stock in religion, be he imagined if he did he'd be praying for patience right about now.

"Fuck you," Mia said and stalked up the porch stairs.

Trotting behind her, Nick reached out and grabbed her elbow. He spun her to face him, his chest heaving and his eye flashing with anger. "That's the second time you've said that to me. I'm getting pretty sick of it."

"Then maybe you should start listening to it," she yelled, yanking her arm free of his grip. "You can't just waltz back into my life like this with your pretty words and big apologies and then make me feel..."

Her mouth worked, but no sound came out. She looked so sad. Angry, of course, but unbearably sad, and he of all people knew that look well. He wanted to reach for her in comfort as much as shake her out of frustration, so he shoved his hands into his pockets. It seemed to be his new default around this woman.

When he finally spoke, his voice was low and quiet. "Are you mad that *I'm* here or that *he's* still gone?"

"That's not fair," Mia said, her throat tightening with grief. Her chest rose as she took a steadying breath and fought back the tears that welled in her eyes, turning them into dark orbs of molten glass.

"When Ewan died, I thought I was dying, too, but he was gone. And you were just..." his voice cracked and trailed off. "I didn't..." he said, stopping again. He cleared his throat and stepped closer to her on the porch. Thunder rolled to accompany the roaring in his ears like the bass in a symphony, the metallic ting of raindrops on the roof overhead the lone triangle player. "I didn't know what to do. For me. For you. I couldn't be around anyone, and then it just got easier not to. If I wasn't with anyone who'd known him, I didn't have to feel so.... helpless."

She seemed so small in that moment, looking up at him from under damp lashes. "You were my friend, too. And then he died, and you left. Like I didn't even matter."

"You mattered," he said, looking her straight in the eye. Then his face changed, and his brows drew together as if discovering something new for the very first time. He said in quiet surprise, "You matter."

Then something shifted in him, like a heavy iron gear rotating and locking into place. The feeling shook him to the core. This woman—this intelligent, beautiful, lost woman before him—was suddenly standing where a friend (and a reluctant one at that) had been only moments before. It was gravity, this pull, and it was stronger than the voice that told him he was betraying his best friend, stronger than his better judgment, stronger than even the gravity holding his feet in place.

Helpless to it, Nick inched closer, cupped her face with his hands, and got to work showing her exactly how much she mattered.

15

———

Mia's eyes widened in disbelief, and a flash of anger speared through her, even as her stomach knotted with desire. He stepped closer to her, so close she could almost hear his heart pounding, and her body clenched mutinously in anticipation. His hands moved to either side of her throat, thumbs pressing in on her jaw, and his mouth descended. She gasped when his lips met hers, a boom of thunder masking the sound, and the long line of his body pressed her into the door. Compared to the heat of him, the door at her back was like ice. Instinctively, her lips parted for his, and his tongue dipped into her mouth, tangling with hers in an erotic dance. He changed the angle of the kiss, his movements jerky and desperate, and she drew in a sharp breath. His hands skimmed down her body and gripped her hips. She moaned and pressed herself against him, her hands skimming up and under his shirt as their mouths mated.

The feel of his hot skin beneath her fingers was as exciting as it was dangerous, and she helplessly reveled in the feel of him against her. All the tiny moments of electricity, all the tension, all the sparks she'd been feeling coalesced into this one moment like a lightning strike. The force of it paralyzed even her thoughts. He nipped at her bottom lip with his teeth, his mouth moving along her jaw and down to her neck.

A crack of thunder and a flash of lightning startled her, and Mia tried to blink away the fog. "We can't do this," she said. Her system raged, the heat building at the center of her. But this was Nick, her friend, her husband's best friend. How could she be so impulsive, so stupid? Drawing in a shaky breath, she put a hand on his chest and pushed him away.

His breathing was ragged, and he blinked like a man stepping out of a cave and into the sun for the first time. He rubbed his hands over his face. "I'm sorry."

"You have to go," she said, crossing her arms over her chest.

He stared at her for a moment, his face an indecipherable mask, and then nodded. He turned on his heel and stomped down the porch stairs without another word. Mia watched him walk through the torrential rain until he disappeared into his house. She rubbed her hands up and down her arms, brushing away the wisps of wet that blew in from the storm. Standing alone on her porch, she touched a finger to her lips and wondered why she wanted to cry. She looked up as the sky turned dark, and the thunder and the lightning and the rain continued. It seemed the sky was crying for her. By the time she turned to slip inside, her shirt and hair were damp. Padding across her bedroom floor, Mia pulled a dry shirt from her dresser, dropping the damp one on the floor where she stood. She suspected it would be another restless night.

But tonight it wouldn't be ghosts haunting her dreams.

MIA WAS STILL FROWNING over Nick's behavior when she shelved books in her shop the next day. More boxes of books, decor, supplies, and signage were arriving every day, and the bookshop was slowly becoming the whimsical reading getaway she envisioned.

He wanted her, there was no doubt about it, and she wasn't exactly fighting him off either. But the fact remained that she was unavailable by choice, a widower who would never marry again, and there were simply too many memories (good and bad) with Nick to change that decision. More than that, she was finally taking steps to get her life back, to move forward after so long trudging in place. She wasn't about to let an ill-advised affair derail all the progress she was making. She didn't want to go back to being that person.

As much as she wanted to *want* to be left alone, her heart and body were of a different opinion. She couldn't stop thinking about the way his hands felt on her or how his skin had been hard and hot under hers. And his mouth, oh god, his mouth. There was no doubt in her mind just what he could do to her with his mouth if he set his mind to it.

Mia tried to convince herself it was because she was in

a dry spell—becoming a widow in your late twenties did that to you—but the excuse fell flat. She hadn't dated at all since Ewan's death, another of her failings according to society's standards. It was that she wasn't interested in men, or women for that matter, but relationships always ended in heartache, one way or another, and she had enough of that to last her a lifetime. Still, the thought of a wild tumble and that delicious release wasn't unappealing.

Fanning her face with a thin paperback in her hands, she reminded herself that she was supposed to be getting ready for the bookshop's opening, not indulging in sexual fantasies about her dead husband's best friend.

Mia bent to cut open another box of books and heard the bell attached to the door ring cheerfully behind her. She glanced over and saw Sarah step in. She wore cherry red lipstick on lips stretched into a brilliant smile, and her arms were overflowing with a large package wrapped in gold wrapping paper.

"Knock knock!" Sarah said.

"What are you doing here?" Mia asked. She wasn't expecting anyone, but that wasn't an excuse to be inhospitable, and at the moment she'd do just about anything to stop thinking about you-know-who.

Sarah set the package on the folding table next to her and said, "I thought I'd drop by and bring you a little business housewarming gift. The book club girls and I were just so excited to hear you're opening up this little bookstore. You know, it used to be a hair salon, but it went out of business about a year ago. By the way, we're hoping to have our book club meetings here if you're looking to do events like that. Wouldn't that be fun?"

Mia nodded and moved to the table where the wrapped package sat. She tried to keep up with Sarah, but listening to her was like getting hit by a southern steam roller, though far more entertaining. It was hard not to be completely charmed by a woman so sweet she likely ushered the flies out instead of swatting them.

"Here now. You open your present," Sarah said, pushing the box toward her.

Mia carefully pulled apart the wrapping paper and set it in a neat pile next to the box. Inside was a modern tea set with a tall tea pot, sturdy dark teal teacups, and a metal stand. Mia fingered the raised vines and leaves that wound up the handle of the cups. "They're beautiful! Thank you."

"I'm so glad you like it! I thought you'd like feminine but not fussy," Sarah said.

"I do. It's perfect. Thank you again. That was very kind of you."

Sarah clapped her hands together. "You're so welcome, darlin'. Now why don't we give that thing a test run, and you can tell me when you started seeing Nick Robinson?" She raised her brows and gave Mia a meaningful look.

"I am not seeing Nick," Mia said with a laugh. She turned and busied herself with the tea, taking it over to the bar along one wall and plugging it in.

"I heard differently. In fact, I heard that not only did you two hit the beach for dinner and a romantic walk, but you were spotted getting kissed senseless on your front porch last night."

"And who told you that?" Mia asked, handing Sarah a mug and leading her to the newly arranged seating area.

"I keep my sources confidential, but I don't hear you denying it," Sarah teased.

"I'm not seeing him like that. He's helped me get settled into the new house, and we're working on a research project together. That's all. The kiss was... a misunderstanding."

"Now that's too bad. Weren't you all pretty close back in the day?" Sarah asked, and Mia remembered that while Brad had run with their pack, Sarah hadn't entered the picture until much later.

"Thick as thieves. We all were. Brad was there, too, especially when there was a spot of trouble to get into, if I remember correctly."

Sarah smiled at the mention of her husband. "Well, I don't remember much of all that. He's pretty buttoned up nowadays. And you're changing the subject. We're supposed to be talking about you and Mr. Smoochy cozying up."

"There is no cozying up going on... now or in the future."

"That's what they all say, honey." Sarah sighed and threw up her hands. "Fine, if you won't give up the goods, at least spill the beans on this project you're working on. I'm shamelessly nosy, and I want to hear all about it."

Mia considered keeping the entire thing a secret—one of the parties involved was Sarah's husband and Mia still didn't know how he fit into all of this—but limited the details she shared instead. "We're looking into the deaths of Brad's son, David, and Emily. Just trying to wrap my head around what happened and maybe understand why."

"Brad's David? Are you two writing a book or something?" Sarah asked.

Mia nodded, hoping she could be assumed to be nodding to the former question without expressly lying about the latter. "It happened right around the time Ewan died, so I'm fuzzy on the details."

"Oh, of course you would be," Sarah said, patting her softly on the thigh. "I expect the whole world stops spinning when something like that happens. Although, I'm not sure if I know of anything that would help. Brad doesn't talk about it much at all. In fact, it's almost like they never even existed. I can't imagine how hard it's got to be to go through that. I'd probably lock it away in my head, too."

"He doesn't talk about it at all?"

Sarah shook her head. "Never. He gets mad if I bring it up, too, so I try not to. It's just too painful for him."

Mia found it strange that a parent and widower wouldn't eventually want to talk about his wife or son at all. Didn't parents often turn their kids' bedrooms into little shrines? Not that she knew whether that was normal or even common, but why wouldn't you want to keep their memory alive and with you? Unless Brad knew more than he let on. Or maybe he was more involved than he let on.

"Yes, it must be hard to go through that," Mia agreed. "Rachel, her sister, gave me her old journal to look through. Maybe I'll find some answers there. Do you think Brad would want it when I'm done? I got the impression that Rachel doesn't want it back, and it just feels wrong keeping it."

"I don't think he would, but I can check and let you know if he does. Otherwise, I think there's an estranged mother on the mom's side who might want it."

"Thanks, Sarah. Now, tell me more about this book club," Mia said, ready to change the subject. She successfully redirected the conversation from dating and David to the book club and began planning the first official meeting. She and Sarah agreed to hold it on the first Tuesday of the month, meaning their very first meeting would be in just three weeks, exactly three days after her grand opening. It seemed her plans for the bookshop were falling into place nicely.

Now, if only the rest of her life would do the same.

16

Mia groaned in her bed and tossed for the hundredth time. No matter how long she closed her eyes or what position she lay in, she couldn't fall asleep. Her mind churned with thoughts of David and of a mother who felt she had no choice but to do the unimaginable. What must be happening inside a mother's head to make that feel like the next logical choice? What could drive a mother to smother her own child? She turned over yet again, glaring at her nightstand as if it was single-handedly responsible for her insomnia. Despite the darkness, she could still see the outline of Emily's journal. She had yet to open it, but she wondered what secrets it held. Perhaps it was time to unveil them.

Mia pushed herself up on her elbow and leaned over to the nightstand. She pulled the bedside lamp's short chain, and the room filled with its soft glowing light. She grabbed the small journal, taking a moment to admire the worn turquoise leather and the tarnished brass clasp, and flipped it open. The handwriting was loose and feminine, and there was care in the spacing and words chosen. The dates appeared on the top right corner of each passage, sometimes weeks or months apart.

As she read, Mia felt herself slipping into Emily's world. Most entries were about the day-to-day, but every so often Emily jotted down a quote she found meaningful. The entries described the menial details of her life, her thoughts on motherhood, progress on projects like a bookshelf Emily refinished for the nursery, and the overwhelming sadness she felt every day. She also wrote about her hatred for her medication and the doctor who prescribed it. It was clear that Emily was having trouble far longer than a few months before her death. In the entries closer to the day she died—David seemed closer to two years old in these—she wrote her husband didn't take her feelings seriously, and her doctor seemed deaf to her pleas for help.

It was here that the journal began taking a darker turn. There were fewer entries about the struggles of motherhood or the frustration of an unsupportive spouse. Mia skimmed through the entries faster now, watching in horror as Emily's life unraveled before her.

Brad is having an affair. I know it. He works late almost every night. He finds any excuse not to come home. He doesn't want to be around me anymore. I'm such a burden. I tried to talk to him, get him to help, but he calls me dramatic and pushes me away. Where did my life go? Why doesn't he love me anymore?

David is sick with a nasty bug, which means none of us are sleeping. Brad is crankier than usual, and it makes me angry. I can't ever just have his support without him making it all about him. He blames me for David getting sick since I'm the one who put him in daycare, but it's only two days a week, and I really need that time. Some days it's so hard to get up, and once I do I can barely function. Dr. Hubert is adjusting my medication, and I'm seeing him weekly again. I hope that will help.

No more medication! I'm losing so much weight that my clothes are falling off. I can't eat. I can't think. I feel like a zombie.

David is acting strange. Brad doesn't believe me. What's new? I saw David watching me from around the corner. He stares at me for hours sometimes. He looks into my soul, and he sees all my secrets.

A woman came by the house today. I almost didn't answer the door. No one comes except for sales people. She said she works with Dr. Hubert and wanted to check on me. It was nice to sit and chat with someone, even if she's probably going to take everything I said back to him so he can push me back onto that awful medicine. At least he believes me now. Why would he send someone if he didn't? She asked a lot of questions about David and Brad, our routines. She also alluded to the affair. Does everyone in this town know??

Brad didn't work late tonight. He's been home on time every day this week. I wonder if the affair is over. I tried to talk to him about David, but he didn't want to hear it. He *says I'm being delusional, but something is wrong. David barely speaks, but I hear him in my mind all day. He tells me what he wants, and his thoughts are dark and twisted. Something has taken over my son. Something evil is living inside him. I won't let it take him! I asked Brad if I could take him to a priest, and Brad got very angry. But I have to do something.*

I have to save him. Forgive me.

THE LAST ENTRY made Mia shiver in her bed. Who knew that two short sentences could make one's entire body run cold? She glanced at the date. It was the date of the news articles, the day David and Emily died, a jarring fact but not such a surprise. There wasn't much doubt in her mind that Emily had killed her son. All the reports she'd read alluded to that. But would Emily have hung herself? Would a woman so disconnected from reality realize what she'd done and kill herself out of guilt? Or was someone else responsible for her death? Rachel said Brad was abusive, but in Emily's journal, he seemed more aloof and dismissive than outright violent. A star athlete in high school, she remembered him always hovering on the periphery, part of the crowd without being part of it. Still, abuse or not, he was certainly physically capable of killing his own wife if Rachel's suspicions were to be believed.

She shook her head and tapped her phone to check the time—it was barely midnight. Whatever she'd read, none of it seemed to explain why she was seeing the ghost of a little dead boy. If his mother killed him, as the media reported, why was he visiting her? What could she add to this? How could she help? They knew what had happened to him. That left Emily, but there wasn't any obvious foul play in her death as far as she could tell.

Mia's phone buzzed next to her as she received a message and interrupted her thoughts. She looked down at her phone as the notification appeared. It was from Nick. She reached out a hand to pick it up, then pulled back. For a moment, she considered ignoring it. She still didn't know how she felt about their kiss, but she wasn't a coward. In the end, she grabbed her phone from the nightstand and opened the message.

"Are you up?" Nick wrote.

Mia thought about ignoring it, but she was curious. "Yes," she texted back.

"Come outside," he wrote.

Mia took a deep breath and considered the message. They hadn't spoken since he kissed her. Since they kissed, really. She may as well be honest with herself. It wasn't like she hadn't fully taken part in it. Even now her body flushed, thinking about it. She knew meeting Nick outside was welcoming more trouble, but she couldn't help herself. Whether she was feeling daring or reckless, she walked out onto the porch clad in a thin gray tank top and black cotton shorts.

The cicadas sang along with the evening crickets and frogs, and lightning bugs flickered as they danced across her lawn. The air felt rejuvenated from the storm and was slightly cooler than normal because of it. There was still the thick blanket of humidity so iconic to the south, but the gentle breeze blew cool against her skin, and it was a welcome relief from the scorching heat of the summer days. Mia saw Nick standing at the edge of her driveway, his face illuminated by the nearest streetlight and the moonlight from above. The crescent rode high in the sky, and Mia wondered what it thought of the comings and goings of the people it watched on the world below.

"I wasn't sure you were awake. Or that you'd come," Nick said. He wore brown shorts and a white shirt, and his mussed hair looked as if he'd been running his hands through it. He walked up the steps and matched her stance on the porch, leaning his forearms on the railing.

"I thought maybe you'd want to apologize face to face," Mia said.

Nick raised a brow and angled his body toward her. "So you've been thinking of me then?"

Mia sniffed. "Not at all." She hugged her arms tighter against her body.

"An apology wasn't exactly what I was thinking about. More of a continuation."

"Nick, this isn't going to happen. I'm not interested in you... or anyone, for that matter."

"You seemed interested enough the other night," he

said, intentionally relaxing deeper into his southern drawl. "I've dreamed of you, Mia."

"The other night was a mistake. And how can you sit there and say you've been dreaming of me when, for the past two years, you haven't given me a single thought?"

He shifted closer to her. The movement was slight, but it set goosebumps dancing across her skin all the same. "I thought about you then, but I'm thinking about you a little differently now." His hand wound around her back, and he pulled her impossibly close, twisting her body so that she was face to face with him. She tried to resist, but her body ignored the commands, and her eyes widened. "I've also been thinking about this," he said, lowering his mouth to hers.

His hands tangled with hers, and he maneuvered them both away from the railing so that the siding of the house was at her back. Without thinking, she made an inaudible sound deep in her throat and melted against him. He felt her relax and groaned into her mouth. Then his hands were everywhere at once, sliding up her torso, moving over her breasts until they finally settled around her neck, and he devoured her. She gripped his hips as they ground into hers. His arousal pressed against her, and she slid her hands up and under his shirt to explore the skin beneath. His hard muscles rippled under her touch, and her fingers dug into his back when he tore his mouth from hers and moved along her jaw and on to her ear.

His tongue left a fiery trail along the lobe. His teeth scraped the side of her neck, and she felt him tremble as she moaned again. Her mind was racing, but she could barely think. It screamed of all the reasons this should not be happening, but she was powerless to act on them as the sensations washed over her in hot waves. Nick captured her mouth again, and she felt his hand dip low on her belly. He moved lower and lower until he cupped her through the thin fabric of her shorts, his fingers moving against her in slow, erotic circles. She was so wet and so aroused she thought she might explode. Throbbing need warred with her muted sense of reason, and all she wanted to do was hike her leg up so he could push inside of her.

"Nick, I... we..." She moaned against his mouth and fought for some semblance of control over her body. "Stop... stop..." she said frantically.

He groaned and ripped himself away from her, his chest heaving with the effort, his arousal clearly visible through his shorts. He ran a hand through his hair and stared at her, but she couldn't guess at his thoughts. All she knew was that she was just as out of breath as he was. She could feel the heat flushing her cheeks, and color rode high on his. Her lips were swollen, her body deliciously aroused and yet unfulfilled, but she couldn't allow this to go any further. She knew him. On some level, she still loved the asshole. Maybe one day she could move past the pain he'd caused her. But sex would complicate something that was already far too complex.

"I can't stop thinking about you. I can't stop wanting you," he said. "I don't know when it changed, but it did." Nick inched closer to her dangerously. "I want to take you to bed, Mia. I want to touch you until you're begging me to fuck you."

Mia pushed her hair out of her face, a hand fisted on her belly. "Stop it," she said desperately. "We can't do this. *I* can't do this." She scrambled for an excuse, any excuse that he might actually believe.

"Why? I know you, Mia, and I know you want me as bad as I want you."

Her mind raced. What could she say that he wouldn't argue with? "Because you were like brothers. I was married to him! This is wrong."

"Ewan?"

"Who else?" she said, throwing her hands up in frustration.

Nick's face flashed with frustration, surprise, and hurt, and then it was gone in an instant, his expression more resolute than ever. "But you're not married to him anymore. And I'm not his brother," he said, his eyes darkening and flashing with need.

Mia's breath caught, and she closed her eyes. He would never understand the real reason she couldn't throw reason to the side and jump into bed with him. He failed to see that her heart would break regardless of how the coin fell. Relationships always ended with death or heartbreak. And death aside, how many serious relationships had he successfully wiggled out of at just the right moment? How many times had she seen him skirt around conversations about marriage or commitment with girlfriends in the past? How many hearts had he broken along the way, including hers? This had to stop, and it was clearly going to be her who had to keep it from happening again. Mia had already buried the love of her life. She wasn't interested in doing so again.

The thought brought fresh pain knifing through her. She remembered so clearly the funeral and the days and weeks after, how it felt like she was dying, too. And she remembered the way Nick had left her, grieving and confused. The unanswered calls and texts, the voicemails, never returned. Hot tears filled her eyes and spilled over to streak down her cheeks. "You have to go," she said, her throat tight and her voice ragged.

His brows drew together in confusion, and he reached for her, but she jerked back. "Mia, what's wrong?"

"Just go!" she said, putting a hand to her mouth and fleeing inside. She shut the door behind her, and rested her back against it, closing her eyes tightly as if to shut them would shut out the memories. After a few minutes, she heard his footsteps down the stairs, and she slipped to the floor, letting the wave of sadness take her under. Lost to it, she rested her head on her knees and let it all pour out.

Mia woke the next morning and realized it was a night without dreams or nightmares or ghosts trying to tell her... something. Why couldn't ghosts be direct, she wondered.

Hey, Mia, I'm dead. The authorities believe I smothered my child and then hanged myself, but actually, I was an international spy whose family was eliminated in a complex plot to force my husband, also a spy, into retirement and leave the villains alone.

See, how easy was that?

Shaking her head at the ridiculousness of it, Mia readied herself for the day, choosing to dress in a white tank top and a pair of wide-legged black linen overalls that looked surprisingly dressed-up when paired with a long crescent moon necklace and flat dress shoes. Looking herself over in the mirror, she kept her wavy hair down and naturally styled. It was her bookshop's grand opening day, and Mia wanted to feel professional yet still inviting and comfortable. She wanted that to be reflected in everything from the decor to the layout to her very person.

For breakfast, she opted for a bagel slathered with cream cheese and sat at the little bar at the end of her kitchen to eat it. She went over her list of tasks for the day, but as she surveyed each item, a different list caught her eye. She looked over at the square cork board hung on the kitchen wall.

Read a book just for me.
Learn something new. *Gardening!*
Eat out alone.
Make a home.
Find yourself.

She considered each item on the list and then looked around her. From the kitchen to the dining area to the living room, her furniture was well lived in, her walls and bookshelves decorated with photos and postcards and other knickknacks she'd collected over the years. There were even photos up of her and Ewan now, photos she'd kept tucked away for years. They still made her sad to look at, but they also made her happy, and that was new.

Mia picked up her pen and crossed an item off the list.

Make a home.

Looking at the remaining items, she murmured, "I'm working on it, Mia."

She polished off the bagel, dusted the crumbs off her overalls, and tossed her bag over her shoulder. Today, she would open her bookstore and take one more step toward finding herself. She might even celebrate with a dinner out alone and cross another item off her list. She stepped outside and took a deep breath. The summer air was already nearly sweltering, but not even the heat and humidity could dampen her spirits. Glancing down, she noticed a potted bush of wild roses sitting next to the door frame with a card pinned underneath it. She bent to pick up the card, stopping to caress one of the deep purple petals before she stood straight and opened it. Inside, a message was scrawled in barely legible handwriting, each letter connecting to its mate in a cramped, half-cursive-half-print style.

Thinking of you.
—Nick

Along with the message was the care and instruction sheet for the flowers growing wild in the dark green pot. Her eyes moved between the note and the velvety blooms, and a small smile touched her lips. The man may be arrogant and pushy, but he certainly knew what he was doing. Now, more than ever, she was determined to keep things platonic, but she had to admit that she enjoyed the gift.

When she drove past Nick's house on her way downtown, Mia saw his car was in his driveway. He was home.

She had the impulse to stop, to thank him for the gift, of course, but she resisted. She needed more time to think, more time to parse out her own feelings and decide exactly what to do about him.

Still, she wondered what he was doing locked away in that house. Would he be writing his next novel, working on revisions with his editor, entertaining a woman maybe? Mia shook her head. He was welcome to do all three, and all at the same time, if he so chose. She had enough on her plate, she reminded herself, and continued driving. It was none of her business what he did in his spare time.

17

———

Nick was not, in fact, doing any of the things Mia imagined. Instead, he was sitting at his desk with a printed manuscript on one side and his open laptop on the other, working on neither. She'd likely be miffed to learn that he blamed her for his current work slump, but it couldn't be helped. He hadn't been able to get anything worthwhile done in days. To be honest, it was more like weeks. Ever since he'd run into her at the bar, his mind was a blur of shame, frustration, intrigue, and desire. Today, the latter caused his troubles. He scrubbed his hands over his face and leaned back in his chair with a groan. Deadlines were approaching, and all he could think about was getting his neighbor into bed. Sexual frustration was turning out to be anything but a muse. In fact, it was actively putting up blocks in his mind.

But as he sat and cursed his lack of bed mate, Nick realized he was feeling far more than sexual frustration. Sure, it started out that way. Mia had come back into his life abruptly, or he into hers depending on your perspective, and the pull of attraction was instant. For the first time in his existence, he wanted to think of her not as Ewan's wife, but as Mia. Just Mia. How lucky was he that he was so deeply attracted to a woman he already cared about so much, a woman who he respected and genuinely liked? Every moment in her presence only reinforced that. However, he was also forced to come to terms with just how deeply he'd hurt her—if nothing else, it explained how guarded she was around him, how careful she was to keep their changing relationship in its own well-defined box. Somehow over the years, he'd been able to convince himself that he was just Ewan's friend, that Mia didn't need him, maybe even was better off without him around reminding her constantly of her dead husband. It was a way to close the door to his own grief. If he didn't watch Mia fall apart, he wouldn't fall apart either, but repairing their relationship was turning out to be more important than he planned.

The more time he spent with her, the more layers fell off the carefully crafted story he told himself. He realized what he felt was more than attraction or a duty to make amends. The love he felt for her was evolving, changing as his feelings changed, and it wasn't enough to acknowledge his attraction to her. For years she'd been one of the gang, the partner of his friend, someone he'd known since his childhood. Now he wanted her for himself. No. Correction: he burned for her. He was hard just thinking about the way she kissed him, how she felt against him, soft and writhing and moaning. Every noise, every breath, was an aphrodisiac. All he could think about was her, and even in his imagination, there was no one who compared.

"Because you're falling in love with her, you moron," he muttered to himself, realization hitting him with equal surprise and horror. Pushing away from his desk, he wished he could pick up the phone and call his long gone friend. He'd tell Ewan he was being an idiot and ask for advice, and Ewan would never disappoint. He'd simply laugh at Nick and walk him through how to un-idiot the situation.

For the first time, Nick wondered what Ewan would actually think of all of this. What would Ewan think about Nick lusting after his wife? Would he believe that he, the man who had successfully avoided the big L so many times before, was falling in love with Mia? Nick shook his head and stood. He didn't know what Ewan would think. He might be happy for him and give his blessing, or he might call him a son-of-a-bitch and deck him. There was certainly a case for both. Whatever Ewan would do, Nick knew he had to see Mia. She needed him, though she was too stubborn to see it.

Today was her grand opening, the big event she'd been planning for weeks, and he needed to be there for her. If she didn't want him around, she'd simply have to throw him out. They had too much to talk about to put it off anymore, he thought. He grabbed his keys and looked at the clock, grateful it was nearing the end of the day. Perhaps the timing of his arrival would increase the likelihood of her actually listening. It didn't matter to him whether he needed to appeal to her using emotion or logic. One way or another, he was going to make her hear him out. He was going to make her see that being together was not wrong at all.

He only hoped that by the time he arrived, he'd have figured out how he was going to say all that. Thinking of Ewan again, he asked his friend out loud, "Any pointers?"

And, of course, there was silence.

MIA SANK into a chair with a giddy laugh. She was finally alone after hours on her feet socializing, greeting what had to have been the entire town, checking out customers, and even dipping into the extra supply of teacher assigned summer reading books she'd stashed away behind the counter. Not every day would be like this, of course, but the town had not disappointed in their support.

Alexis leaned onto the counter in front of her and handed her a bottle of water. "I can't believe how many people were in here today."

"I was just thinking the same. I must have sold 200 books," Mia said with a smile as wide as her face. She took a sip and surveyed her bookshelves.

"I believe it! Sarah and her book club bought up the entire romance display, and your children's section is almost completely cleaned out."

"I know." Mia laughed again. "I can't believe it. Thank you so much for being here. I don't know what I would do without you."

"You'll have to—" Alexis stopped when the bell above the door jingled, and they both watched Nick walk in. Alexis raised her brows at Mia meaningfully.

"I see you got my present," he said, gesturing to the potted roses on the floor next to the checkout counter. He didn't even acknowledge Alexis. He didn't mean to be rude, but his eyes were only for Mia.

"And that's my cue." Alexis grinned at Mia and fanned herself, pantomiming exactly how hot she thought Nick was behind his back. The opening door set the bell to jingling again and gently slapped closed behind her, but neither Nick nor Mia seemed to notice.

"I did. Thank you," Mia said.

"You didn't think I'd miss your opening day, did you?" Nick asked, reaching out to casually tuck a stray lock of hair behind her ear. "Have you been thinking about me?"

"Of course not." Flustered, Mia repeated his gesture and pushed her hair behind her ear, shifting her weight from foot to foot.

"I've been thinking about you."

"Oh," she murmured and watched him move to stand behind her. His hands came to her shoulders, and he kneaded the muscles there. He massaged her back in rolling circles from shoulder to her hip and then up to her neck and the base of her skull. She couldn't help but moan in relief. "If I wasn't so sore, I'd tell you to go away," she said, sucking in a breath as he focused on a particularly tender knot in her neck. She tipped her head to the side to stretch the muscle as he worked.

His fingers splayed out and began working back down her back. She already felt like putty in his hands when suddenly his lips were at the side of her neck. She stiffened, but he only chuckled.

"Let me, Mia," he murmured in her ear even as his

fingers worked her tight muscles. She relaxed again when he moved again to her lower back and hips. As he massaged, his breath was hot in her ear. "I can't get you out of my head. You're all I think about you when I'm awake, and I dream about you at night. I want you, Mia. I know you want me, too."

His hands left her back, and she whimpered, caught up in the spell he'd weaved over her. He turned the chair, so she faced him.

"You're so beautiful," he said.

He grasped her hands and pulled her to her feet, and she let him draw her into a kiss. This time was different. Where there had been desperation, now there was tenderness. One of his hands moved to the small of her back and pulled her to him, the other lovingly cupped her cheek. His lips met hers, only the tip of his tongue stroking hers before he changed the angle of the kiss.

She responded to him instinctively and matched the lapping rhythm he set. Her hands wound around his neck, and she couldn't help but press herself against him. She felt the hand at her lower back fist in her clothing. It had been so long since anyone had pulled at her like this, not since Ewan. The dull throbbing in her heart brought tears to her eyes, and they fell before she could think to blink them away. Nick's thumb rubbed against her cheek and came away wet. He drew away from her, his brows drawn together.

"What is it?" he asked. Mia shook her head and looked down, her face still cupped in his hand. "Mia, please."

"You don't understand. How could you know what it's like?" She pulled herself from his arms and wiped the tears away. She moved to the other side of the counter, putting more space in between them.

"What is *what* like?" he asked, moving around the counter and closing the distance.

"It doesn't matter." Let him think whatever he wanted. She pushed her hair out of her face, crossed her arms, and stared at him warily as he came closer and closer to her. When he reached her, he cupped her elbows in his palms and pulled her to him, this time into a warm embrace. His arms came around her, and she stood stiffly against him.

"I don't understand, Mia, but—" he broke off. He looked down at her, and something flashed in his eyes. He saw her, really saw her. "I want to show you something."

Mia hesitated. "Nick, I'm exhausted. I just want to go home."

"It's important. Please."

With a sigh, she nodded reluctantly and walked with him outside. She listened when he explained they would take her car so he could drive her home after, but she barely heard it. His voice sounded tinny and far away.

They drove toward the beach, but rather than park in one of the main lots, Nick drove further down a winding road and pulled into a small wooded area popular with the locals. Once he parked, he walked around to her side of the car and opened the door. He took her hand and led her through a gap in the old fencing and down a wooded trail. Spanish moss hung from the oaks on either side of the beaten path, and the light of the sunset filtered through in uneven patches.

They walked for several minutes before the trees thinned and gave way to small dunes. Flat wooden planks replaced the path, and the woods became sand. Stairs built into the side of the walkway led down to the beach, but Nick kept hold of her hand and instead led her onto a long pier that stretched out into the water as if daring nature to tear it away.

"Why are we here?" Mia asked.

"This was our place. Ewan's and mine," he said. His pace slowed, and he watched her closely as they walked. Their steps sounded hollow on the weathered wood. "It's where we came to talk or fish or sneak beers. When we were older, it was a retreat from work or women, any of our problems."

Mia said nothing and turned her face to the water. The wind coming in off the ocean blew her hair from her face, and she breathed deep the smell of salt and sand. She'd spent her entire life by the water, and she realized how often she took it for granted. It's beauty, it's power. The waves crashed around her, and she could hear the gulls chattering as they filled their bellies one last time before dusk.

"Once, I came here with Ewan, and he was sure he'd messed up big. With you. You'd had a big fight, the kind that ends couples, and it was right before the wedding. I never knew what he did that was so bad, but he was sure you were going to break things off," Nick said. "When I asked him what he'd do if you left, he said he wouldn't do anything. He told me, 'If I can make her happy and stay, I will, but if leaving makes her happier, then that's what I want for her.'"

"I didn't know he talked to you about that," Mia said. Her voice was quiet, nearly a whisper. She looked down at the hand still in his, at the way their fingers interlocked, her olive skin next to his dusky tan complexion.

"To my way of thinking, Ewan would want you to be happy now. Whatever that means. So, if being alone makes you happy, Mia, then I'll leave you alone, but if what we've started has even a chance of making you happier, then I say we take our blessings from someone we both loved, and we choose to be happy." He drew her hand to his lips and kissed her fingers. Though he wanted to press her to make a choice right then and there, he knew she needed time. "Come on, I'll take you home."

As they drove back, Mia retreated into her thoughts. If she could talk to Ewan right now, would he again be so selfless as that? Would he want her happiness above all else, even if it was this? The answer wasn't a great mystery. His love for her was so strong, she knew there was nothing but truth in Nick's words. Ewan had only ever wanted her happiness, and he'd worked toward that goal his entire life. There was no doubt in her mind that he would support whatever would make her happy for the rest of hers.

She sneaked a look at Nick, considering his words and actions today, wondering what thoughts prompted them. She looked at him again in her periphery, and she couldn't help but admire how beautiful he really was. He had a strong straight nose and high cheekbones with a jawline she knew was the envy of many a man. While he wasn't looking at her now, she knew his eyes were like liquid ink, dark and sexy with thick eyelashes. He was so different from Ewan, who'd been quite a bit more fair with almost red hair. Her attraction to Nick surprised her, considering she'd only had eyes for Ewan for so many years. Mia wondered if that thought ever crossed Nick's mind. Was he as twisted up inside as she was? Or had he made peace with it?

They pulled into her driveway and Nick cut the engine. He glanced at her before he ducked his head and got out of the car. Mia watched him walk around the hood of the car and open the passenger side door for her as seemed to be his habit. She stepped out and allowed him to lead her to her door. He watched her struggle with the deadbolt and turn the doorknob.

"Call me if you need anything," he said. He turned and took only a single step before Mia called to him.

"Nick."

He turned to her, his face emotionless, his eyes shielded. Her thoughts were still a jumbled mess, and she didn't have a logical reason for it, but still she heard herself ask, "Will you stay?"

18

Nick was against her in a blur of motion. He caught her mouth in his and hiked her up. Holding on to his shoulders, Mia wrapped her thighs around him and poured herself into the kiss. He carried her through the door, kicking it closed behind them. He was a man possessed, his lips taking hers roughly as he walked through the living room, but he hesitated in the hallway.

"Bedroom. On the right," she gasped against his lips.

"Finally," he muttered when they made it to the bed, sitting on the edge with her in his lap.

His hands glided up her thighs, and he gripped her hips as she ground herself closer to him. He gasped and broke the kiss, groaning against her neck. His grip on her hips tightened, and she leaned forward and nipped his ear lobe lightly with her teeth. His hands tugged the thin straps of her baggy overalls down, and she leaned back as he drug the shirt underneath off her body. Without pause, he unhooked her bra, and it followed her shirt to the floor. She mirrored his movements, pulling up his shirt and tossing it over her shoulder. Then she stepped back off him and tugged his shorts and boxers down. He was already hard and throbbing for her, and he leaned back, bracing himself on his elbows. Her eyes never leaving his, she stood and pushed her overalls and underwear off her hips. They dropped to the floor, and she was left standing completely naked in front of him.

"Oh my god." His eyes devoured her, taking in every inch of her body. It wasn't as if he'd never seen her body before—they lived in a beach town, after all—but he'd never seen her body like this... or this much of it.

She was built like a Greek goddess, and he appreciated her full figure, the way her breasts sat round and begging for his attention, her belly full and soft, her hips wide and rounded. His blood roared when he saw the tattoo riding high from her left hip to the top of her thigh. It was a black and gray set of flowers bursting open as swallows swooped around it.

"You are so beautiful, Mia," he whispered.

Wordlessly, she stepped forward and pushed his shoulders back. He scooted onto the bed until he laid out fully, and she crawled over him. She straddled his hips and relished the feel of his hands moving up her thighs, hips, sides, and breasts. She leaned forward, and he took one into his mouth, circling and pressing against the nipple with his tongue while his hands cupped her. His fingers traveled down her belly to the very center of her.

As his mouth worked against her breast, he pressed against her center, his hand moving in large circles until she was gasping. She moved a hand over his, drawing his fingers up to the swollen nub at the apex of her, and coached him through the position and rhythm she liked, throwing her head back when his movements against her clit brought her to the peak.

She had to get closer to him. Her need for him was frantic, and she was sure she'd explode if she didn't have him inside her soon. "I need—" she gasped, and she adjusted herself over him.

"I know," he managed, his hand moving to position himself at her entrance, but he hesitated. "Condom... wallet..."

Mia shook her head, kissing him and nipping at his lower lip. "Birth control," she said, her breathing heavy, her eyes clouded with desire.

"Thank god," he said and groaned when she eased down onto him.

She savored the slow feeling of being filled, then rocked against him again and again until he tore his mouth from hers, gasping. She leaned forward on her palms and moved her body up and down, urged on by his pants. His hands gripped her hips as she rode him, and she felt the heat rising within her once again. His eyes widened as he watched her, and she ground down on him, his murmured encouragements stoking the fire within her. He threw his head back as she rode him to madness. The pressure built inside her until she cried out and pleasure exploded from her center and washed over her entire body.

It took everything he had not to slam into her over and over as he felt her wet heat throb around him, and her entire body shook with her orgasm. Nick waited until her climax had ebbed before throwing an arm around her waist and flipping her onto her back.

He rolled over top of her and pushed himself as deep as he could go, relishing her gasp as she took every inch of him. He moved inside her, slowly at first. Again and again he pushed into her, reveling in the feel of her hands at his hips, pulling him to her faster, harder. "I want you to come again. I want to watch you while you come again."

He reached down between them and rubbed her clit in circular motions, and she cried out. His teeth scraped up the side of her neck, along her jawline, and to her mouth again. "Open for me," he said, coaxing her legs further apart.

He felt her clench as she mewed against his mouth, and he knew she was close. He pulled his lips from hers and watched in fascination when she tensed, a cry erupting from her mouth. She arched against him, her insides pulsing around him. He gritted his teeth, his breathing heavy, skin slicked with sweat, and he slammed into her until his own climax rocked his system and spilled into her.

Mia felt his breaths heave in and out of him in time with hers. She couldn't help but stroke his delicious back as he laid atop her. His mouth was hot against her neck where he'd dropped his head, and when he raised it to look at her, she nipped playfully at his lips, a satisfied smile on her face. He shifted his weight off her and propped his head on his elbow, her legs still twined around his. He drew a finger slowly up and down her arm.

"So that happened," he said.

"That happened," she agreed.

Mia considered taking this opportunity to give him a full rundown of the boundaries she knew they would need if this was to continue, to clarify that this was a satisfying physical relationship and nothing more, but she was too sated and relaxed to spoil the mood.

"You hungry?" he asked abruptly.

"Starved," she said with a satisfied smile.

"Good." He sat up, confident in his own nudity, and disappeared into the bathroom where he hunted up a couple of washcloths. She heard the water run, and then he reappeared. She reached her hand out for one, but he shook his head and gently cleaned her with the cloth. He tossed it into the clothes basket across the room. Touched by his care, Mia shamelessly admired his form as he pulled on his shorts, from his broad shoulders to his well-toned chest and abs.

"What are you looking at?" he asked with a grin.

"Nothing. Just some guy I brought home."

"Just some guy, huh?" He surprised her when he vaulted across the bed and pounced on her again. She laughed against his mouth, and he kissed her senseless. "Still some guy?" he asked, pulling away from her. She flipped onto her side, tucked an elbow under her head, and shook her head.

"By the way, this," he said as he drew his hand down and over her tattooed hip, "is so fucking sexy."

"You've seen it before. You were there when I got it," she laughed.

"Yes, but I've never seen it like this before." His hand lingered on her hip. "I'm going to rustle us up some grub."

He grasped her chin, kissed her again, and pushed himself off the bed. Mia watched him walk into the hallway and fell back onto the bed with a sigh. *What am I doing?*

For a moment, a strange sense of guilt threatened her bubble of happiness. From his speech on the beach, she knew he was looking for more than a roll in the sheets now and again, but that was something she couldn't give him. She was finally finding herself again, building a home, building a life of her own. She wasn't ready to give that up. But despite the niggling guilt for starting something she couldn't finish, she couldn't bring herself to stay away from him. And maybe she was wrong about his intentions. It wasn't as if he was dropping on one knee.

She heard the bangs of her cabinet doors and then the refrigerator's suction as it opened and closed. The microwave turned on, and Mia realized Nick found the takeout leftovers. Reaching down onto the floor, she grabbed her tank top and cotton shorts and pulled them on. Glancing sideways, she noticed Emily's journal was still on her nightstand. Not wanting to think of it tonight, she pulled open the drawer and dropped the book inside. She turned just as Nick walked back into the room, holding two steaming plates. He'd piled the beef and broccoli high on mounds of rice, and she noticed a bottle of soy sauce stashed in his shorts pocket.

"Dinner is served, my lady," he said. "I wasn't sure if you like eating in bed, but the occasion seemed to call for it."

Unable to argue with his logic and also a fan of eating in bed, Mia happily scooted back against the headboard and accepted the plate. They ate like ravenous wolves, set their plates aside, and then attacked each other again with equal vigor.

NICK COULDN'T SLEEP. He laid on his back, an elbow propped under his head, and listened to Mia's deep breathing. He tried not to take it personally that she had rolled to the opposite side of the bed as soon as she'd fallen asleep. She faced the opposite wall, laying on her side only inches away from him, but it felt like miles.

There could be a myriad of reasons. She could be used to sleeping alone now. It was even possible she was never the type to snuggle up with someone all night. It's not like he would know. He suspected it was more to do with the wall she'd built around herself than anything else, but he wouldn't let that deter him. He could only imagine how broken her bruised heart was—it was only natural that she should want to protect it—but he knew she needed him. It may take an insurmountable amount of persistence to convince her of that, but he was a determined man. She could keep building up that wall around her heart, and he'd simply tear it down brick by brick.

It was strange, this possessiveness he suddenly felt for her. He supposed he was always protective of her in some way, but it was different now. Now she was his. He reached a hand out and stroked his fingers through her hair, pushing it away from her forehead. He loved how it splayed across her shoulders and onto the pillow in dark waves, how it had draped down over her breasts when she'd ridden him into oblivion. His body grew hard just thinking about it.

His fingers drifted from her hair down over her shoulder and along her side. Her skin was smooth and soft, and he pushed the covers down to see more of it. He splayed his fingers out over her hip, and Mia murmured quietly in her sleep, shifting ever so slightly. Butterflies fluttered in his belly at the thought of being with her again, and he stretched out on his side behind her. His arousal pushed insistently between her legs, and he began stroking her softly everywhere. He pressed kisses to her neck and cheek. His hot breath washed over her ear and his hands moved up and down her hips, over her belly, and into the soft nest of curls between her legs. He stroked her there, pleased when she began to moan and push against him.

She grew impossibly wet, but Nick couldn't take her yet. He needed her to know it was him she was making love to. He needed her awake and begging for him. Patiently, he teased her until her eyes fluttered open at last. She turned her head to look at him, her back remaining flush to his chest, her cheeks already flushed with arousal.

"Nick?" Her brows drew together, her eyes blinking and unfocused.

"Can I have you?" he asked. She moaned in response, his fingers driving her mad. Her body writhed against him, but he needed more. He needed her to say it. "Mia, tell me you want me."

"Yes. Please, Nick," she gasped.

That was exactly what he needed to hear, and he

pushed himself into her from behind, groaning at the feel of her all around him, the curve of her behind pressing against him. He buried himself to the hilt and withdrew over and over, his teeth clamped onto her shoulder, his fingers working her clit just the way she'd shown him she liked. Again and again he pounded into her, and she reached back to grab his hips. She arched her back and gasped when he buried himself deeper inside of her. When he was sure he couldn't hold back any longer, she cried out, and he felt her body clench around him. Nothing could've been more welcome in that moment, and he growled as his orgasm ripped through him.

Breathing heavily, he collapsed on his back, his chest heaving, and pulled Mia to his side. With a contented sigh, he breathed in the scent of her and let his eyes close. Her body relaxed against his, and, even if for only this moment, he believed that was where she would stay all night.

As his eyes grew heavy and his body relaxed, he drifted into that weightless place between waking and sleep when a prickling sensation danced over his skin like someone was watching him. He opened his eyes to slits, the hair on the back of his neck standing on end, but there was nothing there, only the darkness and the sounds of night drifting in from outside the window. He blinked until the sensation was gone and pulled the covers higher.

There was nothing in the dark that wasn't also in the light. Closing his eyes, he focused on the sound of Mia's breaths and forced himself to sleep.

19

The crash from the other side of the house woke Mia with a jolt, but it took her a moment to realize that it wasn't a sound from a nightmare. Nick stirred sleepily beside her, his eyes opening and meeting her worried gaze. He sat up next to her, and they waited, ears pricked for any other sound. When the door —either the front or back door, they couldn't tell which— banged against the wall and slammed shut, they bolted out of bed in unison.

Mia scrambled to throw on a tank and shorts and saw Nick do the same. Grabbing her phone, she followed him out of the room and to the left, down the hallway. To his credit, he didn't demand she go back to the bedroom or stay behind him. In fact, he rightfully assumed that she was already checking the bathroom and spare bedroom across the hall and dialing the police.

"They're gone," Nick shouted from the kitchen.

When Mia reached the end of the hallway, her hand

flew to her mouth as he turned on lights, and she saw the state of her house.

Books littered the floor, thrown about the room and resting in all manner of positions. Some were missing pages while others had fallen open face down and split their spines. Picture frames lay cracked on the floor alongside the broken shards of a glass fairy statue, one of the last gifts Ewan had ever given her. The 9-1-1 operator on the phone told Mia not to hang up, that police would be there soon, but she barely heard it. She wanted to cry, but the shock of it all paralyzed her.

At some point, Nick took the phone and led her outside to a chair on the front porch. He sat down next to her, his eyes alert and watchful, and they waited for the police to arrive. A glance at the clock on the way out would've told her it was just after three in the morning, but she wasn't taking any of it in. She felt Nick's hand rub her back, and she leaned into him for comfort. They were just things, she told herself. Things could be repaired. Things could be replaced. But someone violated her personal sanctuary, and she wasn't sure that was as easily repaired.

The police arrived minutes later, three cars parking on the street in front of her house and showering her lawn with blue and red lights. One officer approached Nick and Mia while others entered her home from the front and the back. They called to one another in short barking commands, the hot breeze carrying their muffled voices outside. More officers arrived, and Mia wondered if she was that important or if they were just that bored. Small-town police work couldn't be that exciting in the middle of a summer night. Well, maybe it could. Someone had killed her husband at night in a small town.

In and out the officers went, and she expected they were collecting evidence, maybe dusting for fingerprints. She wasn't exactly sure. The woman in uniform standing with them was asking a laundry list of questions, but Mia sat numbly through most of the interview. Nick gave most of the details, and Mia was grateful for it. When the officer asked questions about the property and what might have been damaged or missing, Mia spoke up.

Yes, they'd locked the doors before going upstairs.

Yes, she heard the crash and called immediately.

No, they didn't see anyone.

No, nothing was missing as far as they knew.

The officer's brows drew together when Mia said nothing was taken, and he asked if Mia was sure. She handed Mia her card in case she remembered something or discovered anything missing later. It wasn't long before the house was blessedly quiet again, and Mia set to work putting things back in order. Without question, Nick pitched in and began sweeping the floor.

"You don't have to do that," Mia said. Her voice was quiet, flat.

"I know," he said.

When they'd put the room back to rights, they double checked the locks on both doors and walked back to the bedroom together. Nick put his arm around her and pulled her in close. Though the sky was already beginning to turn pink with the impending sunrise, they left the lights burning. They both made a valiant attempt to go back to sleep, but neither could do more than doze.

NICK WOKE groggy and out of sorts over two hours later. It took a moment for him to realize that he wasn't in his own bed, but when he did, the memories of the night before replayed like a movie. It was certainly a night for the books. He wiped the sleep from his eyes and looked over at Mia. He supposed it was too much to hope for her to stay snug against him all night. She was curled up on the far side of the bed, her body huddled into the warm blanket as far as possible from where he was laying.

"Not ready to share the bed with someone again, are you?" he muttered.

He walked into the bathroom, decided against a shower (he lived only two houses down), and attended to his morning needs. He splashed cold water on his face and hair, running his hands through it until it looked less like he'd tumbled out of bed. When he was finished, he peeked into the bedroom. Mia still slept soundly, her body turned over and one arm stretched out. He considered it a good sign that it looked like she was reaching for him.

As he walked into the kitchen to make breakfast, he planned his next move. She was obviously shaken up by the previous night's roller coaster, but he couldn't afford to lose any headway. Like an idiot, he was already falling for her, and it was only a matter of time before she discovered that and booted him out of her life out of self-preservation. He had to convince her she needed him before that happened. He had to convince her that being with him was as important for her happiness (and healing) as breathing. Tapping his fingers on the counter as he thought, he decided what Mia really needed was romance. Romance and constancy. He had to prove to her he would not abandon her again, that she meant more to him than any woman before. And wasn't it a funny thought she did? What a circle they'd traveled. From childhood friends to enemies to lovers. It was something right out of a book.

Nick cracked eggs into a bowl and settled for scrambling them briskly with a fork because he couldn't find a whisk. He lit the burner on the stove, added a pat of butter to a pan, and poured the whisked eggs into the melted butter. He popped two pieces of bread into the toaster and turned back to the stove to stir the eggs. The air filled with the smell of warm bread, sunny eggs, and sizzling butter.

"Morning," he said when Mia walked in.

She rubbed her eyes and ran a hand through her hair. His mouth watered at the sight of her, hair all tousled, her body relaxed and a just a bit wobbly. She looked like a goddess. "Good morning," she replied sleepily.

"How are you doing?"

"I'm alright. I'm trying to go with the flow and not overthink it."

He turned off the burner and moved to her. He wasn't exactly sure how to help, so he went with an alternative approach: distraction. "My plan was to make you a hot breakfast in bed, but I'm afraid we'll have to settle for cold eggs instead."

"Why? Aren't you cooking eggs right now?" she asked, gesturing to the pan filled with scrambled eggs on the stove.

"They'll be cold by the time I'm done."

His hands held her face, and his lips brushed over

hers softly. He kissed her in slow, languid movements, and she felt her heart swell dangerously even as she tightened with desire. With a laugh, she pulled away. "I have to get ready."

"Later," he said, moving his attentions to her neck.

"No, now," she said with a laugh, and pushed him away. "Go finish breakfast."

He playacted defeat, hunching his shoulders and muttering to himself, but she saw him grin as he started building their plates up with toast, eggs, and slices of fresh strawberries. They ate together at the kitchen table and took turns talking about their plans for the day. Mia would spend her day at the bookstore, while Nick would be in editing hell on his laptop.

"What are your plans tonight?" he asked a little too casually.

Mia knew his game, but as shaken as she was from the break-in—or perhaps because of it—she was determined to handle it alone. This relationship, whatever it was, needed to fit inside its own carefully constructed box. Asking him to stay over or even going out on a date was stepping outside that box, and it risked too much.

"I'm probably going to come home and crash. There's bound to be a lot of foot traffic in the shop again today, and I've got mountains of inventory to reorder and restock."

Nick nodded and stood. He leaned down and gave Mia a kiss on the cheek. He wanted to push her, to prevent her from keeping him at a distance, but he also knew she was only waiting for an excuse to give him the boot. "Call me if you need me." He took their empty plates to the sink, where he rinsed them and slid them into their slots in the dishwasher.

They both readied for the day, Nick leaving before Mia so he could grab a shower and change. Mia waved him off, nodding when he told her he'd catch a ride later to go pick up his car from her shop. What a strange morning, she thought as she hugged her arms around herself.

True, she had spent the night having wild sex with Nick, of all people. Even more surprising, he turned out to be not just an accomplished lover but a selfless one. There had been no hesitation whether she took charge or showed him what she liked, or if she was surrendering to him. He cared about her pleasure and enjoyment as much as his own, maybe even more so.

But there was something about their morning together. The breakfast, the little pats and kisses, the casual touches. It was all so familiar. She remembered it being a bit like that with Ewan, that familiarity and the comfort, but it had lacked the desperation. It was as if Nick couldn't stop touching her in any way he could, whenever he could, for fear of never being able to again. She must keep it under control. It was the only way this would work. She finished dressing, threw her hair up into a messy bun and smudged a bit of eyeliner on. She hoped a solid workday would take her thoughts off the mind blowing sex she'd had the night before and a foiled burglary attempt that still made no sense.

What a night.

20

Mia barely made it to the door before her chest tightened, and it became hard to breathe. Her bag slipped to the floor with a dull thud. The world went black around the edges, and she scrambled over to the couch before her legs collapsed from under her. Her body was shaky as she laid out on the cushions, curling into a fetal position. Closing her eyes tight, Mia focused on her breathing.

In the nose.

Out the mouth.

Nice and steady.

Like a chant.

Finally, her heartbeat slowed, and the tightness in her chest subsided. She opened her eyes and rolled to her back, focusing on relaxing every muscle in her body. She stared up at her ceiling and decided she wasn't going into the shop after all. What was she thinking, anyway? A stranger broke into her home only hours after she was at her most intimate with Nick. She couldn't just go about her life like it was any other day.

She looked around the room. Despite their cursory cleaning efforts, it still bore signs of the night before, as if some invisible villain had opened the doors to her deepest secrets, and no locks could keep them shut. Even as the helplessness washed over her, anger was close behind. That invisible villain had the nerve to walk into her home, break her things, and threaten her sense of peace.

But they wouldn't destroy it. She wouldn't let them.

Sitting up on the couch, Mia took a deep breath. It helped to focus on the soft cushion beneath her and the way the wood floor was cool beneath her feet was a welcome grounding force. She was stronger than she gave herself credit for. Mia stood and clasped her hands before her, looking around the room like a queen surveying her kingdom. For a moment, she considered calling Alexis, but she decided against it. This was something she needed to do herself. For herself.

Pulling the chairs and sofa to the middle of the room, Mia gave the floor another thorough sweeping. She dumped a dustpan's worth of dust and dirt and the tiniest glass shards in the trash, then picked up the mop and walked back into the living room where the worst of the damage was. On one hand, she wanted to make sure there were no traces of glass left for her feet to find later. On the other hand, it was important to her she cleanse her space. Someone uninvited had walked on these floors, and she wanted every trace of them gone.

Next, she walked over to the stack of picture frames Nick had carefully piled on the antique desk she used as a television stand. It stood next to the shortest of her book-shelves, a small nod to the eclectic blending of old and new that Mia loved. She sorted the frames into two piles: one for damaged frames where the glass shattered and one for frames with the glass intact. She wasn't sure what she would do with the glassless frames yet, but she could at least repair the others. Mia would hang them as soon as they dried and serve as a sort of victory flag flying high after a battle.

Gathering these picture frames into her arms (there were five in total), Mia walked over to her kitchen table and spread them out, surveying the various states of damage on each. Most were broken at one or more corners, but there was one that was broken at every corner and splintered down the length of one side, as well. Nothing a little wood glue wouldn't fix, she thought. She went digging in the drawer she'd nominated as the official junk drawer of her house.

Success!

With a bottle of extra-strength wood glue in her hand, Mia sat at the table and began fixing the picture frames. As she worked, she let her mind visit all the places in the photos again in her memory. She remembered that camping trip with friends, the sunset on her honeymoon, her twenty-first birthday out with Alexis. They were good memories, evidence of a happy life well-lived so far.

She was pressing two corners of the last frame together when someone knocked on her door. She looked up with a small jerk, forcing herself to stay calm. Burglars didn't knock. There was no reason at all to be startled by the noise. Mia set the picture frame aside to dry and walked to the door, opening it to find Nick holding a can of paint in one hand and a bulging plastic bag in the other.

"What are you doing here?" She blinked and cocked her head to the side. It wasn't bad that he was here, simply... unexpected.

"I didn't see you at the bookstore, so I thought I'd bring you these," he said, holding up the paint and bag he carried like trophies. "I think the paint matches the shade you were talking about for your living room wall."

Mia took the gallon of paint he offered and looked down at the color sample dotted on the lid. It was exactly the shade she'd been dreaming about, because of course it was. Nick knew her well, and clearly the universe wanted her to remember. Considering they were now more intimately involved than ever before, she had to admit there was a great deal of comfort in that. She set the metal can just inside the front door and asked, "So, what's in the bag?"

"Supplies. I wasn't sure what you had, so I grabbed a little of everything you might need." He shrugged his shoulders.

"Thank you, Nick. That was very thoughtful. I'll have to fix up your atrocious flower beds one day in return."

He looked like he wanted to say something—perhaps ask to come in and help. She felt guilty for not offering, but she desperately needed time to process this all alone. She needed to prove to herself that she could. There was also something to be said about drawing a firm boundary around her home improvement projects. Couples worked on their home together.

She and Nick were not a couple, and this wasn't their home.

"Alright, then. If you need anything..." His voice trailed off as he shoved his hands in his pockets. He stood for a moment longer, rocking back on his heels, before he gave her a small salute and hopped down the porch stairs with heavy steps.

Mia stepped back inside and closed the door with a faint click. She looked from the furniture still pushed to the center of the room to the blank wall on the far right.

"I guess I'm painting today, too."

Mia sat on her porch later that evening, exhausted, her arms and shoulders aching. The sun was setting in front of her, and she enjoyed watching the orange ball of fire slowly lower itself below the horizon. She took a sip of water from her glass, and the ice brushed gently against her lips. It was a refreshing end to a day spent working to reclaim her home. Newly fixed picture frames littered her kitchen table, the glue dry but still tacky, and two coats of dark green paint dried on her wall. Repair and renew.

"It's a beautiful sunset today, isn't it?" Ida said, walking across the slim patch of grass where neither neighbor was sure where one yard ended and the other began. She wore bright white capris with a yellow satin shirt tucked into the front. She carried a cake in one hand and a small green basket of strawberries in the other.

"It is," Mia agreed, her chair creaking as she rocked.

"I took a trip out to Washington Farms today to pick

up some fresh strawberries for this pound cake I made and thought I'd bring some by for you," Ida said. She walked up the porch stairs and gestured to the door with her head, her red painted lips drawn into a smile.

Mia stood abruptly and slid in front of her to open the door. "It looks delicious," she said, welcoming Ida in. "I apologize for the smell of paint. I only finished a half hour ago, but I do have the windows open."

"Don't apologize. It's good to see you making this place your own." Ida set the cake and strawberries on the bar at the perimeter of the kitchen, immediately at home. She opened cabinets until she found a cutting board and busied herself with slicing fruit. "Will you be removing that awful wallpaper in the bathroom next?"

Mia followed her in, pulling out two plates and taking a seat on one of the bar stools. "It's pretty bad, isn't it?" Mia said with a chuckle. "I'm surprised you remember."

"Child, you don't forget something that ugly. It was just as hideous the day Nancy put it up," Ida said.

Mia laughed and wondered what the infamous Nancy was like. Despite the easy conversation, the break-in loomed over her as if an elephant filled the living room behind them. She didn't want to tell Ida, not out of any desire to hide the information from her, but because she didn't want to speak of it herself. Still, they were neighbors, and it didn't feel right keeping it from her. Ida deserved to protect herself.

Ida laid a thick slice of buttery yellow pound cake on each plate, topping each with fresh strawberries and a dollop of homemade whipped cream from a repurposed butter container. She slid a plate in front of Mia and moved around the bar to take a seat in front of her own. She picked up her fork and scooped up a bite of cake topped with a plump strawberry. Holding it in front of her mouth, Ida asked pointedly, "So, how long are you going to make me wait before you tell me why the police were here last night?" She took a bite as if punctuating her sentence and looked at Mia with a raised brow.

Sufficiently chastised, Mia gave Ida the condensed version of the night's events, minus exactly what Nick's involvement outside of the burglary had been. "Have you ever had something like this happen on this street?" she asked.

Ida shook her head. "No, not me. I don't recall it happening to anyone else either, though sometimes we get the occasional drunk singers walking from the bar downtown. So prepare yourself for that. Though, that's usually around the fourth of July when there isn't any parking to speak of in this poor little city. One year, Alan Baker—he owns that antique shop downtown—even crawled into bed with me in the middle of the night. Drunk as a skunk, he was."

"He didn't! What did you do?"

"I nearly beaned him with the bat I keep by my bed. It just so happens that the sight of it scared him out of there real quick."

"You threatened him with a bat?"

"You better believe I did, and he's never mentioned it since. Though, I do get mystery flowers on my doorstep every year for the occasion," Ida cackled. "Now, I make sure to lock my doors up tight, especially on holidays when the liquor is flowing out of the bottle as fast as the common sense out of the minds of the men who drink it."

Mia shook her head at the ridiculousness of small town life, but really, she wouldn't trade it for the world. But Ida's comment niggled at her. She thought about her own blunder with locked doors, and her brows drew together. She reassured herself that just because a burglary hadn't happened to anyone before didn't mean that there was any reason to be concerned about it happening now.

"That's a serious face, darlin'," Ida said.

Mia propped her chin in her hand and shook her head. "I'm just tired, is all."

Ida nodded and pushed her plate away from her. "Well, then I'll get on out of here and let you nap." She stood and patted a hand on Mia's cheek, a grandmotherly gesture that made Mia's heart clench. She'd never met her own grandmother, but she imagined this was how it felt to have one.

"Thank you, Ida. I think I'll do that."

21

____

Technically, Nick was writing again. If you considered words typed by a man spending as much time staring out the window as he was watching his computer screen, then his book was coming along nicely. Plus, revisions on his previous book were back on schedule. But while he spun fantastical mysteries on paper, the one happening in front of him was less easily solved. Mia hadn't called him in days, and her replies to his messages were sporadic, delayed, or a few words at most.

He knew she was intentionally keeping him at a distance. When you were intimate with someone, you knew these kinds of things. He figured Ewan was the reason, and he didn't blame her. Honestly, his epiphany at the pier convinced him that Ewan would want them to be happy together, but he wasn't sure if she believed that as firmly as he did. In his more self-indulgent moments, he imagined if Ewan could pick anyone for Mia, it would've been him, but his plan to romance her was failing miserably.

He tried every approach he could think of—sending sweet messages, asking her on dates directly, dropping by the bookshop for lunch, even buying her home improvement supplies. Nothing was working. Simply put, it was impossible to romance someone who was avoiding you. How was he supposed to court the damn woman at this point without seeming like a stalker? He could only think of so many legitimate reasons to drop by before it would appear desperate at best, creepy at worst.

She couldn't keep this up forever, though. Eventually, she'd have to come home early enough that he could catch her. So, like any reasonable person, he positioned his desk catty-corner to the wall so he could see out his window and watch for her car. There was absolutely nothing odd about that, he assured himself. He justified it by saying he was also watching out for someone whose house was recently broken into. That's what good neighbors did, of course.

At long last, her car streaked across his view. "There you are," he muttered.

He watched as her car slowed and pulled into the driveway, and he glanced at the clock on his laptop screen. He'd give her five minutes. That way she had time to get inside, maybe change if she needed to, but it wasn't so long that she'd be in the shower or otherwise occupied by the time he casually strolled by. Whistling at the brilliance of his plan, Nick tossed a clean shirt on and slid his feet into comfortable sandals. He ran outside and intentionally slowed himself down when he began the short walk to Mia's house. It wouldn't exactly look natural if he showed up harried and out of breath. Rather than find her inside, though, he saw that she'd changed into what he liked to think of as her gardening clothes and was kneeling down, pulling weeds from the flower beds.

Mia turned at the sound of his whistling and smiled up at him as he came closer. She stood, brushed her hands off on her shorts, and walked across the grass to him.

"Hey, you," she said.

"Come here." He pulled her to him and brushed his lips against hers. "I missed you."

Mia sighed. "I missed you, too."

"But you didn't want to," Nick quipped. Before she could respond, he continued, "It's okay, though. I'll forgive you if you'll let me take you to bed again." He nuzzled her neck, his teeth nipping at her as he pressed hot kisses up and down it. He felt her pulse quicken, and he grinned victoriously against her skin.

"Fine," she said breathlessly.

"Tonight," he said. He knew he was pushing her, but he couldn't help himself. She smelled of spice and paper and soil and sweat, and it was intoxicating.

"Yes, yes," she agreed.

"Good," he said. He gave her neck a playful bite and pushed his luck again. "Have dinner with me first."

"You know I can't," she said, leaning back in his arms.

"Can't or won't," he said, raising a brow.

"They're the same thing. I'm sleeping with you, but that's all."

"I can wait."

"It's not a matter of waiting, Nick. I don't want to date you. I don't want to date anyone," she groaned.

"You should know that a challenge like that only makes me want to prove you wrong." He put a hand up. "No, don't say anything else. You'll only be that much more salty about it if I win, and I'm in too good a mood to spoil it. We'll just agree to disagree and order takeout instead."

Mia eyed him warily, but she nodded.

"Perfect. So tell me about your week," he said, throwing an arm over her shoulder and steering them toward the house. He smiled inwardly when her hand slid into his back pocket as they walked, a gesture he'd seen her do with Ewan countless times. He wondered if she even knew she was doing it—he hoped so. It wasn't a terribly glorious feeling to be jealous of a dead man.

They decided on takeout from a local Italian restaurant and ate it together at the kitchen table with white wine and talk of the latest gossip. Sarah was in the bookshop again earlier that day and spilled the tea on a whole mess of small town drama. One of the high school teachers was being let go for undisclosed reasons, Brad's nephew's friend's sister—or was it cousin?—was pregnant and not happy about it, and the antique store owner next to Mia's shop (newly widowed) was having a flaming affair with a nurse at the assisted living facility where his late wife had been. When dinner was done and the gossip mill dry, Nick took Mia's hand and brought it to his lips.

"Come to bed with me," he said. Mia nodded, and he led her to the bedroom. She moved to turn off the overhead light and bedside lamps, but he stopped her at the last one. "Leave that one on. I want to see you."

Without thinking, she said, "Ewan never liked all the lights..." Her voice trailed off, and she looked at him in horror. "I'm sorry."

"Why?"

"It seems a little rude to talk about my bedroom habits with one man when I'm having sex with another, let alone his best friend," she said, taken aback. It seemed fairly obvious to her.

He crossed the room, his face a mask of severity. "What if I told her we shared everything?"

Mia punched him in the arm.

"Okay, I deserved that." He laughed and squared himself in front of her, twining his fingers with hers and bringing them to his lips. "I don't expect you to stop loving Ewan. I know you still do, and I know you miss him. I do, too. That's never going to change for either of us, and that's okay. I don't want to pretend he wasn't your husband or try to make you forget about him. He was a good man, and you're a good woman. I know you've got enough room in there for me, too."

The wall around her heart cracked, and she tried in vain to ignore the feelings that poured out. She'd never dreamed Nick, her Nick, could speak with such depth, and she told him so.

He chuckled, pulled her to him, and ran his hands up and down her arms. "I never had much reason to. You were off limits."

Then his eyes met and held hers with near terrifying intensity. "Now you're mine."

He took his time peeling the clothes away from her body as her hands worked to do the same for him. He wrapped one hand around the side of her neck in a gesture that sent thrills of anticipation through her system, and his mouth met hers. She eagerly welcomed him and matched his pace, opening and closing her lips on his, moving as he moved. He felt her hands on his back as he skimmed a hand down the side of her breast. He cupped it and rubbed his thumb over the nipple. She shuddered beneath his touch, and he circled it again. She moaned and arched against him, her lower belly pressing against his arousal.

He drew back from her then and pulled her down to the bed with him, spreading her legs wide so he could see her splayed out. "So beautiful," he said. "I've been thinking of doing this all day." Before Mia could even react, his mouth descended onto the most sensitive part of her.

He positioned himself between her legs, one arm pushing under her thick thigh and anchoring her hips. He lapped at her and languished in the soft folds of skin there. With his free hand, he pushed aside the soft bush of hair and drove his tongue into her slowly. He moved higher to her clit and rubbed it with the flat of his tongue. Again and again he moved his mouth against her until she was gasping and writhing beneath him, her hands wrapped around his head and pressing him down as she pushed herself off the bed and into his mouth. He pushed his fingers into her as he circled her clit with his tongue rhythmically. She was close. He could feel her pulsing around him, hear her pants, and he groaned against her as he worked.

She cried out when she came, and her legs shook against him. Her breathing was heavy, and he watched her hands dive into her own hair as the orgasm washed over her. She was sopping wet, and he couldn't wait any longer. He slid his body over hers and pushed himself into her. She moaned in response and met his gaze as he entered her, gasping at the sweet fullness. When his movements became rhythmic, she urged him on with her words and her hands, grabbing his hips and pulling him toward her. Her nails dug into the skin at his hips, but he wasn't ready for it to be over yet.

Ripping himself out of her, he lifted her by the hips and turned her over for him. "I want to see you from behind. I want to watch your ass slap against me while I fuck you."

Mia propped herself on her forearms and arched her back. He guided himself into her, fascinated by the sight of it. His fingers dug into her hips, and he swore her tattoo made him that much harder.

"Touch yourself," he demanded, one hand still on her hips, the other splayed across her lower back. "I want you to come again."

He watched in fascination as she rubbed herself. Over and over they moved together, sweat beading on their skin, their moans joining, until he felt her clench around him, and she cried out again. It was all he needed to fall over the edge, and soon he joined her in ecstasy. They collapsed onto the bed together, and Nick drew her to him. Spent and satisfied, she snuggled into him, her body sated. It wasn't long before her breathing deepened, and she slept. Nick drew the covers up and over them both. He watched her slip into sleep, wondering just how many walls he'd have to break through to get to her heart. She fit so perfectly against him, he hardly believed she'd ever belonged to anyone else.

Not anymore.

Now she was his.

22

Mia woke the next morning slightly sore and unbelievably satisfied. She turned over as she'd done throughout the night, but the other side of the bed was cold and empty. With a frown, Mia pulled on a t-shirt and walked into the kitchen. Nick wasn't there either, but she found a note sitting on the kitchen counter.

The muse struck. Off to work.
Dream of me.

Dream of him. How could she not? Her entire world was turning upside down, and there he was calmly chipping away at her defenses with the determination of a salmon swimming upstream. She had a feeling that just like the salmon, he'd keep at it bit by bit until he made it all the way into her heart. The worst of it was she was no longer so sure she didn't want him to. She'd forgotten how it felt to curl up in the night with someone—to feel their arms come around you in sleep or even to know you weren't alone—so much so that she was making it a point to separate herself from him in sleep.

Twisting her up even more was the intensity of the chemistry she and Nick had, and just how different it was from anything she'd experienced before. Sex with her late husband was always loving. He knew what she liked, and she knew how to touch him, but nothing they'd done came close to the pure heat of being with Nick. She felt like she'd graduated from the slow and steady pace of a merry-go-round to a full-blown roller coaster complete with steep hills, breathtaking falls, and loops that turned her stomach into knots. There was no comparison. But when she thought about it, wasn't that a good thing? Wasn't it a good thing that she could look back on her memories with her late husband with joy and not feel as if Nick had proverbial shoes to fill? Or that Ewan had somehow missed the mark.

Mia filled a glass with ice and water and picked up a banana from the fruit basket in the center of her kitchen table. She peeled each layer as she walked over to the bookshelf. Taking a bite, she grabbed something from her "to be read" stack, noticing with a pang that her fairy statue no longer sat beside it. Anger wasn't far behind the sadness. How could someone invade her home like that? And why would they? What could she possibly have that was worth invading her home and breaking her things? It felt worse that she knew the statistics, knew that it was likely she would never get the answers to those questions.

According to her internet sleuthing, investigators solved less than twenty percent of home burglaries, so she was better off putting it out of her mind and double checking the locks. (She reminded herself again to fix the sticking lock.) The police were likely right. They believed nothing was taken, so it was probably some drunk tourist or a small-time criminal looking for an easy score. Her door was likely one of dozens tried that night and the unlucky unlocked winner.

She sat down, opened the book, and immediately immersed herself in a world of magic and castles, love and betrayal. She must have been reading for hours when a knock at her door made her nearly jump out of her skin. The irritation was instant, not with her visitor but with the person who'd threatened her sanctuary. Someone had done this to her, made her feel less than perfectly safe in her own home. She was building her life there, and someone disturbed that peace. Vowing not to be undone by fear, Mia took a steadying breath and walked to the front door. Judging by how stiff her neck was, it had to be late in the afternoon, and a glance at the clock confirmed it. She flipped the lock, intentionally avoiding the peep-hole, and opened the door. When she saw Alexis smiling at her, she sent a silent prayer of thanks to the heavens that it wasn't Nick—she simply didn't have the mental energy to maintain her own defenses at the moment.

"Hey, stranger!" Alexis crowed, stepping inside automatically and giving Mia a hard hug. "I heard someone's been a grand success! Maybe that's why you haven't answered any of my texts."

Mia hugged her back, then pushed the door closed

behind her. She smiled a little bashfully and tucked her hair behind her ear. "Yeah, sorry about that. I've been slammed every day this week. I almost felt bad closing today and tomorrow."

"Well, you look exhausted, but you also look really happy. It's been a long time since you looked happy." Alexis sat down on the couch and tossed her brown purse onto Mia's favorite chair.

"It's been a long time since I felt happy, but I think I'm getting there." She sat next to Alexis and folded her legs under her. "So how are you? What brings you over here?"

"Well, for one, I had to make sure you were alive," Alexis said.

"Still here."

"That's a relief," Alexis said. She wore her riot of amber curls down today and tucked a stray lock behind her ear without thinking. She looked around. Though Mia and Nick had done their best to clean the room, Mia had gotten a little side tracked painting, and there were still stacks of broken pictures hanging out of their frames and abused books on the floor and shelves. "Did something happen?"

"Oh, that," Mia said with a sad laugh. "Apparently, I had a break-in, so I repainted. You know, to reclaim my space and all that."

"Hold on. The color looks great... But someone broke in? Why? Are you okay? Did they take anything? Why didn't you call me?" Alexis demanded. Her voice went from concern to irritation.

"It just happened. I was going to call you. I was!" Mia said defensively. She grabbed her glass of water like it was a life preserver. The ice had long since melted, and droplets of condensation soaked the glass. A ring of water pooled on the coffee table around the bottom of the cup. She took a deep gulp.

Alexis made a sound that could only be interpreted as skeptical, but she decided not to push Mia. The last thing she wanted to do right now was fight. She took a breath and softened her voice. "Are you okay? I worry about you."

Mia shook her head. "You don't have to worry about me, Lex. I'm fine. A little shaken up, but fine. They didn't take anything, and the police don't seem too concerned about it. A crime of opportunity is all. Nothing to worry about. Really." Alexis did not look convinced, so Mia tried to change the subject. "How's work?"

"I see what you're trying to do," Alexis said pointedly. "But it sucks so much right now. I'll let you change the subject so I can vent." Mia laughed, relieved, and Alexis continued. "They've laid off a few people—you left just in time to avoid that drama—but instead of hiring any new editors, they've just shifted their workload to the rest of us. So we're all drowning in emails, agents are getting upset that it's taking us longer than normal, and of course, Cathy is acting like it's all on us to fix it."

"Maybe you could come work for me," Mia said. She was only joking, of course, but as soon as the thought was out of her mouth, the idea took root. She couldn't resist how appealing it sounded, how much fun it would be to spend her days surrounded by books with her best friend.

And her nights with Nick.

"Now there's a thought." Alexis took a sip from the iced coffee in her hand, it to Mia next.

Mia shook her head. "No, really. Think about it. If it stays this busy, and I have every intention of doing everything I can to make that happen, I'll need someone to help me, likely sooner rather than later, and there's no one else I'd rather spend all day with. It wouldn't be New York editor money, but it would be decent."

"I don't make New York editor money now," Alexis said with a chuckle.

"Come by the shop the next day you have some time off, and we'll talk more about it."

"Sure! Right now, anything sounds better than spending all day in the office with that woman and every waking moment out of it reading manuscripts. My eyeballs are going to revolt and run away in my sleep," Alexis said. "Now, in other news, tell me everything that's happening with the delicious Nicholas."

"Would you believe me if I said we're still just friends?" Mia hedged.

Alexis snorted and shook her head. "Nay, nay, my dear. Spill it."

Mia took a deep breath, thinking of how to break down everything that had happened since she'd last seen her friend. How could she condense the casual drop-ins, the kiss, walking on the beach, and mind blowing sex into a story that even made sense?

When she waited too long to respond, Alexis said with a cackle, "You've already slept with him!"

"No!" Mia cried, sitting forward. Then, with a grin, she fell back on the couch. "Okay, yes."

"I knew it!" Alexis said, pointing a finger at Mia. "Tell

me everything! Is he the slow and steamy type or rough and ready?"

Playing along, Mia wiggled so that she was propped up on the arm of the couch. She sighed and pursed her lips. "Both? The first time he picked me up and carried me all the way to the bedroom."

Alexis fanned herself. "I love it when they do that. Does he also do the... you know?" Alexis mimed pushing a man's head down between her legs.

"Oh, yeah," Mia said with a laugh.

"Hallelujah! On a scale of one to ten, how is he?"

Mia shrugged her shoulders. "Is it bragging to say that he breaks the scale?"

"Yes! Oh my, you have been busy. So are you two officially a couple?" Alexis asked.

"We're keeping it casual. I get the feeling he wants more, but we're just enjoying each other right now. No strings attached."

"Well, I'll be rooting for you because I'm loyal, but if rumors are true, he's quite the charmer. You'll be lucky if you can hold out against him," Alexis said. "What I really want to know is how did all of this happen without a whisper to me?"

"I'm really sorry about that. I've been so busy with the house and the store and, I don't know, ghosts. It's just got me all out of whack."

Alexis looked instantly concerned. "Nightmares still?"

"Well, yes, but—okay, please don't think I'm insane—I think they might be real," Mia said. She told Alexis about the dreams bleeding into real life, the news stories, the sister, the journal, and even her growing suspicions about Brad's role as Emily's murderer.

"It sounds straight out of a murder mystery," Alexis said. She sipped the last of her coffee and set the cup down on the floor beside them, and the ice jingled musically. "But Brad? You really think he could've killed her?"

"I don't know, maybe. I mean, aren't we all capable of it on some level?" Mia speculated. "Say Emily really smothered her baby, and then Brad came home. Isn't it possible he could've killed her in a blind rage?"

"Or maybe it was a lover trying to get his family out of the way? Didn't you say he was having an affair?"

"Now that would be straight out of a murder mystery. Emily said he was sneaking around, but she wrote toward the end that she thought it might have ended."

"Maybe for one of them. Or maybe she really killed herself. You did say she thought her son was possessed. Not the most stable, I'd say, and honestly, I don't know that Brad is the murdering type," Alexis said. "But what can you do with any of this?"

"I'm not sure. I think they—Emily and David, that is— want me to figure out what happened to them. Maybe it'll help them find peace or move on to the other side or whatever it is ghosts do," Mia said.

"You know, I ran into this cop recently who works over in Candler County. Please don't ask how we met. It's mortifying. But I'm supposed to be seeing him again soon. Maybe I can pick his brain and see what he has to say about all of this," Alexis said.

"That'd be great. Maybe go easy on the ghost talk, though."

"I'll keep it vague," Alexis assured her.

"In the meantime, I'll keep digging through the diary and see if I can learn anything else. Maybe I'll find another clue." Mia took a deep breath and mentally locked that all away, desperate to change the subject again. "Now, tell me more about this cop. Is he a dating kind of friend?"

"Not exactly," Alexis said.

"Wait, I thought you were still dating Amanda?"

"Not really." Alexis shifted uncomfortably. A dusky red flush crept up Alexis' cheeks, giving her brown skin a ruddy, slightly shiny appearance. She blew out a breath and hid her face in her hands when her chin quivered.

"So... the cop isn't exactly a dating kind of friend, and you're not really dating Amanda anymore? I'm confused," Mia said.

"I don't want to talk about it," Alexis answered from behind her fingers, her voice tight from holding back tears.

"Honey, what happened?" Mia shifted closer to Alexis and rubbed a hand in circles on her back as Alexis began to cry.

Mia shook her head sadly. There was only one way to handle heartbreak, a surefire ritual of women, and it called for reinforcements. She stood and said, "I'll make up the spare bedroom," and then walked to the kitchen like a warrior preparing for battle. Only tonight her weapons would be wine, snacks, and romance movies.

23

Mia knew she was tempting the fates when she went to bed with the journal, but the ghosts—there was no longer any doubt in her mind that they were ghosts—had revealed nothing new in her recent dreams, and she was running out of leads.

"If they're always giving away clues in your dreams, maybe you need to figure out a way to dream more," Alexis had said over breakfast that morning.

It hadn't sounded particularly appealing then, and it certainly didn't now, but she was growing desperate. Mia laid the book on the bed next to a spiral-bound notebook and diligently noted all the information she'd discovered in neat bullet points going down the left side of the paper. She underlined information she needed to learn more about, like the abuse claims from the sister, and added question marks next to pieces of information that confused her, like the visit from the doctor's assistant. Along the bottom, she drew a square box and added broader questions.

Did Emily really kill David?

Who was Brad having an affair with?

Did Brad kill Emily, or did she commit suicide?

She was sure if she could work out the answers to those questions, she'd know what happened. "Is that what you want? For me to find out what really happened to you?" she asked the room, but as expected, there was no answer.

She sighed and tapped her pen on the notebook. There had to be someone who could fill in some details. Brad was married again, and happily, by the looks of it, so talking to his former flame was out of the question. And she couldn't very well go asking him if he'd gone and murdered his ex-wife and possibly his son, either. The doctor was probably bound by patient confidentiality laws, so she'd strike out there. That only left the assistant, really. She wondered if those same laws would apply to her, as well. It might be worth looking into.

On her nightstand, her phone jingled at the sound of an incoming text message. Leaning across her notebook, Mia grabbed the phone and unlocked the screen. It was a message from Nick asking if she was still up. Feeling slightly guilty, she sent her phone to sleep and set it back on the nightstand without responding. Maybe it was wrong, but she needed to be alone. It was so easy to relax into him, so easy to envision him as someone to share the load with, but she wasn't about to sacrifice everything for which she was working for a man who was just going to break her heart. Why couldn't he be like every other toxic man-boy and be satisfied with a little sex on the side, friendly banter, and the occasional takeout in bed?

Putting it from her mind, Mia dedicated herself to pretending her phone was not judging her and flipped idly through the journal again. She didn't imagine there was anything left to pick apart in its pages, but she had to try. The entries ended suddenly with that last ominous message.

I have to save him. Forgive me.

It sent a shiver up Mia's spine thinking about it. How sick did you have to be to write that? To feel that? Mia felt like everyone around Emily had failed her. She was seeing a doctor, and she was on medication at one point. Her husband knew well that she was struggling far longer than was typical after giving birth—Mia knew because she'd done some reading on postpartum depression and psychosis. Yet, no one had done a thing, and those who had surely hadn't done enough. It was heart wrenching to live Emily's life through these pages, to feel the isolation and confusion and anger.

Emotionally exhausted, Mia didn't notice when her eyes drifted closed or when the room slowly filled with an eerie fog. The lamp light flickered, and a dark figure crawled through the shadows. Mia slipped into sleep as something else slipped into her bed, crooning a lullaby and stroking her hair.

In her dreams, Mia snuggled down into a soft bed, much like her own. She felt the bumpy ridges of a soft blanket clutched between her fingers as an icy hand brushed at her forehead. A haunting melody floated on the air, but she couldn't make out the words of the song. Suddenly, the stroking on her forehead stopped, and there was the choking feeling again. She couldn't take a breath. Her body bucked against the pressure on her face, but she couldn't dislodge it.

Then, as suddenly as it started, it stopped, and she was standing in a hazy white room. She recognized it from her earlier dream, and she turned in circles, trying in vain to remember where to go. Memories from this dream and others all bled together until it was impossible to tell what was happening now.

Through the fog, she heard two women's voices. One voice sounded calm, the other frantic, but she couldn't make out the words.

"No, Momma," David cried.

A door behind her opened, and Mia turned in time to see blonde hair disappear around a corner, the smell of decaying roses floating behind her. David stood beside her, crying. She reached out to touch his hair, to offer some sort of comfort, and for the first time felt the soft wisps of it. Without thinking, she bent down and picked him up, nestling him into her neck and rubbing his back in slow circles. Mia rocked back and forth with him in her arms, and when she heard the gasping and kicking of Emily suffocating on the ground, she sang a lullaby to cover the sound.

Mia's eyes flew open, and she gasped. She stared at the ceiling, letting her mind drift back to reality, but when she sat up, Emily's grotesque, contorted face was only inches away. Mia screamed and pushed herself back against the headboard, the back of her head slapping against it with a crack. Emily's eyes bulged, and her mouth was open in a death-like scream. The inside was black and cavernous, her lips peeling back from her teeth, and out of her throat came a low ghastly moan. Mia fought for calm, pulling the covers over herself like a shield. Her breath hitched, and her skin prickled. Her mind raced to make some sense of it all, to form some semblance of a plan. How did you fight off a ghost hellbent on terrifying you? And for what? Emily inched closer to her, and a squeak of terror escaped Mia's mouth.

Behind Emily, Mia saw David's tiny body appear in the doorway, dressed in the same pajamas as always and dragging his little blanket alongside him. He knuckled his eye as he cried, his face pale, eyes puffy and tear filled. Sniffling, he said in a small voice, "Momma. Momma."

With a wail, Emily's ghost floated backward off the bed. She turned her face as she stood and sobbed softly, and when she looked back at Mia, her face appeared how Mia imagined she'd looked like in life. Sad, gaunt, hopeless... but not a decaying corpse. Emily didn't open her mouth again, but Mia heard a haunting whisper in her mind say, "I'm sorry." Then the ghostly figures faded into nothing, and the crying slowly died out.

With a hand pressed to her heart, Mia gasped, "Oh my god."

Mia's hand shook as she picked up her phone. She managed to pull up Nick's number. It was only a little after three in the morning, so there was a good chance he was asleep. In fact, he was probably sound asleep, she thought. She hesitated, her finger hovering over the call button. Maybe she shouldn't call him. It was only a nightmare, after all. If she called him over now, he might get the wrong idea. Hadn't she already decided that more separation was best? Yes, it was safer if she put down the phone and sorted this out herself.

She pressed a button, sent the phone back to sleep, and let her body fall back onto the bed.

If only she had an "off" button of her own.

24

In the morning, Mia wasn't feeling as rested, but she was determined. Unfortunately, the ghosts hadn't given her much more to go on, but she was sure about one thing: she had to talk to the assistant who visited Emily in the days before she died. There was something important about Emily at the end, something Emily was trying to show her in the dream, and Mia knew she was missing it.

Why ghosts had to be so cryptic, she did not know. You'd think they'd be the ones scrawling the names of their killers on the wall instead of leading people through hazy dreams or hovering over them with dead faces as they slept. The thought of Emily's ghastly face in those moments was terrifying and not a sight she wanted again.

Gathering the diary and her notebook, Mia decided she needed to get out of the house and stare at a fresh set of four walls. She needed to figure out how to get access to

Emily's doctor without waltzing into his waiting room and demanding an appointment. She daydreamed, just a little, about what doors the credentials of a private investigator could open and even briefly considered hiring one. Then again, a real P.I. would likely hear her story and laugh in her face. Instead, she decided that a trip to the local cafe, where the baked goods were always hot and the tea and coffee plentiful, was exactly what she needed. The cafe liked to think it lent itself to the more colorful folk of her St. John's, the artists and the creatives, but really, it was a gathering place for so many more. She didn't consider herself particularly creative, but she always felt at home there, too. The creative atmosphere might be exactly what she needed to come up with a creative solution around doctor-patient confidentiality.

Mia parked on one of the many downtown streets and walked just over a block to Sweet Bea's. Opened in the early 1900s by Beatrice Smith, the little cafe had a reputation as a hub for writers and artists in particular, and it was a favorite among the locals. Mia walked inside and ordered a lemon tart and black currant tea at the counter. She pulled the strap of her bag up onto her shoulder and waited for her order to be ready.

"Here you are, ma'am," a young man who couldn't be over sixteen said, handing her a travel cup of tea and the tart atop a thin napkin square.

Mia took it gratefully and wound her way through the crowd to a chair by the front door. Some might be here seeking a quiet space to work out of the way, but today, she wanted to be in the thick of it. Mia wanted to see the people who came and went, listen to their conversations, and be revitalized by their energy. She pulled out her notes, and her eyes scanned the page. She bit absent-mindedly into the tart, and the lemon zinged across her tongue, the buttery pastry melting in her mouth. With quiet appreciation, she closed her eyes and thanked the bakery gods for blessing man with butter and flour.

Turning her attention back to her work, Mia looked over her unanswered questions and tried to piece them all together. Based on her dreams, she knew Emily was unwell and probably predisposed to killing her son. That was pretty clear. Although she clearly had no personal experience in the matter, she was positive that the choking feeling from her dream was David being smothered. Despite what Emily's sister believed, there didn't seem to be a whole lot of evidence that she didn't kill him. And while her dreams weren't exactly evidence, the police statements were.

Next, she was sure she'd watched Emily strangle to death, though whether that was by her own hand was yet to be determined, at least as far as Mia was concerned. So if David's death was obvious, what was she missing about it? And what about Emily's death did she still need to uncover? There had to be more to it. Why would they show her how they'd died if it meant nothing? Then again, why reveal any of that without giving her some-thing more tangible? Watching it happen, feeling it, was unnerving. Just thinking about it made her feel as though she was suffocating right now, the nauseating smell of roses and decay filling her nose.

"Mia," a woman squealed. Mia looked up to see Sarah coming toward her from the counter with her arms already open for a hug, and as expected, Sarah pulled her into an embrace the moment she stood. Really, it was amazing how the woman had so much energy all the time.

"Sarah, how are you?" Mia asked politely.

Sarah flicked a wrist with a smile. "Oh, I'm just fine and dandy. I see you've come up for air. Store keeping you nice and busy?"

"Very," Mia said. "I'm excited for the next book club meeting. Have y'all decided on a book yet?"

"We've almost settled, but Jane has to go and read all the reviews first. I swear, that girl reads a hundred reviews about anything before she'll ever part with a dollar."

"If you need any recommendations, you let me know. We've got several new releases coming in the next few weeks that you might like."

"Thank you, I'll pass that along," Sarah said. She glanced down at Mia's open notebook. "So, what are you workin' on?"

"Just a little research," Mia said, speaking slowly, her hands restlessly fiddling with the pages.

"Oh, are you helping Nick out with one of his new mysteries? I heard y'all were getting a little cozy."

Mia took a breath and wondered how she could fly under the radar on this one. She tried not to overthink it and settled on simplicity. "Yes, sort of."

"Hold that thought." Sarah put up a finger and scurried over to the counter to grab her coffee and a muffin. Mia took her seat again, and Sarah joined her, placing her muffin on the table in between them and crossing her ankles under the chair. She talked between delicate sips. "What are you researching?"

Keep it simple, believable, Mia ordered herself. "Mostly medical information, though I'll admit I don't know as much as Nick seems to think I do."

"Where men get their ideas," Sarah quipped.

"I know. I'll never understand." As tactfully as she could, Mia asked, "I don't suppose you know anyone who might let me ask a few questions, pick their brain a bit. I heard Dr. Hubert's still in business. Do you know him?"

"I do. In fact, I'm meeting him here today to talk about sponsoring my niece's softball team, but darlin', he's a psychiatrist. I don't know what kind of help he'll be."

"That's fine. I'm sure anyone with more experience than me could fill in these gaps. I don't even know what to search for online," she lied. Mia noticed Sarah give her an odd look and wondered if her lie was convincing. The last thing Mia wanted was for anyone directly connected to Brad to know what she was all about, especially the woman who was his wife and the town's busybody. If he did murder Emily, she didn't think he'd take kindly to someone poking around trying to bring it to the surface. If he didn't...

Well, she couldn't bear to cause him more grief. She, of all people, knew how hard it was to live normally again.

"Of course." Sarah took another sip of her coffee and nibbled on a muffin.

Mia didn't want to tell Sarah to go away—that seemed rude—but she wasn't exactly in the mood for idle chitchat, either. She looked around and watched the people sitting and standing around the room, what they were drinking and doing. There was a young girl in a crop top and shorts tapping away at a laptop, and a man in neon sunglasses waiting at the counter, sighing dramatically with every passing second. Her fingers itched to flip through her notes again, but she didn't dare do it in front of Sarah. Instead, she tapped her fingers in lyrical patterns on the side of her coffee cup.

"How are things at the bookstore?" Sarah asked.

Mia smiled tightly. It looked like she'd be sharing a conversation with Sarah, after all. "It's going well. I'm actually coordinating with a children's book author and the local elementary about a live reading event for the kids in the fall."

"Isn't that lovely! You know, I once went to the children's theater downtown with my niece. The author came to read and sing, and we just thought it was the sweetest thing. Man went on to become a bestseller, too." Sarah bit delicately into her muffin, reminding Mia of a chipmunk in slow-motion.

"That's the dream, huh?"

"Yes, it certainly—" Sarah said, stopping mid-sentence when a man walked through the door. "Earl! How are you?"

Mia watched as the man, dressed in a blue button-down collared shirt tucked into khakis, leaned in to give Sarah a hug. This must be Dr. Hubert. They exchanged pleasantries, and he walked to the counter to order a drink. When he came back and sat, his cheeks were rosy, and he was blowing over the top of a cup of tea. The string from the bag hung over the side, and Mia could smell bitter notes of black tea leaves and sweet rose.

"And who is this, Sarah?" the doctor asked, a pleasant smile on his face. He looked at Mia and raised his steaming mug in greeting.

"Oh, my manners!" Sarah exclaimed. "This is Mia Clark. Mia, this is Earl, Dr. Hubert."

Mia grasped the hand he held out and shook it firmly. "It's a pleasure to meet you."

"Likewise. Is this one trying to rope you into supporting the local youth, too?" He raised an elbow at Sarah, his eyes glittering with humor behind small, round glasses.

"Actually, I ran into Sarah here this morning, and she mentioned you may be able to help me with some research for a project I'm working on. I wonder if I might ask you a few questions, and then I'll leave you two to your business. Honestly, I could really use an expert's input."

"Well, I'm flattered. Of course. How can I help?"

"Thank you," she said. "Most of my questions are about patients' rights and confidentiality. I'm just not sure what types of scenarios those apply to."

The doctor took a few minutes to go over the applicable regulations, what they allowed and prohibited, and how they could apply in a few common situations. Mia sat and listened like an opponent in a game of chess, carefully planning her next move. She couldn't ask him outright about the mystery assistant without looking suspicious, but it seemed like that woman was one of the last to see Emily alive, and she desperately needed to talk to her.

"What about other members of staff? Ones who aren't the doctor," Mia said, leaning forward.

"Privacy applies to the person and the records. It doesn't much matter who the staff member is or what they do in the office," he said.

"That makes sense." Mia sat back in her seat and considered what this meant.

"I'm glad I could help," he said with a nod. He drew the cup to his mouth.

"One more quick question," she said, the words virtually tumbling over one another. "Would you ever have a nurse or assistant visit someone in their home to check in on them?"

"I suppose there could be cases where I would, if I had one," he said, angling his head as he considered it.

"You've never had an assistant or a nurse to help you?" she asked. She added in a rush, "I mean, you must be so busy. How do you run a practice by yourself?"

He scratched the stubble along his chin. "Nope, nope. Never had one in the office. Like to work alone and at my pace, I do. I've got a receptionist who fields my office line and sets appointments, but she works remotely. I don't think I've seen her in person in nearly a decade," he said. Mia nodded, her thoughts already far away. Dr. Hubert waited a moment, and when it seemed she had nothing else to say, he took a deep breath and slapped a hand on his knee. "Well, I hope I answered all your questions. You tell Nick I said hello when you see him next," he said with a wink.

"Oh, well, alright. Thank you for your time." She gathered up her notebook and bag, nodded her head to Sarah, and gave Dr. Hubert a tight smile. Did everyone in this town know who she was sleeping with?

As she walked out of the cafe, her phone buzzed against her ribs from the side of her purse, and she struggled to pull it out. She looked down at the screen, walking briskly to her parked car. It was another text from Nick. She shoved it back into her bag without reading it. The urge to vent her frustrations into a reply was too great. She was at another dead end with her research, which meant more nights of nightmares and lost sleep. Sarah probably thought she was slowly losing her mind, and her romantic life was the current local gossip.

At least it wasn't also raining, she thought and looked at the sky mutinously. "Don't you dare," she muttered.

Taking a deep breath, she forced her pulse to calm. She was going to take some time to putter around her garden and maybe even get a little adventurous and dive into the overgrowth in the backyard. The last thing she wanted was the sky to decide to ruin her healthy coping mechanism. The alternative was to bury her feelings in a pint of raspberry sorbet and cry over the romantically tragic deaths of fictional men.

Honestly, she wasn't sure what she was more upset about: that she was running out of ideas to solve her ghostly mystery or that she was feeling more and more pushed into a relationship with Nick that she didn't want. Every time she turned around, he was stopping by, texting her, calling.

Logically, Mia recognized it wasn't exactly his fault. He

would probably reach out to her less often if she responded more. As for the town gossip, plenty of people had seen them together, and it wasn't as if their romance was a secret. Emotionally, though, none of that really mattered.

However childish it was, he started this *thing* of theirs, and so naturally, this was all his fault.

25

For the first time in what felt like forever, Mia allowed herself to sleep in. When she did wake for the day, she dressed quickly and casually in denim shorts and an old band tee with her hair thrown messily into a bun on top of her head. Alexis was meeting her at the shop later, and Ida had promised to drop off a few thriving tomato plants that morning. She wanted to get them arranged in her little garden before she left.

She stepped outside shortly before midmorning, thankful to see the beautiful plants from Ida waiting for her. Hard green bulbs, just beginning to redden at the top, already covered the plants, and she contemplated harvesting them now for fried green tomatoes or waiting for them to ripen. She pulled on her gardening gloves and reminded herself not to get too carried away. She only had a couple of hours at most before she was due in the bookshop.

"You've been avoiding me," Nick called from behind her.

Mia sniffed and said, "I have not. I've been busy."

"Mmm," he muttered, walking up the porch stairs. Each step was slow and deliberate. "Liar."

"What brings you to my doorstep today, Nick?" She sighed and watched him approach, her stomach knotting tighter with every step he took. She wasn't sure why he came over originally, but his intentions now were clear. He took another step, and Mia's pulse quickened. Her tongue darted out to wet her lips, and his eyes darkened with desire.

"Ask me inside, Mia," he said, his eyes locked on hers. He reached out and took her hand in his, pulling off her gardening gloves one finger at a time. The slide of fabric against her skin had never felt so sensual. The gloves dropped to her feet, one after the other, and still his eyes stayed on hers. He tucked a hair behind her ear, and the back of his hand lingered on her cheek. He stroked the back of his fingers down it, his hand wrapping around the side of her neck, and drew her closer.

Her pulse roared in her ears. Her breasts pressed against his chest, and she could feel his heart racing. She couldn't resist fanning the flames of his desire, and if she was honest with herself, she didn't want to.

Looking up at him from under her lashes, she whispered, "And why would I need to do that?"

"Because I want to kiss you where I can take my time about it."

He lowered his mouth until it was a breath away, and Mia let herself have what she'd been dreaming of. His mouth crushed down on hers, and she grabbed his arms to stabilize herself as her entire world tilted. His other hand fisted at the small of her back, and he expertly maneuvered them through the doorway. Somewhere in the far corner of her mind, she registered the sound of the door closing behind them, but the noise sounded hollow and far away.

"The lock," she gasped between kisses, and she was vaguely aware of the sound of the lock clicking into place before he was turning them again. He pressed her against the wall, and the hard length of him stretched out along her. His hands cupped her neck, then skimmed down her shoulders and sides to grip her hips, all while his mouth ravaged hers. She felt his muscles bunching as they moved together, her body arching up to meet him.

"Mia, please," he begged. "I need you now."

He raised his head to stare at her, his gaze unfocused, and the depth of feeling in his eyes shook her. Then his lips were at her throat, and his teeth were on her neck as he pushed down her shorts and underwear. He groaned with pleasure when he found her soaking wet and ready for him, and within seconds he was hiking her leg up to his hip and sliding into her. She gasped, arching against him and murmuring encouragements as he moved in her. Nick grunted, and his hand came between them to stroke her. He desperately needed this to be as good for her as it was for him.

"Oh my god, Nick." Fire exploded from her center and pulsed through her body, and she gasped. Her knees went weak, and she gripped his shoulders tightly to keep from crumpling to the ground. She felt more than heard Nick growl against her shoulder, the sound a low rumble in his throat, before he joined her in oblivion. As his orgasm ebbed, he sagged against her, his breathing ragged.

He lifted his head from her shoulder, and the look in his eyes terrified her. It spoke of possession, territory, of feelings deeper than she was willing to go. She responded with a wary smile and gently disentangled herself from him. Blissfully ignorant, he kissed her cheek and walked half-naked toward the bathroom. She heard the flick of the light switch, the water running in the sink, the squeak of the metal towel holder when he dried his hands. Every sound increased her anxiety. These were the sounds of comfort, of making a home together, of "why don't you keep a few things in the bottom drawer?" Her fingers were shaky when she buttoned her shorts and smoothed down her shirt.

"I take it you missed me, too," he said with a grin when he reemerged from the hall. He came to her and reached an arm out, trying to snag her by the waist, but she evaded him and stepped quickly to the side. His brows drew together, and he frowned.

"I've got to get to the shop," Mia said as an explanation, but they both knew she was pushing him away. Hurt flashed across Nick's face. He hid it quickly, but Mia felt a stab of guilt.

"Alright," Nick drawled. "I'll see you later then." He leaned down and kissed her on his way out, his mouth lingering on her lips for a moment longer, his face still set in a frown.

Mia murmured in agreement, grabbed her bag, and followed him out the door. She hurried to her car and didn't realize until she was sitting inside that her under-wear was sopping wet from their frantic coupling, and she was still wearing her gardening clothes. Checking to make sure Nick was out of sight, Mia got out of the car and hurried back up to her house to change. She didn't take a deep breath again until she parked on the street across from the bookstore.

She could barely think through the emotions crowding in on her. It was clear Nick's feelings were developing at an alarming rate, far faster than she'd feared. Why couldn't he keep things simple? A simple relationship based on mutually satisfying activities beneath the sheets and no obligations or expectations outside of it. Surely that wasn't too much to ask. And while Nick may not be asking for more with his words—yet, she told herself—the look in his eyes said it all and more.

Looking up from her steering wheel, Mia saw Alexis walking toward the front door of the shop. She got out of her car and hurried across the street to unlock it.

"Hey!" Alexis said when she saw Mia approaching.

"Hey yourself," Mia said. The keys jingled as she turned them in the lock, and the bells sang overhead when she pushed the door open. Alexis followed her inside, looking around with a smile.

"It's even more beautiful than when I last saw it." Alexis pointed to the children's section. "I see you finished making the lighted clouds. I didn't know you could make those yourself. They look amazing."

"Thank you! The kids love them, too."

"I'll bet." Her chest heaved with a deep breath, and

Alexis smacked her hands on the sides of her jean-clad thighs. "So, where should I start, boss?"

"Here. Let's sit and chat for first." Mia led Alexis to a small seating area furnished with pillowy couches, chairs, and ottomans. Mia sat in one of the oversize chairs and folded her legs under herself as Alexis took a seat across from her and leaned forward. "I'm hoping you coming on to help will mean I'll be a little less exhausted at the end of the day. Ideally, I can also stay open six to seven days a week instead of five. I know there's a million reasons not to work with friends, but I think we could make it work. I just want to make sure you know there are no hard feelings if you say you don't want to do this. Now or ever."

"Hun, if I didn't think we'd make it work and be awesome together, I wouldn't be here at all," Alexis said. "The truth is, I've been feeling restless. Itchy, really. I don't know if I need a new relationship, a new job, or something else, but I need a change. This is my sign."

"Weren't you the one telling me I needed a change? Could it be that the wild stallion is ready for domestication?" Mia asked.

Alexis tutted playfully. "Don't go that far. I still haven't met anyone I'd settle down for. Let's just say that this whole 'find yourself' journey of yours has inspired me to do the same. Only without the paranormal crime fighting."

"I didn't know you felt that way, but I'm happy for you. Speaking of the paranormal..." She explained the latest dream to Alexis, who remarked that it sounded more like a confession than one of her regular creepy dreams.

"Hold that thought." Alexis jumped up with her hand

pushed out as if ready to stop traffic. "I've got something for you."

She streaked over to the front desk where her purse sat and brought back a folded up town magazine. On the cover, printed in bright colors, was a picture of Brad and Emily posing for a photo with David on Emily's hip in front of a newly constructed house. The cover was an ad for Brad's construction company, and from the look of David, the photo couldn't have been taken much earlier than his death. In fact, Alexis said aloud that the magazine's date was two months prior.

"She's beautiful," Mia murmured, not realizing at first that she spoke out loud. Seeing them together and so alive, Mia found it interesting how much David resembled his mother, including her red hair.

"Do you still think he could've done it?"

"I don't know anymore. Did you talk to your cop friend—are you seeing him now?"

"Sort of. About your ghosts, though, he says that if there wasn't a trial, you might talk to the lead investigator on the case, but with no evidence of foul play, there really isn't anything they'll do."

"I was afraid of that. Maybe I'll wait to call him. I'll just sound insane right now, but Emily's journal will be a good segue later," Mia said. "Now, how are things going with the new man? What was his name again?"

"Sidney. Things are... interesting, weird, complicated," Alexis said, blowing her breath out through her lips and tossing her curls from her face.

"But not Amanda-ex-girlfriend-complicated, right?" Mia had never liked Alexis' ex, but after the heartbreak cry session the other night, she liked even her less. Alexis shook her head, and Mia breathed a sigh of relief. "By the way, you never said how you met the cop."

"If I told you, I would die of embarrassment."

"Does it have to do with that drunken bar incident I heard about recently?"

"How did you know?" Alexis demanded, sitting up straight in her seat.

"You have your ways. I have mine."

"It was Sarah, wasn't it?" Alexis groaned and collapsed back into the cushions. Mia smirked but shook her head, not in denial but to signal that she would not confirm the guess, either. "Fine, I'll grill her later. Anyway, complications aside, we're actually going out one weekend soon. You should come and meet him—bring Nick along."

"No, no, no. I think I need to take a step back from him for a while," Mia said.

"Why? What happened? Did you have a fight?"

"Not really." Mia pushed a hand through her hair in frustration and blew a breath loudly from her lips. "Lex, hypothetically speaking, what would you do if your husband died? Would you ever get remarried?"

Alexis laced her fingers together and cupped her knees in front of her. "I think it would depend on how old I was, what happened, whether I wanted to spend the rest of my life alone. But we're not talking about me, are we?"

"Nick gets this look in his eye sometimes, and I know he wants more."

"And you don't want that," Alexis said. It wasn't a question.

"No, I don't. Is that so wrong? I made it very clear

when all of this started. Nothing serious, but he keeps trying to wiggle in."

"Would it really be so bad to let him in, though?"

"Yes!" Mia yelled, and Alexis jerked as if struck. Mia exploded out of her seat and paced the sitting area. "I've already gone down that road once before, and I don't want to again. I can't do it. It... it hurts too much when they go, and one way or another, Nick will go." Defeated and out of steam, she sank back down. "You wouldn't understand."

"I wouldn't understand? I was there with you, Mia. Jesus, don't pretend like you were alone because you locked yourself away. People envy you for just a taste of what you had, even knowing it wouldn't last. I envy you, and you spit in our faces by denying yourself any chance at having that again." Alexis stood and yanked her bag off the floor next to her. At the door, she turned back to Mia and took a deep breath. "I know you've been hurting for a long time, and I've been there with you through it all. But Mia, I'm the only one giving and supporting. I'm always there with a smile and a hug to help you pick yourself up or say something motivating. Somewhere along the line here, you stopped giving that back to me. And now you want to turn your nose up at a chance at love again and stay miserable? I'm sure this is just a silly fight we're having, and we'll make up, but right now, I can't talk to you."

Alexis stormed out, leaving Mia wondering how this had swung so wildly out of control. They'd gone from taking a step back from Nick to her relationship with Alexis. What happened? When had she messed that up so badly? Mia stood and blew out a frustrated breath.

"I didn't ask people to envy me," she muttered on her way to the stockroom at the back of the bookstore. "And it's my business if I choose what parts of myself to share with someone, isn't it?"

Mia lifted a box onto the table that served as her unboxing and sorting area, thinking back on the years she'd known Alexis. Of course, grief consumed the last two years of her life, so if she was being honest with herself, there was some merit to what Alexis was saying. But was she really at fault for that?

Mia sliced through the packing tap at the box's seam a little too forcefully, giving a cry of horror when she opened the flaps and realized she'd murdered the books on top. Picking one up, she groaned at the deep score mark down the center of the cover.

"What are you doing?" she asked herself.

She scrubbed her hands over her face and then lifted the shredded books out of the box and gently set them in a pile to her right, whispering to the book gods a plea for forgiveness. Hoisting an unharmed stack into her arms, she walked back out into the store and began restocking the young adult section. The self-help books were selling well, as were the fantasy romance books. If memory served, several of her bestsellers were the first or second in a series, and she made a mental note to snag the latter books in the series as soon as they were available.

As she moved through the stacks, Mia's physical load lightened, but her mental load only grew heavier. She couldn't think of one time when she'd really been there for her friend lately, and wasn't that something you should know right away? Shouldn't you be able to recall a time when you offered support? She wasn't convinced Alexis was right about Nick—it was definitely better to put some distance between them so she could think about the best way to handle all of this—but after nearly an hour mulling through her thoughts, she finally came around to the opinion that she owed Alexis a gigantic apology. Maybe she could call her that evening and drop by for an emotional support night in.

Yes, that's exactly what she needed to do. Then she could pick her friend's brain about the itchy feeling she mentioned and possibly offer some help and advice of her own for a change. She picked up her phone, typed out a text, and then crossed her fingers. If there was one thing she knew about being friends this long, it was that they always forgave.

Even if they didn't make it easy for each other.

26

More than a week later, Alexis still wasn't ready to forgive Mia. However, she agreed to the girls' night at Mia's place the following day, and that was a sign of success. Apparently, this resentment was brewing for some time, and Mia had a lot of making up to do. The realization only made it that much worse. It sucked to be on the outs with your best friend, but it definitely sucked worse to be the one at fault.

Unfortunately, not having any plans for the present evening meant that her options were to down to scraping wallpaper off her bathroom walls or giving Nick a call. That she wanted to do the latter made her double down on the former, so off to scrap wallpaper she went.

For several hours she continued that way, steaming away the old paper, scraping it from the wall in curled strips, and tossing it into a damp pile on the floor. When her arms and shoulders were burning, she unplugged the machine and grabbed a cold bottle of water from the refrigerator.

Taking it outside, she surveyed her front yard. Inside and out, the fruits of her labor were apparent. Blooms covered her azalea bushes so that there were barely any green leaves showing. At the far corner of her porch there was a tall grouping of black-eyed Susans that jutted proudly into the air, their dark faces staring straight up at the sky with yellow petals that sank back toward the ground. They looked like beautiful women with their faces turned up to the sun and their arms stretched back to bask in its warmth.

Mia walked down her porch stairs and pulled a few errant weeds from her beds, singing quietly to herself as she crawled along the curving bed.

"Mares eat oats and does eat oats and little lambs eat ivy. A kid'll eat ivy, too. Wouldn't you?" she sang.

When the weeding was done, she knelt to find the perfect blooms to cut, clipping a handful of choice black-eyed Susans and bringing them inside. Stroking the blooms, she mused that tending your flowers was a lot like tending your relationships. They required love and care and attention, and they wouldn't give back such beauty unless you invested that care in them. Resolutely, she vowed to tend her friendship better and get things back on track with Alexis. If a garden could be weeded and fertilized and brought back to life, she could mend their friendship.

If only she could so easily sort out Nick. Mia thought about the looks he gave her lately, the ones that said, "You're mine." One hot enough to burn through her.

Mia needed to reset their boundaries, to fertilize the garden in the right way, so they could continue enjoying each other without stepping over the line she was desperately trying to keep drawn in the sand.

She finished arranging the flowers in a vase filled with water when a knock on the glass at the back door had her jerking her head up. There was Nick, smiling at her through the panes and giving her a small wave.

"I was just thinking about you," she said as she opened the door for him.

"Were you really?" He stepped into the room with his hands suspiciously tucked out of sight. He kissed her on the cheek and moved past her awkwardly, hiding his back from her.

"Yes, you numskull. I said so, didn't I? Now what's that behind your back?" She closed the door behind him and slid the deadbolt home.

"Not so fast." He danced away from her. "This is not a gift. It's a trade. You can have it if... you agree to go out to a movie with me tonight."

Mia watched the irritation flash over his face when she hesitated. He hid it behind a charming grin, but she saw the tightness hiding in his expression. "Nick, I'm tired. It's been a long day," she said. She made a half-hearted attempt to pinch her nose and rub her temple as if exhausted, but they both knew it was a lie.

"Alright, present first then," he said briskly.

First, he brought out one arm, and Mia saw a beautiful bouquet of burgundy roses. They weren't the carefully sculpted type either, but the wild variety whose stems twisted together and apart, like the bush he'd given her.

Their petals fell open and beckoned you to press your face into them and inhale—which is exactly what Mia did as she took them into her arms.

"These are beautiful." She pressed her face into the blooms. Their scent was light and fresh, and she could even smell the leafy scent from the freshly cut stems. "I'll have to get another vase out."

"One more thing," Nick said before she could get sidetracked.

Mia turned back toward him and saw his other hand appear from behind his back. Her precious glass fairy perched in his hand, every piece reattached with care. The flowers dropped from her hand to the counter, and she covered a small gasp with a hand over her mouth. Another crack in her well-crafted armor. Tears rolled down her face without warning, and she looked from the fairy statue to him. "How did you...?"

Nick shrugged. "I saved the pieces and put them back together."

"But why?" she said, moving closer to stroke her fingers over the barely visible cracks. There were a few nicks here and there that hadn't gone as seamlessly back together, but it was perfect as far as Mia was concerned.

"I know how much it meant to you."

Mia took the fairy in her hand, memories of Ewan flashing before her eyes, and cradled it in her arms. "I don't know how to thank you," she said. She held it close a moment more and then set the statue on the counter next to the flowers.

"Come out with me, Mia. Please." He gripped her hips and pulled her against him gently. He nuzzled at her neck and kissed her, his lips a whisper across hers. "Please," he said again, looking into her eyes.

"I can't," Mia said, bringing her arms up between them.

Something flashed in Nick's eyes—temper, anger, hurt —but just as before, it was gone. "Then I supposed we'll just have to stay and eat in." His fingers worked the band of her pants over her hips.

"We can't!" she squealed, grabbing at her shorts in vain.

"You say that too much." Before she could protest again, he hiked her up onto the table. This time, he wasn't soft or gentle, and he certainly wasn't in a hurry as he knelt between her legs and feasted. Instead, he was possessive, hellbent on driving her mad and watching her as he did it, as if claiming her physically would force her to open her heart to him.

But as he ravished her on her kitchen table, the statue and roses in the center of her view, Mia wondered if that's not what she wanted after all.

SITTING out on her front porch the next evening, Mia considered her sore muscles penance. She'd spent the day shining up the bookstore to prepare for Alexis' start the following week. If she would still consider working there, that is, it needed to be perfect. She took a sip of a wine spritzer she'd made earlier, the ice clinking in her glass, and rocked back and forth in the rocking chair.

When Alexis pulled her car into the driveway, the knot

in Mia's stomach tightened. Alexis stepped out of the car and walked up to the porch as Mia stood. She noticed her red-rimmed puffy eyes. "You've been crying," she said, setting down her glass and opening her arms instantly.

Alexis nodded and gripped her hard in a hug, tears streaming down cheeks that were barely dry. "I'm so sorry I said such awful things to you," she said. "They were true, and I meant them."

"Well, that's nice to know," Mia said with a laugh.

"But I shouldn't have unloaded it all like that," Alexis finished.

"You have nothing to be sorry for. I've been an awful friend." Tears pricked at Mia's own eyes. They held each other until the muscles in their arms and shoulders tired before separating and wiping their hands over their faces. Sniffling, Mia wrapped her arm around Alexis' waist and rested her head on her shoulder. "Do you forgive me for being the worst?"

"Always," Alexis said, leaning her head on top of Mia's.

"I'm glad you got mad at me so we could have this moment."

Alexis laughed and said, "Anytime. Now, where's the wine and the strippers?"

They walked inside together and took seats at the kitchen bar where Mia had laid out platters of their favorite deli meats, cheeses, crackers, and fruit, along with a chilled bottle of white wine and a stemless glass. Mia refilled hers with wine and ginger ale as Alexis plucked a cube of cheese off the tray and popped it into her mouth.

"Alexis Donnely, did you get your hair cut?" Mia asked suddenly.

Alexis' hand flew instinctively to her hair. "It's my therapy. Sarah did it for me. You like?"

"I love!" Mia said. "She did a great job. It looks fantastic on you."

"Thanks! I'm loving it, too. Who knew that woman could give me a proper cut?" Alexis remarked. The cut really did look phenomenal on her. Where her tight brown curls had fallen to her shoulder in almost one length before, they were now slightly shorter and layered so that they bounced playfully away from her face with more short pieces to frame it. The whole look was fresh and vibrant, and it suited Alexis to the ground. "You should drop in on her. You could use a refresh, too."

"Maybe once I figure out if her husband is an ax murderer or not."

Alexis poured a glass of wine and took a sip. "Better you than me. I'm glad to leave all the ghosts in your head."

"Oh, thanks for that."

"Speaking of people who aren't ghosts, are you and Nick going to come out with us this weekend?"

"I'm thinking about it," Mia hedged. Alexis raised her brows skeptically, and Mia squeaked, "I am!"

"Have you even told Nick about it yet?" Alexis asked.

"Not yet, exactly," Mia said. Alexis muttered under her breath, and Mia could've sworn she heard something about being stubborn as an ass. "What about your guy? Is he sticking around for a while?" she asked, effectively changing the subject.

Alexis recognized the tactic, but she ignored it for now. "I haven't decided, but I like him enough to see where this goes."

"But you're still feeling itchy?"

"Yeah, I don't know what it is. I thought maybe it was the guy, but the guy is great. Working with you sounds fun, but I still feel restless, like I'm supposed to be doing something, and I can't figure out what that something is."

"Well, I'm really glad you'll be with me at the shop. It gets kind of creepy in there when it's quiet during the day. When we're slow, you'll have time to explore more and maybe figure out what's causing that itch," Mia said.

"Maybe," Alexis agreed, and they fell into silence. Mia took a sip of wine, and Alexis asked abruptly, "Have you ever thought about writing a book?"

"Me? Absolutely not. I was happy enough editing them and happy now to sell them, but I don't want to strap myself to a computer for hours on end, trying to drag magic out of my brain and onto paper. Why do you ask?"

"I do." Alexis looked wistfully out the window. She turned her gaze back to Mia. "I've been thinking about it a lot lately, actually."

"What do you want to write?"

"Oh, I don't know," Alexis said, but it sounded as if she very much knew. "Maybe I'd write romance or mysteries, or both. Wouldn't that be fun?"

"It sounds like it might be for you. Have you written anything yet?" Mia asked.

Alexis nodded bashfully. "I have."

"Maybe that's why you're feeling restless. You've got a book locked away, and it's begging to get out. You can't keep that inside." Mia picked up the bottle of wine and refilled both of their glasses. "How far have you got?"

"About half."

"Of the outline or a manuscript?"

"Ha! You know better than to expect me to have an outline, but the first draft is about halfway there," Alexis said. "Would you mind giving it a read when I'm done, maybe giving me some editing notes?"

"Of course. Lex, this is so exciting!"

"Hold your horses, Mia," Alexis said breathlessly. She put a hand to her chest to slow down her racing heart. "I'm still getting used to the idea. I wonder if Nick knows of a quality agent. Someone tough, but who isn't going to make me cry when they need round nine of edits done."

"I'm sure he does. Call him later. We'll have to do a big event when you finally publish, too! You know, celebrate a local debut author." Mia tapped her finger on her chin, her mind already going through all the possibilities.

"It's not even finished yet, and isn't Nick a local author, too?" Alexis asked.

"Technicalities, my friend! And now we drink to your success! May the book of your heart become a bestseller."

"I'll toast to that!" Alexis said, clinking her glass against Mia's.

27

M ia looked around the room, her skin tingling with goosebumps, her breath curling through the air in wispy clouds. She sat on her bed with no real memory of how she'd got there.

Her legs hung over the edge, back straight, hands resting in her lap. She wore an oversize white shirt and gray leggings. Her feet were bare, and the cold dampness of the room made them feel numb. A shuffling noise behind her had her turning to look toward the doorway.

There David stood with his pajamas and blanket, and she couldn't help but feel a maternal tug when she saw his heart-broken face. He whimpered, but this time he reached out to her with tiny hands. Mia stood and went to him, scooping him up and snuggling him into her as if she'd been doing so his entire life.

She rocked slowly back and forth, shifting her weight from side to side, and hummed softly until his cries stopped. The *sound was a hollow echo in the dim, cold room, but he seemed comforted by it.*

"Mares eat oats and does eat oats and little lambs eat ivy. A kid'll eat ivy, too. Wouldn't you?" Mia sang.

She looked down at the little boy in her arms. His cheeks were flushed pink, and teardrops dotted his dark eyelashes. It was curious how little he weighed. Her eyes scanned his body, noticing a few stains where food or drink had colored the fabric pink or yellow. It didn't register in the moment that he was no longer alive, that all of this was a dream. He was so tiny, so sweet and warm. Except that he wasn't. He wasn't warm at all, though her mind expected him to be. Her gaze shot back to his face, and she jerked in shock.

David's face was no longer flushed pink and lively. Instead, it was as pale as death, his lips tinged bluish purple, and no breath passed through them. His chest did not rise or fall. But the worst was his eyes. Cloudy and gray, they stared through her without moving or blinking. Mia shivered and turned and laid the little boy on the bed, his body settling limply into the cushion of the bed. She brushed a lock of hair from his forehead and brushed her fingertips down over his eyes, closing the lids. He looked to be peacefully sleeping now.

"You're not listening!" Emily's voice suddenly screeched from behind.

Mia whirled around the see Emily clawing her way through the doorway, some invisible force pushing back on her and keeping her from fully entering the room. Her nails dug deep, jagged grooves in the wall, and her mouth contorted with rage. Her eyes bulged from their sockets, bloodshot and crazed. Mia took a step back, holding an arm out as if it would protect the child on the bed.

"Look at my words! Listen to me! Why doesn't anyone listen to me?!" Emily yelled.

Fog rolled off her body in thick tongues of black that licked the floor and slithered toward Mia, and she vibrated with uncontrolled rage. Mia's skin crawled, and her bones felt as if they'd jump from her skin as she fought the urge to run.

"I don't know how to help you," Mia cried.

With a long shriek, Emily broke through whatever barrier held her at bay and crawled hand over foot along the floor to Mia. Her movements were jerky and broken, her body bending over itself, and Mia screamed as she grew closer, pressing herself against the wall so hard she was sure she'd go right through it. Emily's hand clamped around Mia's ankle, and the damp stench of death filled her nostrils. Mia's heart was beating hard against her chest, and she held her breath, her fingernails digging into the wall behind her.

With a jolt, Mia jerked awake in her bed and scrambled back against the headboard. She inhaled a jagged breath and pressed a hand to her heart as if that would slow it down. Her eyes darted around the room, analyzing every shadowy corner, but she was as alone now as when she'd fallen asleep. She leaned over, pulled the cord on her lamp, and lit the room with a warm golden glow.

With one hand holding the covers to her breast and the other stretched out to her nightstand, she pulled open the drawer and rifled through it until she found a pen and her notebook. She hastily jotted down what she remembered of the dream, a shiver zigzagging up her spine as she recounted it.

Maybe once it was out of her head, it would feel less real, she thought, though she suspected that was wishful thinking. If nothing else, putting it down on paper made it that much more real, but there was also a chance it could also give her information. That was ultimately the reason she was keeping the dream journal, anyway. She simply couldn't go on like this anymore. What had started as nightmares of a crying little boy was now a near nightly occurrence with regular horrific appearances by Emily herself. Mia had to figure out how to stop them, and soon.

For their sake and for her own sanity.

Perhaps it was time to pay another visit to Emily's sister, Rachel. Dr. Hubert didn't have an assistant, so who exactly was it that had been checking in on Emily? Was it possible the assistant was as much a figment of Emily's delusions as David's demonic possession? Rachel might not be in the best shape of her life, but she mentioned being close to Emily. Surely she'd know the truth.

MIA TAPPED her thumbs on the steering wheel and bolstered her resolve as she parked her car in front of the rundown ranch where Rachel lived. She was trying hard to manage her expectations. It wasn't like Rachel went above and beyond to be helpful last time, though in the end she had given Mia the journal, the most valuable source of information yet. It wasn't every day that two strangers showed up on your doorstep asking about your dead nephew and sister years after their deaths.

She almost stopped to call Nick. It seemed fitting since he was there for the initial meeting, but she settled for a quick text. That was more casual. "I miss you. Meet up soon?" she texted, setting the phone to silent.

It was one step closer to everything she wanted to avoid, but trying to keep him completely at arm's length was making her miserable, and she was tired of denying she actually enjoyed spending time with him. If it made their relationship more complicated... Well, she was working her way up to dealing with that.

She pushed open her car door and started walking up the gravel drive when her phone buzzed in her hand. It was a message from Nick with a winking face. Clearly, he missed her, too. The thought made her smile to herself, and she wondered if his constant pushing was a sign that he'd grown beyond the type of man who ran away from a serious relationship and into the type who ran towards it.

Mia climbed the sagging porch stairs, her hand gripping the rough paint of the rail. Flakes of it peeled off and stuck to her palms, damp with sweat. The dog was barking madly before she even knocked on the screen door, but she only waited a few seconds until she heard heavy boots walking across the floor on the other side. Rachel barked out a command to the dog, opened the door, and raised her brows in surprise.

"You again? What do you want now?" Rachel asked.

"I'm sorry to bother you. I had a few more questions about Emily, and I'm wondering if you might have time to talk now," Mia said.

"Hmm," Rachel considered that, then nodded. Stepping back and pushing aside the dog to allow her inside. "I don't see why not, but I don't know what else I can tell you."

"I just have a few questions. I promise I won't take much of your time," Mia assured her.

"Time's about the only thing I've got these days. You're as welcome to some of it as the next person," Rachel said.

They made their way through the living room. This time, it seemed, Rachel preferred their talk in the kitchen. It was surprisingly clean compared to what she'd seen of the rest of the house, with minimal dishes in the sink and counters that looked recently wiped down. The laminate floor tiles were dingy and peeling up at the corners, their off-white patterns faded from time and countless passes of boots across them, but they were swept and appeared recently mopped.

Rachel pulled two stools out from a counter overhang and walked over to the refrigerator. Mia sat on one stool, pulling her bag off her shoulder and setting it on top of the counter, while Rachel grabbed a can of beer.

"Do you want one?" she asked Mia. When Mia shook her head, Rachel shrugged and let the refrigerator door slap shut behind her. She boosted herself onto a stool, cracked open the can, and drank from it with a wet slurp. She swallowed and angled her head at Mia. "So, what would you like to know now?" Rachel reached a hand down to pet the dog, and it flopped down at her feet with a huff.

Mia cleared her throat, wondering where to begin. Straight to the point, she decided. "Did Emily ever have hallucinations?"

Rachel thought for a moment, rubbing her palms on worn jeans that were streaked with dirt and black grease. She leaned an elbow on the counter and shook her head.

"No, I don't remember that she did. I mean, other than what she said about David. I guess you could say that counts as hallucinating."

"I guess you could," Mia agreed. "I read in her diary that she knew Brad was having an affair. Did you know?"

Rachel shook her head. "Not at first. I don't live close, and I don't exactly get filled in on town gossip. But she told me about it, eventually."

"Do you know who it was with?" Mia asked.

Again, Rachel shook her head, her mouth folding into a frown. "Nope. I doubt Emily did either."

"What makes you think that?" Mia asked.

Rachel shrugged. Her body language was still relaxed, but her voice sharpened when she said, "I don't know. Just a feeling. But who knows? Maybe she did."

"Maybe. Did she ever have any friends that would come by and visit with her and David?"

"I think she was pretty isolated at the end. If she did, she never mentioned them to me. Why do you want to know all of this? How is any of this going to help anything?" Rachel asked abruptly.

Mia sat for a moment and tried to come up with a satisfying answer. It was a sudden turn into hostility, and she was unprepared. More than that, beyond the idea that figuring out what happened to Emily and David might set their souls free, she had little clue why this information would be helpful. Even that theory was shaky at best, but other than dropping into the local church and begging for an exorcism or a house blessing, she didn't have any better ideas. So instead of trying to plead her case or create a believable reason for her questions, Mia used the same tactic that had worked before. She was brutally honest.

"Do you believe in heaven or the afterlife?" Mia asked. Her voice was low and quiet, and all the sounds of the room went still at her question.

Rachel pushed a hand through her hair and pulled awkwardly at her neck. Her shirt shifted, and Mia glimpsed bruises along her collarbone and track marks on the inside of her elbow before the sleeve of her shirt fell back down to cover them. "Seems to me God wouldn't let someone suffer like this if he existed, but I think I believe in something that happens next, yeah."

"I do, too, and I don't think Emily and David are resting peacefully there," Mia said.

"You really think you're seeing their ghosts?" Rachel leaned back slightly on the stool, the side of her mouth turned up in a half-grin.

"Either that or I'm truly going insane."

"Aren't we all?" Rachel said with a quirked brow, and Mia wasn't sure whether it was good or bad that she agreed.

28

Nick pushed a stack of poker chips into the center of the table and fidgeted with the cards in his hand. Whenever he could, he joined this band of misfits for poker or tabletop games, and it was especially good to know that whatever else had changed while he was away, this hadn't.

This month, he was the host, so they'd all packed into the living room of his house, pushing his furniture against the walls and moving the kitchen table into the center. Chips, pretzels, and bowls of nuts sat on the bar, and there was cold beer in the fridge.

He looked down at his cards. Two sevens. Not such a great hand, especially when Clint was grinning like a fool across the table at the cards in his own hand. "Clint, you've got the sorriest poker face I've ever seen," Nick said.

"Yeah, but you never know if he's grinning over a pair of twos or a royal flush!" Perry teased.

"Oh, ha, ha, ha," Clint said, making a valiant effort to wipe the grin from his face.

Nick grinned to himself. He was not about to win with this sorry pair, so he folded on the next round and sat back to consider his friends. Clint and Perry sat off to his right, forever heckling one another, probably because they were twin brothers and couldn't help it. On his left was Michael, quieter than the rest of them, but he was wickedly clever when he spoke up. Brad was another quiet type, but he made up for it with his consistency. The group once included Ewan, of course, and the ache of his loss throbbed even more now.

Alas, this was the crew that was left. Not too bad a group of friends, all things considered.

"A little birdy told me you've been cozying up to Miss Mia Clark," Michael said, picking up a new hand of cards.

"Mia?" Perry asked. "Ewan's Mia?"

"Yes, that Mia," Clint said, rolling his eyes. "How did you not know about that?"

"Does everyone know?" Nick asked them all. Perry shook his head, but Michael and Clint nodded.

"Was it a secret, then?" Clint asked.

"No. She just prefers to stay out of the gossip mill, that's all. I didn't know so many people had seen us together."

"Only takes one," Brad said. Nick found it an ironic statement considering he was married to the one it often was.

"Those are some big shoes to fill," Perry said. "She was with Ewan since, what, middle school?"

"I've got my own shoes," Nick muttered. The last thing he needed was to compare himself to the man who'd come before him. Against someone like Ewan, he'd never measure up.

The banter eventually turned toward other topics. They gave each other hell over their wives, talked about who was having babies or which parent was currently in the thick of the terrible twos, and, of course, bet like it was their last night on earth. Unfortunately, their conversation whirled back around to the subject Nick wanted to discuss least: Mia.

Not that he couldn't gush about her endlessly. It was that the woman was so goddamn stubborn and closed off. Every time he brought up anything beyond getting her in bed, she backed off. It was infuriating. He assumed it was because going from friends to enemies to lovers was jarring, to say the least, especially when that friend had also been as close as he was to Ewan. But as simple as that explanation was, he didn't feel like it was the entire story, and he couldn't quite put his finger on why.

"So other than making the terrible mistake of dating you, how's Mia doing? How's the bookstore?" Brad asked.

Nick said, "She's good. It keeps her pretty busy, but I think buying a house and opening that shop are the first big things she's done since Ewan died. It's good for her."

"I can imagine," Brad said meaningfully. Of everyone sitting at the table, he knew exactly what she went through and more. "How does she like the neighborhood?"

"She lives here?" Michael asked.

Brad nodded and grinned. "Just a couple of houses down, right?"

"What are you doing with our sorry selves then? Why aren't you cozying up with her down the street right now?" Clint asked.

"Wait, what happened to her husband again?" Perry asked.

Clint elbowed him, glancing up as Brad folded his hand and excused himself from the table. He stage-whispered (badly), "Remember that carjacking at the pier a couple years ago?"

"Ohhhh," Perry said, snapping his mouth shut and looking awkwardly at Nick before burying his face in his cards.

Michael placed his bet and deftly changed the subject. "Will she do a book signing for your next one?" he asked.

"Maybe," Nick said with a shrug. "I haven't even really thought about it to be honest, but it would be cool to hit up a few indie bookstores, including hers, to kick off the next tour."

"Must be hard to rub elbows with the peons, Mr. Hollywood," Perry joked.

Nick smiled at that and took a swig of his beer. "We do what we can. Now, are you going to play or sit there staring at your hand all night?" he said.

IN HER KITCHEN, Mia poured herself a late night glass of wine, not knowing that she was currently the subject of Nick's poker night conversation two doors down. The pale yellow liquid sparkling in the lamplight from the living room. Mia took a sip from the stemless glass and walked back over to her favorite comfy chair. There was something to be said for curling up with a book while a storm raged outside.

Her bare feet slapped quietly on the wood, then padded softly over her new living room rug. It was a recent purchase, but the room needed it, and it helped her forget the night when broken glass and books littered the wood floors. She picked up a book from the pile on her end table and sat, curling her legs under herself in the chair and drawing a thin blanket over her. It may be nearing midnight, but there were several books debuting later in the year that she was considering carrying. When she had the time, she was making her way through the advanced copies before finally deciding which to order. They all seemed so promising it was hard to choose, and she suspected she'd likely end up with every book in her pile.

Wouldn't it also be lovely to find some local authors? She wasn't the busiest place in town, but opening month was promising so far, and she was confident she could host a decent author event given enough preparation time. It crossed her mind that Nick might even be interested, but she disregarded the idea immediately. It would be one more thing to tie them together. Some days, that knot felt like a quaint bow bound harmlessly around her wrist. Others it was a noose.

Mia sipped her wine and thumbed through the opening pages of the book, settling in to read about a woman with a past who was already on the run in the first few paragraphs. The story was so vivid that she swore she could feel the icy wind biting across her skin, and the hair on the back of her neck stood up. She read on as an eerie fog crept over the ground where the woman hid, bark scraping her back. The woman in the book was breathing heavily. Whatever chased her was almost upon her, and she was sure she wouldn't get away in time.

Lost in the story, Mia jumped when she heard a scraping noise outside her back window. She pressed a hand to her chest and laughed at herself. The wind was picking up outside, and thunder rolled in the distance.

"Giving yourself the heebie jeebies," she murmured. It was probably a branch falling from the trees above or even a raccoon or possum scampering for cover from the storm.

Mia nestled herself back into the chair, adjusted the blanket once again, and turned her attention back to her book.

Out of the corner of her eye, something caught her eye outside her kitchen window. Movement. She swore she saw a shadow cross it, but when she squinted her eyes and looked closer, there was nothing. Thunder rolled again, and a flash of lightning burst across the sky, illuminating a figure standing outside her back door. Mia jumped to her feet as the knob of the door turned back and forth slowly, and she screamed. The dead bolt held firm.

She grabbed her phone, and her fingers fumbled with the unlock screen. More thunder, another bolt of lightning slashed open the sky, and the figure was gone. Wide-eyed, Mia hesitated and stopped dialing 9-1-1. She tried to settle her nerves, telling herself she was worked up over the book and imagining things. Her entire body on high alert, the blood roaring through her head, she shuffled slowly over to the backdoor. Falling rain doused the glass panes, shining droplets dancing down the slick surface in the moonlight. Mia checked the deadbolt on the door and verified it was locked tight. She twisted the lock on the knob and flipped the light switch for the back porch with a jerky movement.

Yellow light slid over the wet grass of her postage stamp sized yard. Her stone patio glistened with wet from the drizzling rain, its surface untouched by any footprints, human or animal. With a snap, Mia shut the thick wooden blinds on the back door and moved to the kitchen window to do the same. She shoved her phone into the front pocket of her cloth shorts.

She was just imagining things. There was no one out there, no one who could have any motivation to come into her home. It was just the recent break-in, the nightmares, and her book all cooking inside her head and making her jumpy. Grabbing her glass from the end table, she walked back into the kitchen and tossed the remaining wine into the sink.

"That's enough of that for you," she said.

Vowing not to give the boogie man any more power, Mia walked into her bathroom and splashed cold water on her face. She pressed a soft gray towel to her cheeks and neck, looking at herself in the mirror. Her eyes were still wide, and her pupils were so dilated that her brown eyes were almost completely black. A deep red flush rode high on her cheeks, and her neck still bore splotches of the same color. There was no way she was going to fall asleep now, though that was nothing new.

Mia felt more than heard her phone buzz in her pocket. She pulled it out and glanced down at the screen.

"Wanna sneak over and make out?" a text from Nick read.

She smiled despite herself. While it would've felt like too big of a step to call Nick when she panicked that an imaginary monster was at her back door, his invitation was the perfect excuse to get out of a house that was, frankly, giving her the creeps.

Willing herself to play along, Mia texted back, "Are your parents home?"

"Sleeping," he responded. "The front door is unlocked."

Mia walked into her closet and grabbed a sweatshirt off the hanger, forcing her hands to stop shaking as she pulled it up and over her head. She slid her feet into flip-flops and grabbed her keys, locking the door behind her.

Outside, the thunder and lightning split the sky overhead, but the rain had lightened to a drizzle. The street lights burned brightly as Mia moved quickly down the sidewalk to Nick's house. Despite the late hour and the short walk, she couldn't shake the feeling of being watched and found herself glancing over her shoulder more than once. Of course, nothing was there, but the hairs on the back of her neck stood on end until she was finally inside Nick's house.

She pressed her back against the door and took a deep breath, telling herself she was being silly. Still, she twisted the deadbolt behind her and was grateful for the lamp Nick left burning for her in the corner of the room.

Mia realized this was the first time she was stepping inside Nick's house. She noted the sparse furnishings with only a few comforts scattered around the living room. Most of the furniture that was there was awkwardly pushed against the walls. The television was honestly smaller than she'd expected, but the bookshelf was where he clearly cared the most. Enviable wall-to-wall, floor-to-ceiling shelves filled an entire wall of the room, each packed with books.

There was, of course, half of a shelf of his own work, but the remaining shelves held books from every conceivable genre. Walking past the shelves, she ran her fingertips along the spines of the books. Mia noted that scattered throughout were books on history, true crime, ghost stories, and unsolved mysteries. There were also books on human anatomy, botany, modern archaeology, and even one particularly gruesome sounding one on decomposition. She supposed he used these as research as much as pleasure.

She left the living room, noted a dining room table pulled into the center of the room littered with empty beer bottles, playing cards, and poker chips, and turned toward the stairway. She walked up them slowly, listening for any sounds outside of the creaking of the stairs. As she reached the top, she heard the indistinct murmur of voices and wondered what movie he was watching. She followed the sounds to a bedroom off to the right and pushed the door open gently.

Nick propped up on the bed, covers gathered around

his waist, his subtly muscled chest bare. A light scattering of dark hair dusted it and danced in a line down his stomach and under the blanket. Her mouth watered at the sight.

"Hello there," he said. Then again in a seductive caricature of his voice, "Hello there."

Mia chuckled and shoved her hands in the front pocket of her sweatshirt. She glanced at the television mounted on the wall behind her and asked, "What are you watching?"

"Nothing as good as you. Come here." He clicked the remote and black filled the screen.

Mia moved toward the bed and shook her head. The urge to play with fire was inescapable, and the desire in his eyes only emboldened her. She wanted to drive him wild. Her fingers teased the hem of her sweatshirt, and she slowly drew it and the shirt below it up and over her head. She wore no bra beneath.

"What are you doing, Mia?" Nick asked, his voice husky and strained.

She shook her head again, running a hand through the loose waves of her hair. She looked up at him from beneath her lashes and slowly began pushing her shorts down off her hips and over the luscious curves of her thighs. Eyes watching Nick intently, she wiggled her way out of them, exposing simple black cotton underwear that rode low on her hips. She gave him a satisfied smirk when his fingers bunched the covers over his pelvis.

Enjoying herself, Mia turned her back to him as the shorts dropped to the ground, watching Nick over her shoulder. He sucked in a breath when she grabbed hold of the sides of her underwear. She arched her back, knowing that the cheeky cut of them was particularly flattering on her backside.

"Mia, please. I need to see you. I need to touch you," he begged, and she could hear him shuffling beneath the bedcovers.

"Shhhh. Your parents are sleeping, remember?" she whispered playfully. She pushed the underwear slowly down her legs. Bent over, she turned her head to watch him again, her hair falling in a cascade around her face. Nick's jaw clenched, and she saw his hand moving beneath the covers. Finally, she closed the distance between them, letting her body sway seductively with every step. "I like when you touch yourself like that."

"Come here now, so I can touch you," he growled, and the second she was even slightly on the bed, he grabbed her, pulled her down, and covered her body with his. He ground himself against her, his hands cupping her breasts, his thumbs circling her nipples. His mouth met hers, and he pushed his tongue into her mouth. She met him stroke for stroke, just as aroused as he was.

Encouraged by the way her body wiggled in response to him, her hands gripping his hips, Nick tore away from her long enough to position himself at her entrance and pushed into her. The sudden fullness had her gasping, and then his mouth was covering hers, swallowing her moans as he moved inside of her. But where she would've assumed their loving would be hard and fast and rough, he was inexorably slow and deliberate. He took his time building her up, moving a hand down below to rub her clit in circles as he worked in and out of her. Mia moaned and pushed against him, her hips meeting his with every thrust.

He raised his head from her shoulder and gazed down at her, his eyes boring into her as he watched her climb with him.

"You feel so good," he groaned.

He kissed her again, and then his lips were against her cheek and at the lobe of her ear. His breath was hot, his whispered words encouraging her to pull one of her knees up, telling her how wonderful she was, how perfect she was made.

Sweat bloomed across their skin until they were both slick with it, and Mia felt her body grow hot as her release drew near. She tensed and cried out, her entire body trembling as the climax rushed over her in a wave. Nick's cry joined hers, and he plunged once, twice more, before slamming into her as deep as possible and shaking as his own orgasm spilled into her.

Mia felt his breath heaving against her neck, and she stretched out beneath him like a sated cat who'd just finished lapping up a bowl of cream. As Nick's breathing returned to normal, he rolled off her and to his side. He grinned at her in a way that had her blushing despite already being shamelessly exposed and pulled her to his side as had become his habit. When he drew the covers up over them, Mia snuggled in, enjoying the feel of him and the sound of his heart beating beneath her cheek. She closed her eyes, breathing in the scent of him, and within moments, she felt herself drifting towards sleep.

"Will you stay with me, Mia?" he asked. She nodded

against him and felt his lips graze the tip of her head. His breath whispered over her hair. "I love you."

He didn't notice when her breathing stopped or when her body tensed against him. His fingers continued to stroke circles across her shoulder, side, and back as her mind raced. He couldn't possibly love her. This was not in the plan.

True, he'd brought her little gifts, and they shared meals and conversation together. She enjoyed his company and was drawn to him in a way that excited and terrified her. But love was not supposed to happen. There was no denying that they had a history, but it didn't mean their relationship had to be anything more complicated that good sex between people who cared for one another. Love was not part of that equation.

Oh god, and he was probably expecting her to say it back, to return his affection with equal ferocity. Damn him. Why did he have to keep changing things on her? Why couldn't she just have comfort and safety? After everything she'd been through, was that really too much to ask? Mia kept her eyes closed and prayed he thought she was already asleep. She cared for the idiot. Even if he couldn't get it into his thick skull that love was not in the cards for her. She didn't want to hurt him. Selfishly, though, she didn't want to leave his bed right now.

Best to deal with this in the morning when they were both well rested. They would wake up together as if it never happened, and if he brought it up, they'd have a civilized conversation and redraw the boundaries.

If that didn't work, she would have no choice but to break things off and let him down as easily as possible.

She wouldn't risk her heart again, even, as cold as it seemed, if that meant breaking his.

But as she thought more about it, she wondered if she really could so easily walk away. Could she really deny her growing feelings? Their connection? Mia shivered and not from the cold, and Nick's arms tightened around her. She squeezed her eyelids shut and focused on keeping her breathing slow and steady, forcing herself to enjoy the moment for what it was. Everything else could wait until tomorrow.

29

Morning sunlight streaked into Nick's bedroom, and he carefully peered out from between slitted eyelids. While he didn't think he consumed too much alcohol the night before, it had been poker night, and one could never be too careful when waking after a night of beer and betting. When the sun didn't send him fleeing under the covers like a vampire and the chirping birds outside his window sounded harmless, he breathed a sigh of relief. Stretching from his outstretched arms down to his toes, he brushed against the warm body curled up next to him.

Mia was still asleep, but she stirred briefly at his movements and snuggled deeper into the bed. He thought rolling over and waking her up with his mouth was a phenomenal idea and, glancing down at his erection, it seemed he wasn't alone in that.

Grinning to himself, Nick turned onto his side and slid

the covers down Mia's body. Her skin was soft, and her body relaxed under his fingers. She wore nothing, so there was nothing in between his hands and her delicious curves. He traced the tattoo on her hip, moving from her hip to her belly and lower, and allowed his fingers to dip into the very center of her.

She sighed at that moment, arching against him as her eyelids fluttered open. She looked at him first with confusion and then with what he could only describe as amused tolerance, and he knew he was grinning like a fool.

"I was sleeping," she said. Her voice was thick and like gravel, but he found it that much sexier.

"Not anymore," he said, and he slid down her body to nuzzle her with his mouth.

One leg on either side of him, she pushed at his head and wiggled away with a laugh. "I don't think so! I've got way too much to do today for all of that."

Thwarted, he smirked at her and propped himself up on his elbow. For a moment, he just looked at her. Her dark eyes were swollen from sleep, and her mouth was pouting and begging for his. Okay, that last part was probably a fantasy of his, but it was a good one. A flush dusted her cheeks with pink, and her hair was a rioting mass of locks. His chest felt full, his heart nearly bursting with all this love.

Love.

It was a curious thing to feel it for someone you'd known forever, especially when you already loved her in other ways first. It was a pleasant turn of events, and he wondered if his heart had simply been waiting all this time for her. Telling her he was head over heels in love with her, though, hadn't exactly been in the plans, and it had spilled from his mouth the night before against his better judgment. He didn't expect her to return the emotion right away, but he admitted he hadn't thought she would stoop so low as to ignore his proclamation completely. She thought he hadn't noticed, but he had. He'd said the words, and she'd feigned sleep.

Still, he figured love would be more of a roundabout journey for her anyway, and he wasn't above more shameless maneuvering on his part to get her to admit that she loved him, too. Even if she didn't realize it yet.

"Are you going into the bookshop today?" he asked. She nodded, reaching out to brush a few stray locks of his hair from his forehead. He was sunk. "Come out with me tonight."

It was like drawing a curtain down over the sun. The light in her eyes dimmed, and her body visibly stiffened. "I can't tonight," she said evasively.

"Sure, you can. We'll grab some dinner on the strip and then walk down to the pier." He tried to keep his tone casual, but he felt his lips tighten. God, the woman was so frustrating! What was so bad about going on a simple date together?

Mia sat up and started pulling on her clothes with brisk movements. She didn't look at him when she said over her shoulder, "I really can't. I'm going to be at the store all day today unloading boxes. I'll be wiped. Maybe you can come over, and we'll enjoy some dessert together instead."

"That's bullshit, and you know it," he said, letting his temper get the better of him. He sat up and pushed himself off the bed. Shoving his legs into gray sweatpants, he stood and stalked over to her.

"Excuse me?" She blinked at him.

"You heard me," he said. "Why won't you go out with me, Mia?"

"We don't need to go out. We do things together all the time," she said with a wave of her hand.

"Yes, we do things together, but we don't go out. We don't date. You'll let me share your bed, and you'll share mine, but you won't be seen with me in public."

"Exactly! And don't you dare throw that in my face." She stood and poked a finger into his chest to drive her point home. "I told you from the start that I wasn't interested in dating you. If you hadn't been so pig-headed and stubborn, maybe you'd have actually listened to me and gotten it into your thick skull."

"The only reason you won't date me is because you've got some backwards idea in your head that you're betraying your dead husband," he said, emotion making his throat feel hard and tight.

"You've got me all figured out then, huh? You cross a line, Nick," she warned.

"And I'll cross more! I want more, Mia. I want you. All of you. I told you I love you, and you pretended to be asleep." Anger and frustration boiled over as his heart broke.

Here, Mia. Stomp on it right here. Yes, harder! Just like that. Make sure it stops beating now. There can't be anything left.

"I can't give you that. It's not in the cards for me. You were the one who pushed for this! You kissed me. You pushed me into bed. You opened all of this up inside me, and now you're telling me not to put it all back and stop myself from hurting?" Tears welled up in her eyes, but he couldn't find it in himself to acknowledge her pain when his own was so great.

"There were two of us jumping into bed, Mia. Remember that when you're blaming me for pushing you there."

"It's about more than that!" she said, her fingers tearing at her hair in frustration.

"Why can't you see Ewan would be happy for you? You're so scared to let yourself be happy," he said, pacing back and forth in front of her.

"Of course I am, and I have every right to be!" Tears streamed down her face, and for a moment, Nick's resolve faltered. "I've done this all before. I was married to a man I loved, and I lost him. You have no idea what it's like to go through that, to go days without sleeping or eating because it feels like you'll die, too. To walk around feeling like an empty shell for months."

He silently took in her words, and while his body stayed in the present, his mind was right back at that funeral. Tears rolled down his cheeks now, too.

Quietly, he said, "I know exactly what that's like, Mia. I may not have been his wife, but he was my best friend, my brother. I grew up with him, and it was just as hard for me to lose him as it was for you."

"And then you left! When I needed you most, you left,"

she cried. She swiped the tears away with the back of her hand. "You run from everything! Every fight. Every hard thing in your life. Every woman who's ever wanted more. Well, guess what? This woman doesn't want more. I'm taking control of my life, and I won't let anything or anyone else break me again. Even you."

The silence was heavy around them, and the warm glow of the morning sun felt cold and sad. It illuminated nothing but the deep resentment Mia felt, resentment that strangled Nick.

"I guess now I know what's been holding you back," he said, shaking his head in disbelief.

It had nothing to do with Ewan. She wouldn't open herself to him because she was already preparing for him to leave. She couldn't have the light without the dark, happiness without grief, so she would deny herself all of it. Nothing he did would change her mind, and he knew no amount of time she spent waiting would satisfy her. How could he have fallen in love with someone who didn't trust him?

"I guess so," she said.

"Well, if you won't give me more, then I don't want any of it," he said.

He couldn't do it. His heart felt like it was being wrenched out of his chest. He strode out of the room and started down the stairs. Before he was even halfway down, he heard her footsteps scurrying across the creaky wooden floors above. So this is how it ends, he thought.

"You selfish bastard! You think you're making this dramatic point when all you're doing is exactly what I said you would. Your girlfriend starts talking babies and marriage, you run. Life gets hard, you run. Someone dies, and you run. I won't give you what you want, and you run. Every single time, it ends the same. Relationships, in a nutshell: either someone leaves or they die."

He looked up at her from halfway down the stairs. His eyes were sad, his spirit broken. He wanted to say something, anything really, but he couldn't find the words. And wasn't that a kicker? He, the man who literally spent his career putting words to paper, couldn't find the ones that might save them now.

"You really are running, aren't you? Right in front of me," she said incredulously. There was disbelief written all over her face, as if despite everything she'd said, she hadn't believed until that moment that he was actually walking out.

He felt paralyzed to change course now. Even his face registered no changes as he looked up at her.

She said, "I told you what I could and couldn't give when you started this. You're the one who went and changed everything. So, fine. Run. Go. I won't cry another tear for you."

In a flurry of motion, she dried her eyes with both hands and flew down the hallway. She swept past him down the stairs, stomping across the room below and out of sight. Her scent wafted behind her, a mix of light floral notes and the clean scent of freshly washed laundry, and he heard the front door slam behind her.

He sank down on the stairs. Well, that's how you fall in love with a woman and chase her away in twenty-four hours or less. It should be a concept for a reality television show. It would be an entertaining one if it wasn't currently his life.

He was heartbroken, but more than that, he felt empty. Completely bereft of substance. He propped his arms on his knees and lowered his head onto them, letting his body sag against itself. The stair tread dug into his back, but he didn't move. The pain couldn't come close to what he was feeling inside, his anger bubbling as fiercely as the heartbreak. She'd predicted what he would do before they'd even kissed for the first time, he expected, and all she'd done since that moment was create a self-fulfilling prophecy.

Of course, he would leave when faced with a woman who wanted what was essentially a booty call with emotional support! Who wanted to live like that?! He'd been arrogant enough to believe he could heal her. Because at the root, he had wanted more for the first time in his life, and it was his mistake to think she would love him enough to let herself give it to him. She'd married Ewan, for all his faults. Was he somehow not good enough to take that risk?

Dejected, Nick stood and trudged back upstairs to his bedroom. His shoulders slouched, and he shuffled his feet along the floor. He had to get out of here. There had to be some place he could go tomorrow, today even. Glancing at the calendar on the wall, he saw the days marked off for the beginning of his next book tour. He would start in New York and then zigzag down the East Coast, across to Texas, and then up the West Coast. It was going to be several weeks of hell and not set to start for another month, but if there was any place that he could kill some time in for a month, it was New York City.

Perfect, he thought. He'd set out for the big apple as soon as possible. He needed distance from Mia and this ridiculous situation she'd put them in. They said absence made the heart grow fonder.

He wondered if it could also kill it.

30

"Ugh!" Mia growled as she stormed into her house. How dare he push all of his own ideas and plans onto her and then make her feel as if she'd set him up for failure? She'd been nothing but clear every step of the way about what she wanted, what she was willing to give. Just as she'd told Nick, it was about so much more than Ewan.

There would always be a part of her that loved him, that still felt married to him, but she had to figure out her life alone. She had to figure out who she was and what she wanted. Finally, she felt like an individual person with wants and desires and needs all her own. She wasn't ready to step aside and let someone into her life again, to be part of a unit again. She wasn't ready to tear down all of her carefully constructed barriers.

It wasn't her fault that Nick refused to understand. Even in their latest argument, he missed the point completely. He kept trying to boil it down to one simple, easy to solve problem when it was anything but. She wasn't only processing the realization that Ewan likely would've been happy for her. She was equally dealing with the fear of losing yet another husband and fears that Nick would run away any time life got hard, a fear that he had already validated twice now.

And life would get hard. Mia wasn't the naïve heroine of one of her fairy tales, and she had been married before. She knew also what types of problems would arise. She wasn't interested in dealing with those again, especially with someone who had a history of running away from his problems.

Stalking to her bedroom, Mia threw on clothes for the day, barely paying attention to how she dressed, and swept her mass of hair into a ponytail. She slid her feet into shoes, tossed a handful of her favorite pens and high-lighters into her bag, and braced herself for the wall of humidity outside. They were finally nearing the end of the summer, but temperatures were still well above swel-tering during the day.

No matter, she'd be at her bookshop shortly, where she would spend the day happily restocking books, serving customers, planning the next book club meeting, and helping Alexis get started on her book edits. Nick and his nonsense could take a back seat. She had a life to keep building, and she wasn't about to let some arrogant man who refused to listen to the most basic of boundaries make her feel broken for being clear about her wants and needs because he thought he knew better.

$\sim$

Weeks later, Mia was rearranging a tabletop display she'd set up specifically for local authors, trying to her best to keep her mind busy and off thoughts of Nick. His driveway had been empty since the day they'd fought, and she had too much pride to call or message him to ask where he was. Not that she thought he'd even take her call. It wasn't like he was reaching out to her, either. The bell jingled cheerfully as the door swung open, and Mia looked up with a grateful smile. Alexis was more radiant than ever, and a deep red flush of happiness rode high on her golden brown cheekbones.

"You sure look happy today," Mia remarked.

Alexis virtually danced over to her, slid in for a one-armed hug, and then promptly fell back into a comfy chair close to where Mia stood. "I am," she said in a sing-song voice.

"And why is that? Other than you're writing your dream book and clearly still seeing Sidney," Mia said.

"Nope, that's about it," Alexis said with a laugh.

Mia narrowed her eyes dramatically, and she watched Alexis squirm just enough to give her away. "You had sex this morning!"

"Guilty!" Alexis kicked her feet.

"No bragging," Mia said. She pushed the last book into its home and took a seat in the chair next to Alexis.

"Why? It's not like you're not getting any." It was a casual comment, but the look on Mia's face had her jerking back. "Aren't you?"

Mia shook her head, careful to keep her face emotionless. "We'll talk about it later."

Alexis nodded slowly. She knew what that look meant.

It was the look of heartbreak, and she knew what would happen when those floodgates opened. It would either be a river of tears or a landslide of anger. Clearly, Mia wasn't taking a chance on either.

Mia cleared her throat and said, "So, tell me how the writing's coming."

Alexis took the hint and smiled slowly. There was nothing quite like the feeling of writing your first book and having people ask you about it or offer a piece of encouragement. Writing was hard, but support made it so much easier. "It's going really well. I'm finding it hard not to write a self-insert wish fulfillment novel, though. I know we usually warned new authors about it at the agency, but it's just impossible not to do it."

Mia shrugged. "I think authors always leave a piece of themselves inside their books. That's normal. And you're only on the first draft! You've got plenty of time to polish up your characters and tone anything down later if you want to. I think the important thing is that you get it out."

"True."

"If it makes you feel better, remind yourself that all first drafts suck."

Alexis chuckled. "Also true."

"Are you writing a romance or mystery then, or did you go with something a little more off the beaten path?"

"Contemporary romance. Honestly, it's loosely based on how Sidney and I met."

"Yeah, how *did* you two meet? Did you get arrested and not tell me?" Mia teased. It had become a sort of running challenge, trying to get the information out of Alexis.

"Ha, that's a story for another day," Alexis said,

evading the topic once again. "Suffice it to say, he gave me a ride home one night and things escalated from there."

"Well, I'm happy for you, Lex. Really happy for you." Mia put a hand on Alexis' thigh and gave it a comforting squeeze.

"Thank you. Though now it's your time to spill. Any updates on the ghost family?" Alexis asked.

"I don't know if you could call them updates, but I learned something interesting."

"Oh, do tell."

"Hold that thought."

Mia got up and walked over to the minibar, where she kept the coffee and tea supplies. She filled two mugs with hot water from the tall silver dispenser and dropped a tea bag and two cubes of sugar in each. She brought them back over to the sitting area and held one out to Alexis, who gladly accepted it and blew over the rim of her mug. It gave her a moment to collect herself and refocus on the ghostly drama hanging onto her life like an unwelcome parasite.

Sitting back down, Mia said, "So, I ran into Sarah and Dr. Hubert at the cafe, and it turns out not only was Dr. Hubert Emily's doctor, but he didn't have an assistant who would've gone to check on her."

"Didn't you say someone was visiting her? If it wasn't the assistant, then who was checking in on her?" Alexis asked.

"Yes, exactly! I feel like Emily keeps trying to show me something about it, but I'm just not getting it."

"Why do ghosts always have to be so cryptic?" Alexis asked rhetorically, echoing Mia's own thoughts exactly.

"Who knows? Maybe for the same reason that they give mediums the first letters of their names instead of just saying, 'Hey, I'm Charles. Tell my wife I'll always love her.' Anyway, I went back to the sister's house to ask a few questions about the affair or if Emily had any friends who could've been over, but I got nothing."

"Maybe she was hallucinating," Alexis said, taking a sip of her tea.

"That's what I was thinking. She was already having hallucinations about her son. It wouldn't be too far-fetched to say she made up a caregiver or assistant," Mia said.

"Poor woman."

"Poor family."

"I'm going to call you the next time I'm with Sidney. This sounds like it's going from strange to dangerous."

"What do you mean, dangerous?"

"Think about it, Mia. You start looking into this for real, start talking to people like Emily's sister and the doctor, and then suddenly your house is broken into, and you start seeing people walking around outside at night. That can't be a coincidence."

"I hadn't thought about it like that. But who would care enough about it after all this time?"

Alexis made a sound between her lips. "Obviously, the killer."

"Who might be Brad," Mia said flatly.

"Maybe. Better not to have to find out, though, right?"

"I guess," she said. "He's not going to be weirded out?"

"You won't be his first go around with this kind of thing. He won't be phased at all," Alexis said cryptically.

Mia missed Alexis' tone and nodded, taking a small sip from her mug. Several minutes passed as she sat in thought. She could absolutely drop all of this searching, especially if it was going to put her life in jeopardy. The fact remained, though, if she didn't find out what really happened to Emily and David, she feared they would haunt her dreams forever. Something told her that a psychotic ghost wasn't about to quit because Mia gave up. Mia looked into her tea, trying to think of a better way to go about this, but she couldn't come up with anything.

"You okay, hun?" Alexis asked. Her voice was quiet and concerned. She looked at Mia with her brows drawn together and lips pursed to one side of her mouth.

Shaking herself out of her thoughts, Mia nodded and gave her a smile. It felt like plastic on her face, and it didn't fool Alexis.

"Are you going to tell me what happened with Nick now?" Alexis asked.

"Well—" Mia started to say. The bell above the door jingled, and they glanced over to see Sarah striding in big as life. Now that she thought about it, she reminded Mia of a pared-down version of Dolly Parton. Big blonde hair, a touch heavy on the makeup, and figure hugging clothing. It was a good look on her.

"I hope I'm not interrupting," Sarah said.

"Not at all," Mia said. "Are you here to pick up your books?"

"Yes! I thought I'd come by and check if they're in. Brad and I are on our way out of town for a few days, and we'll pass just about everyone's house on the way."

"You're in luck," Mia said. She stood and walked to the

sales counter, her eyes flitting to Alexis when she heard Alexis' phone ring.

Alexis answered it. She pointed to the phone and whispered to Mia, "Cop." Alexis walked to the other side of the store, and Mia could hear snippets of her conversation. It looked like maybe she'd be meeting the mysterious Sidney soon.

Behind the counter, Mia bent down to grab a box from underneath. She sat it on top of the counter and looked up to see Sarah eyeing her intently.

"They just came in yesterday," Mia said.

"Wonderful!" Sarah clasped her hands in front of her face and moved to stand in front of the counter.

"Would you prefer the box, or would you like me to put these into a bag for you?" Mia asked.

"Oh, this'll be fine, thanks." Sarah leaned in conspiratorially. "So, is this a new man Alexis is talking to? And a man in uniform at that?"

"You're a shameless gossip, Sarah."

"If that's not every woman's fantasy, I don't know what is," Sarah said. When she moved to pick up the box, the sleeve of her shirt rose to nearly her shoulder, and Mia gasped at the large purple bruise on the side of her arm.

"What happened?" Mia asked, and she reached out reflexively.

Sarah laughed uncomfortably and wiggled her sleeve back down as she hefted the box up. "I had me a nice little fall down the porch steps the last time it rained. Maybe now Brad will finally replace those old things," she said, adjusting the weight of the books. "Alright, well, I'm off to play book fairy with the girls. Y'all have a nice rest of your day."

Mia hurried over to open the door for her and waved her off. She turned back to Alexis with furrowed brows and waited for her phone call to end. Sarah's story didn't add up. The last rain storm was weeks before, wasn't it? And that bruise looked fresh, maybe only a day old.

"What's put that look on your face?" Alexis asked, tucking her phone into her back pocket.

Mia looked at her with her brows drawn together, her face warring between disbelief and the horror of realization. "I think he did it."

"Who did what?" Alexis asked.

"When did you say Sidney could meet me?"

31

Nick had been in New York nearly a month, but his book tour was still a week away, and he was already tired of the city. The noise and the lights that never slept were once the starting signal of an exciting adventure. Now, they were only reminders that he wanted to be anywhere but here. No, not anywhere. Home. He wanted to be home. With Mia.

Tucking his hands in his pockets, Nick walked down the street and let his thoughts wander. His heart felt as if it was torn out of his body, a throbbing hollow space left behind, and he had no one to blame but himself. Somewhere between the end of his first week in New York and his second bottle of whiskey, he'd moved past anger and into depression. Well, maybe not quite through the anger. He still had plenty of that.

Mia blamed him for the way things had heated between them, but there were two people driving that train. She'd wanted him just as desperately as he wanted her. But as much as he wanted to put the blame solely on her shoulders, he couldn't bring himself to do it.

Because he had pushed at her.

He'd known from the start where she stood on their relationship, and still he'd pushed for more. Somewhere along the way, he'd even convinced himself he was doing it for her happiness, that he was fixing her. That he knew what was best for her, better than she did. It was pushy and arrogant, he thought, and he cringed inwardly.

He'd been arrogant to assume he could charm Mia into changing her mind and blind at how much more was at stake for her. He'd oversimplified her feelings, chalking them up to the equivalent of, "It's about time to get remarried, huh?" He wondered how many others had done the same over the years. Nick knew her mother well enough to imagine some pushing from there, but it wouldn't surprise him if friends or coworkers or even the pressures of society at large did so at some point, as well. Nothing made people more uncomfortably pushy about dating again than someone becoming a widow.

Like a blundering idiot, he'd only added to that.

He walked down the street with his shoulders hunched over, turned into a stone archway, and pulled open the door to a small restaurant. He waved the host away politely when he saw his agent, Nora, already seated at a small table near the window. She was an older woman with a diminutive stature that disguised just how fierce and stubborn she was. Dressed in a bright red suit, she picked at a bowl of salad in front of her, large diamond earrings glittering in the afternoon sunlight with every movement.

"I hope you're not upset that I started without you," she said when he sat down.

"Not at all." Out of habit, he grabbed the pristine white napkin off the equally pristine table cloth and laid it across his lap. To the server who appeared at his elbow, he said, "A water, please."

"Not hungry?" Nora asked.

Nick gave her a small smile. "Not today. Now, what's this big news you wanted to share with me?"

"Right down to business, I see." She pushed aside her empty bowl and laced her fingers together on the table. "Alright, we'll get the immediate business out of the way. You know we were going to start shopping *In the Dead of Night* around for a potential movie deal. Last week, a producer requested to option it. I've got the paperwork for that here for you. He'd also like to know if you want to be involved in any part of the casting or screenplay."

"That's great, Nora. You're amazing, as always. And no, I'm not interested in becoming a screenwriter or anything else. I wrote the book, and now my work with it is done."

He leaned back in his seat and took a sip of water. There were tiny droplets of condensation that glittered on the outside of the glass, and he was reminded of the way Mia's body looked slicked with sweat beneath him. He shook his head, giving himself a sad, self-deprecating smile. It wouldn't do him any good to think about something that would never happen again. That kind of thinking didn't heal broken hearts, though at this point he'd stopped believing anything did. Alcohol certainly wasn't working.

"Nick," Nora said in a way that made him suspect it

wasn't the first time she called his name. "Where'd you go?"

He snapped out of his thoughts, shaking his head and blinking. "Right here, ma'am."

"Mmm." She looked unconvinced. "Are you going to tell me what's wrong?"

"Nothing. I'm just in a slump right now," he lied. He took another sip from his water glass.

"Well, snap out of it, boy. You've got a book headed to the silver screen and a tour starting next week," Nora said. Their server set a plate of grilled chicken, rice, and roasted vegetables in front of her, and she made a sound of approval as she picked up her fork. "Are you sure you don't want to eat?"

While he admitted her food looked objectively delicious, Nick shook his head. He had little an appetite. Having your heart ripped out and stomped on did apparently did that to a guy. Nora said something to the effect of "suit yourself," and they went through the process of signing paperwork. Nick tried to focus on gratitude and positivity as they did so. Nora had worked as hard as he to make this all happen.

In the spirit of trying to enjoy the gifts of the day, he even tried to do some sightseeing after their meeting, but he couldn't seem to enjoy anything. Every experience reminded him of Mia. He compared (and found lacking) every passing woman to her. Finally, he made his way back to his hotel. At the elevators, he contemplated going directly to his room and staring at the ceiling until sleep claimed him. But the downstairs bar held a certain appeal tonight. At least there he could stare at different walls with people moving about. Maybe he could even convince himself he wasn't moving through his days like a zombie after the apocalypse.

He found an acceptable place at a corner of the bar overlooking the small, low-lit room and leaned against the gleaming wood. Signaling to the bartender, Nick ordered a drink. "Whiskey. On the rocks."

"Nick, is that you?" a woman said as she sidled up to the bar next to him.

She wore a black dress that clung to every curve and exposed a dangerous amount of cleavage. He recognized her instantly, an old flame he'd stopped seeing earlier that year. Not for lack of attraction, that was for sure. They simply had little in common outside of the bedroom.

"Nora said you'd come to New York early, but I didn't realize you were staying here," she said. She slid a finger seductively toward his arm, looking up at him from under lashes coated in thick black mascara.

He doubted that. If Nick remembered correctly, there wasn't much that got past Lena. If someone was in for a visit, he'd doubt if she didn't know the exact coordinates where they were staying, along with their arrival and departure times down to the minute. Not that he was insulting her. Lena was an unashamedly sexual creature and wild fun, to be sure. During their brief romance, they'd appreciated the culture of the city as much as each other.

"How long will you be in town?" Lena asked. She angled her body so that her breasts pushed out toward him.

"Only a few more days before it's off to the next city."

He said swirled his whiskey and watched as the liquid slid around the inside of the glass. "What about you? Are you in town for business or pleasure?"

"Oh, a bit of both, but right now I'm just thinking about pleasure," she purred. Her hands slid up his forearm, and she moved closer to him until the length of her pressed against his side.

"Really?" He could smell the spice of her perfume and the subtler scent of shampoo and hair spray wafting off the blonde hair she'd styled into effortless curls. It was obvious why she'd sought him out, and he wondered if allowing himself to be a passive pawn in her scheme would at least give him something else to think about for an hour. While not the perfect plan, he was just depressed enough to prefer it over drowning himself in alcohol for the next few hours. With a nod toward the archway, he pushed himself from the bar and led her to the elevators by the small of her back.

They barely made it through the door of his hotel suite before she was on him, and he remembered just why they had burned so hot and heavy. She was as slippery as an eel, her body gliding over his and pressing against him in all the right places. He allowed her hands to roam over him and groaned when she stroked his hard length through his pants.

"I've missed you," she said on a moan, her mouth locking with his again. She nipped at his bottom lip and pulled him along with her to the bed. "I want your hands on me, Nick."

The sound of his name was foreign and... wrong. It penetrated the roaring of his blood, and the reality of what was happening hit. He blinked and inhaled sharply, realizing that he simply couldn't do this. He froze. As much as his body was raring to go—and boy was it—he couldn't make his hands move, and he didn't want to. The woman before him, as beautiful and tempting as she was, wasn't the woman he wanted.

She wasn't the woman he loved.

"I can't do this," he said, his voice barely a whisper.

"What?" Lena asked. She leaned back from him, a line forming between her brows and tilting her head in confusion.

Nick looked at her helplessly. His mouth worked for a moment before any sound came out. "I can't do this," he said again, closing his eyes and drawing in a steadying breath.

The corner of her mouth raised in a smirk, and she rubbed a hand hard against his arousal. "It looks like someone thinks you can." Her breath whispered across his lips, and she moved to his ear with a husky moan.

His entire system was on fire, his arousal throbbing with need, but it was wrong. He wasn't thinking of Lena. He was thinking of Mia. Mia, the woman he loved and wanted nothing more than to be with at this very moment. Not Lena.

"He's wrong," he said, taking her by the elbows and pushing her from him gently.

She pouted, part of her waiting for him to change his mind. When he didn't, she shook her head and bent to slip her feet back into mile high heels. As much as she wanted a roll between the sheets with Nick for old time's sake—the serendipity of running into him when she was already on the prowl for entertainment was simply too delicious to pass up—Lena wasn't the type to poach on someone's territory, and clearly, someone had claimed this one.

She took a deep breath and looked up at him, her eyes filled with disappointment, regret, and a hint of pity. "You must have fallen pretty hard, huh?"

"Too bad she didn't," he said, feeling guilty that he'd even thought about going to bed with Lena.

She considered him for a moment and wondered if it was a circumstance of unrequited love or one where he'd royally screwed up. From the sadness in his eyes and the slump of his shoulders, she decided it was likely the latter. "Throw you out?" she asked.

"More or less." He walked to the door and held it open for her.

Lena crossed the room and had just walked through the doorway when she turned back abruptly. "You know, sometimes you love someone so much you think you should let her go if that's what will make her happy, but that's not always true. Sometimes it means you've got to get to work and do the hard thing, the growing and changing, so she doesn't want to go."

"Are you saying I'm not a grown man?"

Lena reached out and patted his cheek with a smirk. "Honey, you may be a grown man on the outside, but you've still got a lot to learn in here." As she spoke, she drew her hand down to his chest, pushing a finger pointedly into his heart.

He huffed out a breath, his feet shifting uncomfortably. "How do you know I haven't already done the work?"

"Are you in bed with your woman or holed up in a hotel hiding from her?" she asked, arching a brow.

"Touché. I didn't know you were so wise."

Lena flipped her hair over her shoulder dramatically. "I have my moments," she said. With one last heated look, she turned and walked down the carpeted hallway. The door shut with a quiet snap behind her, and Nick sat on the bed in silence.

Was he avoiding doing the hard thing? He told himself he'd left to give himself space, to give Mia space, but now it seemed like an excuse even to his own ears. What had he been thinking? If he was being really honest with himself, he left so he wouldn't have to deal with the consequences of his actions. He left so he wouldn't have to face the fact that he was pushing her, and it was wrong. Turning his head to look out the window, Nick smelled Lena's perfume on his shirt and looked at it in disgust. He ripped the shirt off and threw it into the far corner of the room. Standing up, his pants and briefs followed, and he decided it was the perfect time to take a shower. Nothing like blistering hot water to scour the feeling of betrayal from his skin.

32

<hr>

Mia knew she was dreaming this time. She wasn't sure how or why, but there was an awareness within her. She wondered if this was something the ghosts controlled. In the dream, she stood in the middle of a cemetery where gray had washed over all the colors of the world. Everything was a hazy white, and in the middle of it all stood Emily and David. She realized it was the first time she was seeing the two together as mother and son. The top of David's head reached barely mid-thigh on Emily, his hand held in hers high above his head.

Unlike the place where they stood, both of them were full of color, and it was color like she'd never seen on them before, even in pictures. The unmistakable flush of life touched their fair skin, and even the shadows under their cheekbones and jaws were less gray. Their eyes were bright and sparkled as if a light shone directly at them. She could even see the color. Emily's were blue, and freckles dusted her cheeks and nose beneath them. David looked like Emily but had Brad's olive coloring and *hazel eyes, though his hair was blonde and tinged with red where the light hit it. She imagined Emily's eyes were the same as a child.*

Emily looked down at David and smiled. Her gaze moved to Mia, and the smile stayed in place. It was a sad smile, though, like the kind you give to someone at a funeral when you don't know quite what to say.

"You're so close to where you need to be," Emily said.

"Close to what?" Mia asked, but Emily didn't answer. She wondered whether Emily meant she was finally getting close to learning the whole of her story. Or could she mean getting close to resolving her feelings about Nick? Did ghosts give out unsolicited love advice? Because she didn't feel like she was getting close to anything, romantically or otherwise.

"Can't you give me more than that?" Mia begged. "I want to help you."

Emily just smiled sadly, and she and David faded into nothing.

AFTER A FEW LAST-MINUTE CANCELLATIONS, Mia was finally about to meet Sidney Neal, the hunky police officer of Alexis' dreams. She supposed the two had been seeing each other on and off now for a while, and so far, Alexis had said nothing but good things about him. If she was being honest, though, that only slightly calmed her nerves.

Apparently, Sidney was perfectly good with the weird and mysterious, but Mia doubted he regularly encountered the kind of weird that had someone who appeared perfectly ordinary claiming to believe their nightmares were actually restless ghosts desperately trying to make someone (namely her) solve the mystery of their deaths. Only in this case, their deaths were technically solved. Case closed.

Mia walked into the cafe and chose a little nook with a high back club chair in the corner and two other chairs across from it. There was a low table in the middle of the seating arrangement, and Mia laid her purse and notebook on it while she waited. Her stomach was too jittery to eat or drink, and she repeatedly clicked the end of her pen in and out while she waited to keep her hands busy.

"Mia! How are you?" Alan, the antique store owner next door, said as he bent down to hug her. He straightened as best he could, but his back kept the slight curve that betrayed his age, despite his spritely nature.

"I'm doing well. How's business?" Mia asked politely.

"I can't complain. Meeting Angela here in a moment. It was good to see you," he said and walked away as quickly as he'd appeared. If memory served, Angela was the flaming affair, and Mia smiled at that. Flaming affairs at his age. It was scandalous and equally wholesome to know that humans still craved connection and a dash of excitement, no matter how old they were.

Mia inhaled deeply, turned her attention back to the door, and hoped no one else would come talk to her. Why had she agreed to meet at Sweet Bea's to begin with? She should've told Alexis they needed privacy. She needed it. Mia worried the skin around her cuticles as she waited. She shouldn't be so nervous about this meeting—she requested it, after all—but it made the whole story more real than ever before. Rather than feeling caught up in a ghost story, she was caught up in a web of murder and deception... only she was the fly and Brad Williams the spider.

She was still watching the door intently when the spider and his wife walked through it, and she couldn't help but jerk slightly. Her visceral reaction was understandable given the circumstances, she reminded herself, and she eyed Brad warily as the two saw her and walked over.

"Hey, doll! I'm surprised to see you here today. I figured you'd be at the bookstore," Sarah said. "We were just getting back into town and thought we'd swing by and say hello to everyone we missed."

"Hey, Sarah. Hello, Brad," Mia said slowly. She stood and returned the hug from Sarah. "Did you have a good time?"

"The best!" Sarah said, tucking herself into Brad's side with a smile. "We needed it, didn't we?"

Brad nodded and said, "We sure did."

They didn't look as if they'd been traveling any length of time. Sarah sported colorful yoga pants and a loose fitting top, not a wrinkle in sight, her hair in a perfectly pulled back ponytail. While Brad stood casually in jeans and a t-shirt, his hands tucked into his front pockets. Did they ever not look perfectly put together? Mia looked down at her casual summer tee and shorts and felt oddly self-conscious.

"Are you meeting someone?" Sarah asked, looking around quickly.

Mia jumped at the chance to exit the conversation. "Yes, I am. Alexis is meeting me."

Thinking about the break-in, she purposefully left out that her police officer boyfriend would accompany Alexis. She hoped he wore plain clothes. She wasn't actually sure what type of clothing investigators wore. Did they wear plain clothes, a suit and tie, or a police uniform? Did it matter? Whatever he wore, the last thing she wanted was Brad seeing her meeting with an obvious cop after all the poking around she'd been doing lately. She wondered what Brad thought of it. Did he know? Did it make him nervous?

"Say no more. We'll leave you to it, then. It was good to see you," Sarah said cheerfully.

Mia smiled politely as they walked away. She slumped back into the cushion of the chair and heaved a sigh of relief when she saw Alexis and a man, in street clothes, thank goodness, walk through the door. Alexis scanned the room and pointed at Mia. She smiled, and she and the man wound their way through the sparse crowd over to her. They sat in the unoccupied seats.

"Mia, this is Sidney Neal. Sidney, Mia Clark," Alexis said, gesturing to each of them.

"It's good to finally meet you," Mia said. She held out a hand in greeting.

"Likewise," Sidney said, taking her hand and shaking it firmly. "I hear there's something I might be able to help you with, too."

Straight to the point, Mia thought, relieved that they could skip the small talk today. "I'm certainly hoping so."

"Why don't you start at the beginning, then? I can't

promise anything, but I'll listen and see what I can do," he said.

Mia took a deep breath and said, "The dreams, or nightmares really, started just after my late husband died."

"Wait. They started right after he died?" Alexis interrupted.

It wasn't an accusation, but Alexis sounded surprised. Mia looked from Sidney to Alexis. "Yeah. In fact, the first one was the night they told me Ewan was dead. Two officers came to my door with the news, and my world fell apart. That night was the first time I saw David, the little boy. I remember because it felt that much more unfair, that even in my dreams Ewan was gone. I guess I've never really thought about that being significant, though. Those first few days were kind of a blur," she said apologetically.

"That was the night they died, too," Sidney said, his eyes narrowed in thought.

"I didn't realize," Mia whispered.

"Tell me about the dreams," he said.

"They started as dreams about a little boy in pajamas crying and holding his blankey, but they've gotten worse, especially lately. More gruesome, you could say. When I moved, I dreamed of the mother, and then I started to see them when I was asleep and awake."

"I'll bet it's terrifying," Sidney said.

"You have no idea," Mia said off the cuff, but she considered how little surprise was actually showing on his face. Frowning, she said, "Or maybe you do."

"More than you know. But please, continue," he said. He leaned forward, his elbows on his knees, and Mia realized why Alexis was drawn to him. He completely tuned into her when she spoke, like he was genuinely interested in every word, and it didn't seem to be a great effort. It seemed a natural way of being, from his leaned in posture to the way his blue-gray eyes looked at her like she was the only person in the world.

"Alright. I'm sure Alexis has told you what happened next. By pure coincidence and hints from the beyond, I stumbled into a case where a little boy and his mother both died. The picture of them matches who I see in my dreams. It's them."

"David and Emily Williams," Sidney said.

"Yes," she confirmed with a succinct nod.

"From what I know of the case, it was officially ruled a murder-suicide. Mother with a history of mental instability smothers her son and commits suicide. Pretty cut and dry as far as the police were concerned. Do you have any evidence that something else happened?" he asked.

"You mean other than the testimony of a dead woman?"

Alexis stifled a giggle. "Sorry," she said, covering her mouth with her hand. "Humor is how I cope."

Sidney smiled and gave her knee a squeeze. The familiar gesture made Mia's heart clench. "Yes, something besides the dead woman," he said without missing a beat.

"The sister talked about Brad, the husband, abusing Emily, so there's that. And she gave me Emily's diary. It's... disturbing. She writes about a lot of normal things, then some struggles with postpartum depression and medication. Near the end, she talks about David being possessed and it goes off the rails after that," Mia said. "Oh, and she also wrote about seeing her doctor, Dr. Hubert, and an assistant visiting her to check in just before the day she died. But I talked to Dr. Hubert, and he's never had an assistant. Given what else she was writing, I guess it could be a hallucination..."

"Or it could be a solid lead. That's good work. Do you still have the diary?" Sidney asked.

Mia nodded and reached into her bag. She pulled out the thin book and held it in both hands. It was strange to be handing it over now. This book, the words inside of it, had brought her closer to a dead woman than she ever could've imagined. Not that she'd ever imagined doing that in the first place, but that was beside the point. Before she could pass it to Sidney, Brad and Sarah appeared at her side, and Mia scrambled to cover the diary on her lap.

"I just wanted to say a quick goodbye, Mia, and a hello-goodbye to you, Alexis. See y'all at the next book club meeting!" Sarah said with a wave. Brad simply tilted his head, and they both walked out.

Alexis leaned over to whisper in Sidney's ear, presumably to explain who Brad and Sarah were. As the door closed behind them, Mia's board straight posture visibly relaxed. Sidney didn't remark on it, but he could tell she was terrified, even if she wasn't ready to admit it to herself.

"I'd ask you what you think happened to David and Emily, but from your reaction just now, I think I have a pretty good idea. So, I'm not going to ask," Sidney said. He pulled a card out from his wallet and handed it to Mia. "If you ever feel you're in danger or you learn anything else from the living or the dead you give me a call, okay?"

Mia felt a wave of relief. Despite having Alexis and Nick along for the ride, this was the first time anyone with any proper authority was pitching in to share some of the load. Emily had said she was close to where she needed to be. Mia wondered if this was the last step. The mystery may not yet be solved, but someone besides her believed in them. Someone cared and was trying to find the truth. The weight on her shoulders eased slightly, and she relaxed into the chair. Alexis reached out and rubbed a hand on Mia's thigh.

Sidney looked at her intensely and said, "I can't promise that I'll come up with anything more than what you've already got, but I'm sure as hell going to try."

The next day, Mia drove home from the bookstore far earlier than usual. Despite the respectable amount of foot traffic in the shop and Alexis' help, she closed early for the day. She told herself that she simply needed a break. Between her fight with Nick, her ghosts, and the everyday grind, so much had happened that it was everything she could do to roll out of bed and survive the day.

She turned her car down her street and saw that Nick's was still missing. He still hadn't texted or called her. Not that she'd reached out to him, either, but that was to be expected. She was the one in the right. The person with the high ground wasn't the one responsible for groveling.

At her driveway, she hesitated. Instead of turning in, she continued down the street. A right, a left, and a long winding road later, and she turned into a slender drive that was newly paved. She drove through tall black gates and under a wrought iron sign that read, "Cemetery."

Mia parked in the small lot and started walking down the farthest path. She passed a small duck pond and bench that marked the baby section, an area of the cemetery where the tiniest of graves laid row after row. Just ahead there was a live oak tree with giant sloping limbs so thick and long they touched the ground. Spanish moss hung from in tapering clumps. Ewan's grave was on the other side of that tree. She'd come to think of it as his resting place, something peaceful, rather than the location of a body in a grave. It was a part of the cemetery that was fairly vacant, and she imagined he liked the solitude. Or would have if he'd been able to offer an opinion.

"Hello, my love," she said when she sat down cross-legged on his grave. She picked a clover flower and twirled it between her fingers. "Have you missed me? I miss you. God, I miss you so much. Some days it feels like that's all I can do. Just think about you and us and how unfair it is that you're not here."

Her throat was hot and tight. Tears pricked at her eyes, but she blinked them away resolutely. It was a little silly to be sitting here in the late morning talking to grass and stone, but graves were for the living, and she needed it.

She cleared her throat. "I have a confession, though I expect you already know. Something's happened between me and Nick, something that I didn't expect. I could say that I don't know when things changed, but that would be a lie. I know when they did. I don't know that I wanted them to at first, but it happened, and now I think I've made a muck of it."

Tossing the clover flower down, she blew out a heavy breath and yanked a handful of blades of grass out of the ground. "It was all his fault. I told him I wasn't ready for a relationship," she said and paused. "Alright, maybe I didn't say I wasn't ready, but I told him I didn't want one period. Why couldn't we just have great sex and leave it at that? And how am I sitting here telling that to you, of all people?"

She looked up to the sky as if it would offer any sort of guidance, but when none came, she gingerly laid down on the ground, her head beneath her arm. She curled her knees to her chest and pulled at the short blades of grass, wondering what Ewan would say if he could. He'd probably laugh and tell her to stop overthinking it and just be happy. He wouldn't have understood that was exactly what she'd been trying to do. *Look how that worked out for you*, she thought.

"Okay, so maybe it backfired on me, but that doesn't mean I was wrong," she said to the headstone.

She angled her head up, and her eyes scanned his name, his birth date, the date he'd died. Such a short life and so abruptly taken away.

Mia pushed memories of his last day from her mind. She didn't want to remember him like that, but the heartache was still too much to bear. In fact, that ache was exactly what she'd been trying to avoid by keeping Nick at a distance. Sadness knifed through her, and she realized that she'd stopped nothing by doing so. It hurt as much to be sitting here miserably alone, keeping company with a piece of ground and a slab of concrete.

"Okay, maybe I was a little wrong, but he would've left anyway," she said, but that rang false, too.

In reality, she'd been waiting for him to leave her

again, and in the end, she'd made it so he had no other choice but to go. Maybe she had a right to be angry for being pushed, for being made to feel guilty for having boundaries, but she was just as responsible for the way things ended as he was.

"Ewan, I really have made a mess of it," she murmured. "Now I've lost him, too."

And she let herself cry. Wholly and completely, she allowed the outpouring of emotion that her soul so desperately needed.

She cried for the husband she lost. She cried for the future that would never be. For the guilt and the regret. She let the tears and the sorrow and the heartache wash over her like an angry wave over a boat in the middle of a storm. It took her under, tossing her through its waves with violent abandon, and she sobbed until her tears ran dry and the sun rode high in the sky above her.

When she was empty, she scooted up to the headstone, touched her fingers to her lips, and laid them quietly on Ewan's name. The pang in her heart was as vicious as the day she'd put him here, but she supposed that was the nature of grief. People often said time healed everything, but she believed differently. She'd lived with it enough to know better. Grief never really went away. It only got easier to live every day with.

She made the drive home, thinking about how to keep herself busy while she waited for Nick to get back in town. Something physical and time consuming. Perhaps the patio set she'd found for a steal at a yard sale the weekend before would be a good contender. She could refinish with a little paint and elbow grease. Thanks to an impending storm, the temperatures were not quite angry, and the cool wind swept away the humidity so that working outside in the middle of the day didn't sound like the nightmare they usually expected at this time of year.look how that

However, when she pulled into her driveway, it wasn't the project waiting for her at home that pulled at her. Mia looked down the road at the empty drive just two houses down. Nick clearly employed a lawn service, as the grass was mowed despite his absence, but she could see from here just how many weeds were invading his flower beds.

She'd promised to do some gardening in exchange for his help recently. She supposed now was as good a time as any, so she walked down the sidewalk, settled herself in his beds, and began pulling the invading weeds. Mia wasn't yet an expert on which plants were weeds and which weren't, but she figured if she could fumble through well enough in her own yard, she could do so in his, too.

Once she plucked the weeds away, she realized how sparse the flower beds were to begin with. He also desperately needed fresh mulch, at least a few bags, by her amateur estimate. With a sigh, she brushed her hands on her denim shorts and made a mental list of everything that was needed. She wasn't sure if he'd thank her or curse her for the gesture, but she believed in tit-for-tat and all that. At least that was the story she told herself.

She focused on the task at hand and made a quick trip to the garden center. She skipped the specialty store downtown purely because she didn't want to get roped into going back into the bookstore. Plus, she needed a few supplies, like basic non-organic affordable mulch, that she knew they didn't carry. She filled her cart with everything she'd need, including a tray of summer blooms and a few bags of dahlia bulbs she thought would be a perfect surprise. In the fall, they would bloom a velvety red on the outside and nearly black in the center.

Back at Nick's house, she worked in the sun with a glass of sweet tea on the porch next to her. She filled in the beds with the smaller flowers and carefully scooped dark brown mulch all around each. She imagined it was like tucking them into bed. The dahlia bulbs she planted near the back where they could spread out wide and grow tall year after year. When everything was in the ground and fresh mulch spread, she hunted up a hose on the side of the house and gently watered the new plants.

The ritual of planting and watering and tending reminded her of marriage. In the beginning, you went into it with this brilliant vision of what you wanted it to turn out like. Just like gardening, sometimes things worked out according to plan and other times they didn't. Flowers bloomed and died, weeds invaded and were fought back. Still, you tended it all with care and hoped for a beautiful season, even knowing that some flowers might never bloom at all. Marriage was like that. A lot of trust, a lot of work, and a little hope.

Her thoughts turned to Nick, and she wondered what he thought of marriage. Had he thought much about it at all? Was it something he hoped for in his future? It was unsettling, the not knowing. You'd think if someone was in your life for as long as she'd been in his, she would at least have a general idea of his thoughts on the matter.

Maybe she wouldn't know so much about his thoughts on marriage to her in particular, but maybe in general.

She walked over to the water valve and twisted the knob until it stopped flowing. She bundled the hose back up on the wall mount. Hands fisted on her hips, she surveyed the result with a satisfied nod.

"That's some good work you got done there. That boy better be paying you the big bucks," Ida said from her porch.

Mia laughed and said, "Thanks, Ida. I've got some dahlia bulbs along the back, too."

"That'll be a pleasant surprise."

"I'm hoping so." Mia walked across the yard. "Ida, can I ask you something?"

Ida looked surprised but nodded, of course. "What have you got a bee in your bonnet about?"

"When you were married, what did you do when you'd made a huge mistake?" Mia asked.

"I take it we're not talking about planting flowers, are we?" Ida eyed Mia with an intense look that made her feel like she was a child being questioned by the school principal.

"Not quite," Mia said.

"Well, I'd always make sure I knew what I was going to apologize for before I actually got around to it. Talking, taking your lumps, owning up to your mistakes, allowing yourself to be needy and demanding sometimes, fixing the broken parts together. It's all part of it. You've always got to find your way back to each other, even when it's hard, because you're walking that life together. Hand in hand, every day. That's the only path forward when you're stuck together. And I'd say the look of terror on your face right now says you're thinking about getting yourself stuck to that boy over there."

"What if you're not sure you want to be stuck together? Or that he'll want to stay stuck? Or how it'll all turn out?" Mia asked, fidgeting with the ends of the hair that was swept up in a thick ponytail.

"Same way as you did before," Ida said simply.

"And that is?"

Ida shrugged and gestured to the garden. "Like your garden here. You plant and you tend and you work at it, and then you trust."

Mia stared across the expanse of plants.

"Let me give you a piece of advice about our Nicholas," Ida said, leaning her elbows onto the porch railing. From where Mia stood below, she looked like a southern goddess. "In the time I've known him, I've never seen him waste his time or energy on anything that he didn't feel was right for him. It seems to me that a man like that doesn't so much run away from being stuck with someone as he does run to the right one to be stuck with."

Mia took a moment to consider that. Was he running from her, or had he been running to her when she pushed him away?

"Are you always right?" she asked.

Ida laughed and threw back her head. The sound was deep and throaty, with a harsh maturity brought on by age. "If I haven't been, I'm not telling you about it. Now go on and get out of this heat so you can figure out how to get that boy back in town for makeup sex."

"Ida!" Mia's cheeks flushed with embarrassment.

"Don't think I don't see you two sneaking down the road at night. Now, go on. Get."

Mia laughed and did as she was told. As she cut across the grass, she wondered just what Nick was doing at that very moment. Was he thinking about her? His book tour should've started by now if she remembered correctly, and she knew it would last a few more weeks, but she wasn't so sure he would come home after.

More than that, she had no idea what she was going to say if he did. It wasn't as if she could just blurt out, "Oh, oops, Nick. I'm sorry I ripped your heart out and set it on fire, but actually, I'm thinking I might be head over heels in love with you. And even though you're as pushy as you are charming, maybe we could forget the whole heart ripping deal and see how it goes. Just, um, please don't die on me."

Once inside, she flipped on the shower and stepped in before it was even warm. The cold was a shock to her system, but a welcome one. The icy water soaked her hair, turning it from dark brown to black, and ran down her body in thick rivers. She washed the sweat and dirt from her body and turned off the nozzle just as the water was barely warm. She squeezed her hair until it was barely damp and stepped out of the tub. Wrapping a towel around her, she opted to forgo pajamas and walked into the living room to choose a new book to go to sleep to. It was barely dinner time, but her muscles were sore and her mind was exhausted. Tomorrow was soon enough to sort through it all.

Back in her bedroom, Mia let the towel drop on the floor and crawled naked and damp onto the bed and under the covers. She snuggled in and began reading what looked to be a solid mystery about a family haunted by something "other" on the Oregon Trail. It might not be the best choice of books when ghosts already haunted her sleep, but it wasn't like they gave her much peace when she read a happily ever after either.

Her eyes moved over each word, traveling down the page until they grew heavy, and she welcomed the warm blanket of sleep.

34

I t was early afternoon when Nick finally arrived home. By all accounts, the book tour was a success, and he should be excited.

Instead, he was physically exhausted and emotionally spent. He opened the trunk of his car and hauled his suitcase out, throwing his small carry-on backpack over his shoulder. He glanced toward Mia's house, disappointed when her car wasn't in the driveway. It's not like it mattered anyway, he thought to himself. He still didn't know what he was going to say to her. It wasn't like he could very well march over impulsively and stare at her like an idiot. He needed a plan.

Walking into his house, he dropped his bags in the foyer and headed straight for the kitchen. He popped open a cold beer and drank half of it in a few gulps, still standing in front of the open refrigerator. He closed it with the heel of his foot and took the stairs two at a time.

All he wanted to do was fall into his bed and sleep for the next two days.

He set the beer on his nightstand, kicked off his shoes, and aimed to do exactly that, but the second he collapsed onto the bed and closed his eyes, his mind was instantly working at full speed. His thoughts volleyed from wondering when Mia would be home again to what she'd been doing while he was away. He had questions about her ghosts, and he wanted to know how it was going at her bookstore. It didn't escape his notice that none of his thoughts included anything about him or his own life. Apparently, there was room in his brain for only Mia at the moment. He might be happy with it if he hadn't gotten himself booted in the ass by the very woman monopolizing his thoughts.

A quick glance at the clock next to his window told him it was barely two o'clock, but his musings stopped there when he saw a familiar car streak across his window.

He was off the bed and standing faster than he would ever care to recount, watching as her car slowed down and pulled into her driveway. Sliding his feet back in his shoes, he raced down the stairs. Whether she was ready to hear it, there were things he had to say to her. Again, what words he might use to say those things had yet to be conjured, but he'd always been good at winging it, so he was sure he could figure it out.

Actually, he admitted, that wasn't exactly true. He was terrible at winging it, but he imagined he could fumble his way through it well enough. She knew him. She'd get the gist of it.

He hurried out the door so quickly that he almost missed the radical changes to his front yard. Stepping down from his porch, he noticed far more colors than he remembered in the flower beds below him. Upon closer inspection, there were definitely more flowers—beautiful flowers, in fact. All throughout his flower beds.

The weeds mysteriously disappeared. And was that fresh mulch? He wondered if Ida had taken pity on him. The urge to run to Mia was strong, but he was a gentleman through and through, and Ida was technically on the way. It would only take a moment to stop by and say thank you. After all, it was the neighborly thing to do, and it would give Mia more time to settle in. It wouldn't do to pounce on her the second she was home.

He walked across the lawn and climbed Ida's porch stairs. He confirmed that Mia's car was still in her driveway and knocked briskly on his neighbor's door, fidgeting and glancing toward Mia's house every few seconds despite his rationalization.

Ida opened the door and gave him a toothy smile. She'd swept her long, silver hair up into a casual bun at her nape and dressed in a floor length sunny dress with thin straps and a pattern of bright yellow sunflowers. Nick couldn't help but think that was very fitting for her. Age and a lifetime of living on the beach had tanned her skin and covered her shoulders and chest in freckles, both tiny and large.

"So the world traveler is back," Ida said. She pulled him inside before he could object and ushered him over to a cream colored antique couch with roses printed all over it. "Sit. I'll bring us some sweet tea, and you can tell me all about your book tour."

Damn his politeness. Nick sighed and resigned himself to more than a quick visit. Honestly, he should've known better. He sat back against the couch. The couch appeared recently reupholstered, and he thought a few paintings on the wall were new.

"Did you do some redecorating in here?" Nick asked.

"Oh, yes. I got tired of seeing the same old things day after day. Needed something new to look at," she said. She came back into the room carrying a tray loaded with a plate of chocolate chip cookies and two glasses of sweet tea filled to the rim. From experience, he knew the sweet tea would be delicious and the chocolate cookies, if they were homemade, dreadful. Despite that, he would dutifully eat one and take any others she offered him to-go.

"You didn't happen to do any redecorating in my front yard, did you?" he asked.

"Are you really going to come here thinking that I'd be one to go and pretty up those flower beds when I've been hounding you about doing them yourself for months?" she asked, taking a seat on the couch next to him.

"I guess not," he said with a grin he hoped would charm her out of fussing at him.

"Good. Then it's safe to assume you're on your way over to thank the real culprit and fix whatever it is you broke with her." She arched a finely penciled brow and cocked her head at him accusingly.

"Who says it was my fault?" He shoved the cookie into his mouth, chasing it down with a deep swig of cold sweet tea. It was, in fact, exactly as inedible as her last batch and every one he tried before it.

She leaned forward with a gleam in her eye. "Well, was it?"

"Maybe a little." He shifted uncomfortably in his seat.

"Mmm." She looked as if she wanted to ask him more, or maybe she'd already gotten the other side of the story from Mia and was considering how best to chastise him. Suddenly, she stood. "Before you go, I've got something for you."

"Ida, I'd really love to stay, but as you pointed out, I've got some groveling to do," he said, raising a hand as if to stop her.

"Nicholas, when you get to be my age, everyone makes time for you, and if they don't, you tell them it might be your last day on this earth so they feel good and guilty. Now, don't make me say that to you." Without waiting for his answer, she walked out of the room.

"You'll outlive us all," he called after her, and he heard her cackle in answer.

He took her absence as an opportunity to crumble the rest of his cookie into a nearby plant, scooping dirt over it quickly before she returned. He wondered what she'd come back with, but when Ida shuffled into the room again, the blue velvet ring box she held was the last thing he expected.

She stood in front of him and opened the box with fingers that shook with age. The paper thin skin of them showed the purple and blue veins running underneath, knuckles swollen with arthritis. But despite the swelling and her age and the fact that she'd been widowed some time, she still wore her wedding and engagement rings.

Inside the box, nestled in between two rolled up pillows, was one such ring. It was a deep purple amethyst set in the center of a circle of delicate flower petals sculpted in gold. More leaves of gold decorated the band, and the effect was that the ring was dainty, feminine, and intricately crafted.

"Why are you showing me this?"

"I'm not showing it to you. I'm giving it to you. It was my grandmother's ring, and now it's yours." Ida pushed the box at him.

"Doesn't your daughter want it?" he asked. His eyes were wide, his pupils dilated in mild panic. He wasn't yet ready to reach out and grasp the thing.

Ida shook her head. "She's already married and has enough family heirlooms to fill an antique shop when I die. I want you to have this. You go on and give it to Mia."

"Nope. I—no. I, uh… not ready for that," he stuttered, standing and putting his hands out in front of him as if they formed a sort of anti-matrimonial force field.

"Are you really going to sit here and tell me you're going to go to Mia with only an apology and a 'let's kiss and make up?'" she demanded.

"I'd planned to use better words, but that's pretty much the gist of it," he said, cringing at the disappointment already written on her face.

"That's your idea of groveling?! Do you have a screw loose, boy?" she asked, propping one fist on her hip.

"You're doing an awful lot of insulting today."

"Then perhaps you should show that you've got some intelligence in that squirrel sized brain of yours so I can stop questioning it." She pushed the open ring box at him again. "That girl has been betrayed by life already. More than love, she needs promises made and promises kept. Promise her you'll stay."

More than love? What more was there? Honestly, he'd spent so much time planning how he'd get her to fall in love with him, he'd given little thought to what would happen after. Nick let her words sink in and took hold of the ring box with shaky hands. He stared inside it, watching as the purple gem sparkled in the center and wondering if this was what he wanted. Ida made a good point, but it didn't do him much good if he was offering Mia a solution that he didn't want. And if he decided he wanted to take this step with her, would this make his reunion with Mia more complicated or less?

"I know that look. Go do your thinking. Then go do some showing and telling. And don't wait too long. That girl's decided she's done waiting for her life to fix itself. Don't miss your chance," Ida said.

She pushed him out the door as quickly as she'd pulled him in, and he was left standing on her porch in the middle of the afternoon with no idea what to do next.

He took a deep breath and pulled the ring out of the box, shoving the box back into the side pocket of his shorts. The sun hit the amethyst stone and sent bright purple explosions of light in every direction as he twirled it between his finger and thumb. He pocketed the ring and agreed with Ida. He desperately needed to think.

Rather than impulsively dash to Mia's house, he walked to the left and got into his car instead. He needed time to work through it all, and there was only one place he knew of where he could do just that.

35

Relief flooded Mia when she saw Nick's car in his driveway after weeks of staring at an empty rectangle of concrete. She was long past thinking, done mulling things over and trying to muddle her way through to a decision that made sense when none of her feelings made sense anymore. Everything was a jumble of fear and worry and frustration, a situation that forced her to conclude she didn't know what would happen, and trying to script it out and plan for every possibility exhausted her.

She was as ready as she'd ever be. It was time to talk to Nick and move forward, whatever that looked like. Like ripping off a bandage. She didn't know what would happen by the end of the day, but one way or another she was going to tell Nick she was in love with him, and she supposed they'd figure it out from there. Whether that meant he would decide he wanted to kiss her or kill her, she couldn't be sure.

She walked outside and was halfway to his house before she realized his car was no longer in the driveway. Brows drawn together, she wondered where he could've gone.

Then she knew.

Without wasting another moment, she got in her car and started the drive toward the beach, winding her way down a narrow road until she reached the secret entrance to the pier. She walked through the forest of trees and the swaths of moss hanging from their branches. Her feet crunched on the dry leaves and debris beneath them.

Finally, she reached the beach and walked across the sand to where the pier stretched out into the water. It was there she saw him, standing near the end, the wind running its fingers through his hair. His back was to her, and he stood motionless as he looked out over the ocean. She walked slowly over the gray weathered boards, listening to the crash of the surrounding waves. She wasn't sure if he heard her coming or felt her presence, but he turned around and their gazes locked.

"I thought I might find you here," she said. He said nothing, just watched her intently. "When did you get back?"

"Today," he said.

Mia nodded and moved to stand next to him. She turned toward the water and waited. There were things that needed to be said, but there were things she needed to hear first.

They stood side by side in silence while the gulls called overhead, and the ocean churned below them. Small waves lapped at the support posts, and a thin froth of bubbles formed on the top of the water. Tiny fish darted back and forth just below the surface, and Mia wondered if they were bothered by the constant motion of the ocean around them.

Every now and again, the roar of a motorboat would drift by. Then it would be gone and there would be only the ocean and the seagulls.

"Do you remember when Ewan and I found that long vine hanging from the old oak in the woods behind his house?" he asked her abruptly. His voice sounded rough, as if he hadn't spoken in some time.

"Yes, I remember," she said. She folded her arms and leaned on the rail, looking sideways at him before turning her gaze back to the ocean. The setting sun cast a rippling glow of yellow and orange over its surface.

"We thought we were pirates that day, swinging from our ship to the one we captured. Other days, we pretended we were Tarzan. Ewan was on that vine the day it finally snapped. I thought his momma would skin my hide when she found out."

"So many stories."

"More than I could ever count, good and bad."

Mia looked at him again, his features washed with gold in the afternoon light. He didn't look sad exactly, but he was certainly ponderous, and there was a tightness around his jaw and mouth.

"I remember the day Ewan told me he loved you, but I didn't really understand what he meant until recently," he said. "When I thought it was over between us, I knew exactly why he was so willing to let you go. Because when you love someone, you don't fight to keep them with you if it's going to make them miserable. You're supposed to do whatever you can to make them happy, even if that means letting them go. Ewan was a good man, the best. He was the kind of man who could do that for you."

Nick shook his head and looked down at his hands. "But I must not be as good a man as him, because I can't walk away this time. I couldn't do it even if I thought it would make you happy. Mia, I'm sorry I pushed you into this. I didn't listen to what you needed and didn't take the time to understand why. But now we're here, and I can't imagine being with anyone else. I can't breathe without loving you. And you love me, too. I know it. I feel it. If I have to wait a hundred years until you're ready, I'll do it. If I have to show you a hundred ways that I'm here to stay, I will. I'll spend a thousand years proving it to you, if that's what it takes. Just don't ask me to let you go. I can't leave you again."

Tears glittered in her eyes, and when he reached for her, she let him pull her in close. He buried his face in her hair, and the tears she was holding back fell down her cheeks. There were things she needed to say, but right now, she just needed to feel him around her.

"I thought you weren't going to cry any more tears for me," he teased.

"Shut up and kiss me."

And he did.

He kissed her with everything he had, pouring all of his love into that kiss, and she responded in kind. The coward in her wanted to leave it at this, to bury her fears and her feelings and bask in this glow, but she was no longer that woman. Somewhere in all this, the move and the store and the love, she'd found herself again. She was strong, and she was brave, and she didn't hide from her life or her feelings any more. When she pulled back, she rested her forehead against his.

"Mia, tell me you love me. I need the words."

She sighed and closed her eyes. "I love you."

"But you don't want to," he said slowly. He stroked the back of his hand down the side of her face, and she opened her eyes to look at him.

"I have a confession to make," she said. She took a deep breath and tried to quiet the restless butterflies in her stomach. "I'm so scared. I'm scared of losing someone else. Of not knowing if I'd survive it again. It hurts so much, like something ripping open your chest every minute of the day. It's unbearable. I thought if I made sure I didn't let myself get close to you—or anyone, for that matter—I wouldn't fall in love, and I'd never have to go through that again."

"And then I came in and mucked it all up."

"Yes! It's easy for you. You fall for someone and the biggest complication is what drawer will you share and where will you leave your toothbrush or when will she move in? It's different for me. I did all of this before—the friendship and the falling and the marrying—and it was ripped away from me. Now, I'm building this life all on my own, and it's beautiful, and I'm finally figuring out who I am. What I want next."

"Why does it have to be all or nothing? Why can't you have that and let yourself be happy and in love?" he asked. With me, he wanted to add.

"I don't know. I don't—" Her throat was tight with

emotion, self-doubt creeping into her consciousness. She shook her head and turned toward the water again, giving herself time to relax and gather her thoughts.

He cupped her cheek with both hands and tipped her chin up to him. "You're not the same woman you were before," he said, echoing her thoughts.

"I'm trying to remind myself of that, but I'm worried it won't be enough," she said, closing her eyes and focusing on the way his fingers felt against her face as the wind blew over them.

"I told you, Mia. I'll wait as long as you need. But if you're so worried, why did you come?"

"Because I'm more terrified of becoming a woman who walls up her heart out of fear and lives her life based on what might happen. Life is a risk, and so is living. I'm trying to be okay with that, to accept that you can't have the good without the bad. And if I can be blessed with this kind of love twice in one lifetime, maybe it's a risk worth taking."

"Does it help if I tell you I'm scared, too?"

"A little."

"Mia, I've never loved anyone the way that I love you."

Tears fell from her eyes again, and she swiped them away with a laugh. "I'm like a faucet now," she said.

"But a beautiful faucet," he said.

He pulled her in close, and she stood for a moment enjoying the feel of being against him. She snuggled her face into his chest, fairly purring as his fingers stroked circles over her shoulder. The ocean breeze blew her hair around her face, and she inhaled the salty scent of the water mixed with the unmistakable smell of a man. Her body clenched at the memory of him against her, inside her, and she turned her face up to his. He was obviously having the same thoughts, because his gaze was hot upon hers.

"I love you," she breathed.

"I thought you'd never say that," he said, and he crushed his mouth on hers again. Her tongue stroked against his, and she matched his rhythm, their lips opening and closing against one another as their bodies responded in kind and pressed together. When he broke from the kiss, he held her face in his hands again, and his thumbs stroked her cheeks. His mouth was but a breath away from hers, and he smiled that devilish smile.

"Your eyes say you're up to something. I swear if you throw me into this ocean, I'll take back everything I said and never speak to you again," Mia teased.

"However tempting that may be, it'll have to wait another day. I have a present for you."

"I don't deserve another present," she said.

He shook his head and put a hand into his pocket. When he pulled it out again, she froze. Held ever so gently between his thumb and finger was a thin band of metal. In the center was an amethyst stone circled by golden flower petals. More golden leaves decorated the rest of the band, making it look as though it was cast directly from the plants that inspired it.

"At the risk of being pushy again, I'm asking you to marry me. Not because I want more from you, but because I want to give more to you. I want to wake up every day with you, the good days and the hard days. I can't picture walking through my life without my best friend beside me. We can spend the rest of our lives engaged if you need me to wait until you're ready to take this step again, but I realized that the promise is important to you. And I want to make it to you. I promise to be right here beside you for the rest of your life as long as you let me spend the rest of mine making you happy. Be my wife, Mia."

He didn't get down on one knee. Instead, he took her hand, raised it to his mouth, and kissed her knuckles one by one. It was as if he kissed away all that was left of her fear.

"Yes. Yes, I'll marry you," she said, as surprised at herself as he was hearing it. Her gaze shifting quickly from him to the ring and back again.

With a laugh, he picked her up by the waist and twirled her around. For a moment she was weightless, and she gripped his neck tight. Never had she believed she would experience this again. When he set her down, she raised her left hand and allowed him to slip the ring over her finger. It was only slightly loose, and the practical side of her was already mentally flipping through her schedule for the following week so she could get it sized right away.

"Does this mean you'll elope with me next week?" he teased.

"As romantic as that seems, I do want to enjoy being engaged and maybe even go on a few dates before we plan the wedding," she said.

"Is that what you want? The full shindig?"

"I don't know. The whole big production with two hundred of your closest family and friends—I did it once. I'm not sure if I want to do that again, but this is your first time around, so it feels selfish not to consider it. What do you want?"

They started walking back down the pier, their feet scraping and pressing on the old creaking boards. Nick looked at her and said, "I'd be happy with anything so long as you're the one at the end of the aisle."

"I don't deserve you," Mia said.

Nick gave her a lopsided grin and shook his head. "You don't, but it's okay. You've got plenty of time to make it up to me."

When they reached their cars, Nick turned to her, and his smile couldn't possibly stretch any wider. He looked like a kid in a candy store, and she told him so. "I am a kid in the candy store. Only I just realized the lollipop I wanted was in my pocket the whole time. Now, back to the subject of dating," he said. "How about we get started on that right away?"

"That sounds like a plan. I need to change clothes first, and then I'll walk over to your place," Mia said.

Nick nodded, and they drove home separately but together. Maybe it was slightly backwards to go on your first date after your fiancé proposed, but their situation wasn't exactly typical.

As she drove, she let her mind wander. The trees and houses and cars she passed were as endless as the thoughts in her head. How lucky was she to have experienced love like this?

First, there was Ewan. They'd frolicked as children and then adventured into adulthood together. Now there was Nick, and he was as passionate and possessive as Ewan was kind and dependable. Opposites of one another, truly, but then she was a different woman then and now. There were tragic moments to go along with the joy, but in this moment, there was no life she'd rather have.

Mia arrived home, parked, and pushed her key into the front door lock. She cursed when it stuck again and chastised herself for not dropping by the hardware store for a replacement yet.

Finally, she got the door open. The sun was nearly set, and the room was dim. Funny, she could've sworn she left the living room light on. She dropped her purse on the floor as a familiar scent filled her nose, a scent she couldn't quite place. Frowning, she walked across the dark room to where the lamp sat on a side table. Mia pulled the cord...

And realized she wasn't alone.

36

Even in the dark Mia saw the gun pointed at her. Its dark barrel looked wet in the low light. The figure sat in the shadows in her favorite chair, legs clad in dark pants and spread wide. A hand held a bundle of something, rope maybe, and rested on one leg.

"Lock the door. Slowly or I'll shoot you," the figure said, the voice a low whisper.

Mia's mind was racing, her heart slamming against her ribs with every beat, but she did as she was told. Her palms were slicked with sweat. She turned around and risked a glance at the back door. The dead bolt was undone. Mia turned back around slowly and waited for instruction. The blood roared in her ears, and she fought for calm. Every nerve in her body told her to run, but she knew that was suicide. She needed a plan.

The figure used the gun to gesture toward the chair across from her, and Mia sat down stiffly. She asked, "What do you want?"

"You think you're so clever, don't you? A regular Nancy Drew, solving mysteries and poking your nose where it doesn't belong," the person said. Their voice was so familiar, but it was barely audible, and Mia couldn't put a face to it. Then the figure stood and walked into the fading light, and Mia gasped.

"You?"

"So close, weren't you?" Sarah said. She paced in front of Mia, gesturing with the gun even as its aim never wavered. "You figured out what happened, or so you think, but how is that working out for you now? I was one step ahead of everyone then, and I've been one step ahead of you now."

"Did you kill Emily and her son?" Mia asked in a whisper.

Sarah exploded in a flurry of movement. "Of course not!" she said, her chest heaving. "But Emily found out about the affair. Not about me, of course. We were too careful for that, but Brad still threatened to end it with me. Me?! Not her! After all the promises, all the plans we made! All because Emily wasn't 'doing well.'" She spoke in a mocking tone, her lips turned down in disgust.

"That must have hurt you." Mia forced herself to be calm, sympathetic. She scanned her periphery for anything that would be useful. If she could make it to the bookshelf, she may be able to grab a pair of scissors from her pen cup. It wouldn't do much against a gun, but it would be something, at least.

"You have no idea! I knew I had to get rid of them before he got rid of me. I planned a dozen ways to do it, but in the end Emily proved more useful than I'd imagined," Sarah said.

Mia scooted to the very edge of her seat, slowly positioning her body a millimeter at a time, like a coiled spring ready to release at any moment. She needed to keep Sarah talking long enough to make a run for it. If she was fast enough (and if she caught Sarah by surprise), she could grab the scissors and get to the back door.

"What did you do?" Mia asked.

"What I had to! You have to understand, he's mine! We're meant to be together. I couldn't let her steal what was mine. I knew the 'illness' was an act just to keep him from me. At first, I was going to make her my friend and convince her to leave Brad," Sarah said. "I visited her and pretended to be her doctor's assistant. Everyone knew she was seeing Hubert. All I had to do was sit and listen to her, and of course she could call me whenever she needed."

"And did she? Call you?"

"Why wouldn't she? I didn't think it would be in a panic, but of course I came right away, and I came prepared. She was ranting about demons and David and voices, and I realized she really was crazy. I saw an opportunity, and I took it." Sarah put the hand holding the rope on her hip and stopped her pacing.

The gun was still casually pointed at her, and Mia swallowed the lump in her throat, doing her best to keep her voice steady. "You did what you thought you had to."

"Exactly! I never touched that boy, only gave her a nudge. She was already going to kill him. She was insane by the time I got there, convinced he was possessed, and she needed to save him," Sarah said, raising a hand in a gesture of helplessness. There was a gleam in her eyes, and an evil giggle escaped her mouth. She smothered the sound with the back of her hand, the rope dangling in front of her face. "I only agreed with her."

"But why? Why not just persuade her to leave Brad?" Mia asked, forgetting she was supposed to be sympathizing with Sarah. She realized that something about Sarah's mind was not quite right.

"Because I realized could help Brad get rid of all of his baggage. It was perfect! No crazy ex-wife, no child caught between them, no alimony or child support. No strings. We could start our life all over again, together. And he would never know," Sarah said. "Of course, I'd planned for Emily to go a little more painlessly, but she completely lost it after she killed David, and I had to act before she did something stupid like call Brad or the police. It was her fault she suffered! But I took care of it, and I made it so it was like I was never even there."

Despite the horror of it, Mia steeled her resolve and pretended to understand Sarah, even agree with her. "It sounds like you went through a lot of trouble to help Brad."

"You can't imagine what I did for him, for us. I had to haul in a ladder, nearly skin my hands getting her onto that rope, and make it all look like she'd hanged herself. But it was worth it. It was worth every scratch the bitch gave me, every sore muscle, every rope burn. Wouldn't you do that for the man you love? Wouldn't you do anything?!"

There was a desperate tone in Sarah's voice, and Mia's mind scrambled to figure out how she could use that to her advantage. She needed to get to the back door before Sarah's tenuous hold on reality snapped. She wondered if she could get to the phone in her bag. Her eyes flicked to it, but Sarah didn't miss the look and kicked the bag to the far side of the room. "You won't be needing that."

"Please, Sarah. I know why you had to do it. I understand. Just let me go. No one needs to know our secret," Mia begged, her eyes wide with desperation.

"And no one will. I'd hoped to get the diary back before you learned too much. I didn't know Emily kept a record of her madness. But that went over like a lead balloon. Your lover proved to fuck up my plans to get it as good as he fucked you," Sarah said, her brow arched in disdain.

Her stomach knotted as realization hit, and she imagined Sarah sneaking around her home, watching her at her most intimate. She pushed the feeling down. She had to stay calm. "You don't have to hurt me. We'll go back to our lives, and it'll all be just as it was. You'll get your dream life back."

"My dream wasn't in jeopardy, until you went putting your nose where it didn't belong, just like your husband."

"My husband? What did Ewan have to do with any of this?"

"Oh, don't pretend like you don't know," Sarah scoffed. "That crackhead sister gave you the diary, and I know you met with a cop. You've already told him everything. Pity. I liked you, always have. But now I have to kill you, just like I killed Ewan."

"What?" Mia's hands gripped the arms of the chair so hard the tips of her fingers went white.

A piercing ringing filled her ears, and she couldn't draw in a breath. Horror and confusion warred within her as she frantically tried to remember the day Ewan died. Many of the details were hazy and faded after so long, but bits and pieces stood out. The police officers coming to her door. The man explaining what happened. They'd said he was the victim of a botched carjacking, keys missing, two gunshots to the chest at close range. It was the best explanation they could come up with, and the case was closed almost as soon as it was opened. His funeral had followed shortly after.

"It was all going perfect until my car broke down and your hero husband had to be the knight in shining armor. Ewan wouldn't take no for an answer, even going so far as opening my trunk to look for a spare tire. Too bad he found the step ladder and rope instead," Sarah said with a flip of her hand. She relaxed the hand holding the gun as her tone became irritated, and she resumed her pacing.

"Why? A ladder and rope are meaningless alone." Mia's voice was barely a whisper. Her shoulders slumped in defeat, her head lowered.

"Why did I kill him, you mean? Brad called to tell him what happened, and I couldn't be caught just two streets away from his house," Sarah said with a callous shrug. "My arms were covered in scratches, and it was only a matter of time before Ewan put the pieces together. I had to get rid of him. I'm sorry, Mia. It's nothing personal."

With her head still facing the ground, Mia tried to pull her thoughts together. She needed to focus on getting out. She could deal with this revelation later. Looking to the right, she noticed a book sitting on the end table. She adjusted her hand and sent the book tumbling to the ground. Sarah looked down and stepped back quickly, and Mia sprang into action. She couldn't afford to miss any opportunity. She bolted out of the chair and ran toward the back door with every ounce of speed she could muster. If she just could get enough of a lead...

Without warning, she was yanked back by the hair, and Sarah backhanded her hard across the face with the gun. Pain blasted over her cheek, mouth, nose, and eye, and her vision went white. She was thrown to the ground, her face throbbing. Thick blood dripped down her cheek and into her hair as she curled into a ball and groaned.

"I did what I had to do to keep what was mine, and I'll do it again. Any woman with a backbone would do the same."

Mia looked up from under a mass of bloody, knotted hair. She gritted her teeth against the pain and the nausea as her vision swam in and out of focus from the force of the blow. "I wouldn't," she said, her voice low. "I wouldn't have killed his wife. I wouldn't have killed his son."

"I didn't touch him!" Sarah screamed, tearing at her hair in frustration.

"You didn't pull the trigger, but you loaded the gun," Mia said. Keep her talking, she ordered herself. She propped herself up on her elbow, inching closer to the back door as she did so. "And then you moved on to Emily. How did you do it? You're barely bigger than I am. Did you knock her out and hang her? Did you strangle her first?"

Sarah opened her mouth to answer, but a voice from the hallway, eerie and ethereal, drifted in on a wave of cold air.

"She strangled me and then hung me up like a slab of meat," Emily said, her voice a sing-song whisper.

They both turned to see Emily floating into the room, her body outlined in a gray aura that pulsed as she moved. Her red hair whipped around her as if she was underwater. Red-rimmed eyes bulged from their sockets, and her mouth was drawn back in a wide grimace. Her head lolled back and forth, hands outstretched, as she glided closer. Sarah screamed and pressed her back against the wall, and Mia struggled to clear her head enough to stand. Her arms shook when she pushed herself up, but she couldn't hold her own weight and collapsed back onto the floor, helplessly watching as Emily floated closer.

Emily was a breath away from Sarah when her voice turned menacing. When she spoke, her voice was deep with an echo that sounded as if there were many voices speaking at once. "I was sick, and you took advantage of me. I called you for help, and you stole my son. You stole my husband... and then you stole my life."

With a ghastly scream, Emily reached for Sarah's throat. Her hands locked around her, and Sarah struggled to push away from an entity that had no physical form. The gun and the rope dropped to the ground, and Emily pushed Sarah up the wall, lifting her into the air. Picture frames crashed to the floor. Sarah's feet kicked at the wall desperately, the heels of her shoes gouging chunks out of the drywall, and her screams turned into choking gasps.

Mia scrambled across the floor, glass cutting into her fingers and palms as the room spun. She slipped on the blood that covered her hands, and her arms and knees splayed out as she fell. Her chin cracked hard against the wood, and stars exploded across her vision. A roaring sound filled her ears, and she slid on her belly, half-blind to where the gun lay on the floor. She grabbed it and the rope and scampered backwards until her back was against the front door, watching as Sarah struggled against Emily.

Out of the corner of her eye, she saw David step out from the hallway. He'd been crying again, and he gripped the little yellow blanket against his chest and face tighter than Mia had ever seen. Sarah slumped unconscious in Emily's grip, and Emily screamed again, her grip tightening on Sarah's neck. It was a high-pitched sound that cracked, filled with grief and torment and rage.

"Emily, you have to stop!" Mia cried desperately. "Stop, Emily! Your son is watching. David needs you."

Emily's face jerked, and she stared at Mia as the sound of David's cries filled the room. Her head cocked to the side, the movement reminding Mia of an animal listening for the call of its herd. A shiver ran down her spine. Emily turned with a cry and went to embrace her son, releasing Sarah, who crumpled in a heap onto the floor.

Mia watched as Emily gathered her tiny son into her arms, his head laying on her shoulder, and when she turned, the light that pulsed from them was warm and white. Their faces were no longer gaunt and pale but flushed and lifelike, just as they had been in Mia's dream. The air in the room warmed around her.

Emily smiled, and her voice was soft when she said, "Thank you." And then they disappeared, fading into nothing and leaving behind only silence and darkness.

Mia took a moment to catch her breath before crawling over to Sarah's body and checking her pulse. It was weak, her breathing ragged and irregular, but she was alive. Mia wrapped the rope tightly around Sarah's wrists and ankles, tying knots as tight as she could manage, her hands leaving streaks of bright red blood on the twisting cords. When the lights went on above her, Mia looked up and cried out in relief as Nick stepped into the room from the back door.

"Mia!" he said. He dropped to the floor beside her, his hands racing over her body, checking for injuries. "What happened? Are you hurt?"

He cupped her jaw, and she nodded miserably. The truth was, everything hurt. Her head, her cheek, her mouth, her hands, all of it throbbed, and every muscle was rigid and as taut as a bowstring. A black shadow hovered around the edge of her vision.

"Call the police," she whispered as the darkness took her under.

37

Mia slipped in and out of consciousness over the next several hours. She felt her body being lifted onto a flat, bed-like surface, and she glimpsed the lights of an ambulance as she was driven to what she assumed was the hospital. Darkness enveloped her again as someone stitched and bandaged the gash along her cheekbone. Throughout, she felt Nick's hand warm in hers, and she heard his voice whispering in her ear. The blurry face of a woman floated before her, asking her questions in a faraway voice before she went under again.

In her dreams, she heard the voices of people all around her, the beeps of machinery, and the shuffle of footsteps. There was the prick of something on her arm, and someone touched her face. At first, she dreamed of Nick and Alexis and of the sweet sound of a mother singing a lullaby in the distance. Then the dreams slipped away and there was only darkness.

Light was streaming in when Mia woke in a quiet hospital room, groggy and disoriented. She blinked slowly, grateful that the overhead lights were off and the curtains drawn. Her head was pounding, as was her cheek, and her tongue felt thick and dry in her mouth. She looked over and saw Nick slumped in a chair, his face smashed against the heel of his hand. She shivered under the rough blankets, of which there were several layered on top of her, and noticed an IV line taped to her left hand.

"You're awake," Nick said with a deep breath. He yawned and pushed himself off the chair, coming to her side and smoothing the hair back from her forehead.

"How long have I been out for?" she asked. She tried to prop herself up, but the room spun dangerously and she slipped back down onto the pillow.

"Two days."

"What happened after...?" she asked. Her voice trailed off.

"The police came and arrested Sarah. You got loaded up in an ambulance and taken here. There's about ten stitches on your cheek, and it'll probably be a nice little battle scar one day. The doctor says you can go home soon," Nick said.

Mia took a deep breath and closed her eyes again. Her head felt fuzzy, like her brain itself was slightly out of focus. She laid it back on the pillows and said, "That's nice."

"Apparently, you put up quite a fight. Sarah's neck was black and blue, and you gave her a concussion," he said.

Mia peered at him from under her lids when he grasped her hand, and her mind flooded with flashes from that night. She saw Sarah point a gun at her, heard the horrific things she said, watched Emily attack her. It was all too much. She didn't want to know any of this. She didn't want to feel any of this. The machine beside her beeped loudly as her heart rate shot up, and Nick began stroking her again, murmuring tiny shushing noises. A nurse came in and checked the machine with a tut. She handed Mia a small cup of water with medication for her headache, and Mia dutifully (and gratefully) swallowed it.

When the nurse left, he asked, "Can you tell me what happened?"

At his frown, she took a deep breath and tried to think of a cohesive way to put it all together. How could she describe it when she could barely understand it herself? Sarah's greed and selfishness destroyed two families, so many lives lost, so much pain.

Mia's throat tightened, and she closed her eyes tightly against the tears that welled in them. She felt Nick's hands slide over hers as they bunched up the covers in them, and she looked up at him, a world of sadness in her eyes.

"She killed him," she whispered at last.

"What? David?"

"Ewan. She killed Ewan," she said, and then sobs wracked her body. Nick lowered the side rail of the bed with a snap and slid in next to her. His arms came around her, and she buried her face into him, her body shaking with the force of her cries.

"Shhhh," he said. He stroked her hair and held her as the worst of it subsided.

Mia sniffled and swiped the blankets over her face to

dry her tears. She leaned her face against his shoulder again and blew out a heavy breath.

"Sarah was the other woman. She killed Emily, may as well have killed David, and then she killed Ewan to keep Brad from finding out." There was more, of course, more details that made it all make sense, at least to Sarah, but Mia couldn't say anything else. Tears closed her throat.

"It's okay. We have all the time in the world to talk about it," he said, his voice a soft whisper against her head.

"I have to tell someone," Mia said, her voice hitching.

"An officer said he'd be by to see if you were up to giving a statement. Alexis said Sidney might drop by later, too."

He was still running his fingers through her hair when she suddenly realized just how long it was since she took a proper shower or brushed her teeth. She eyed the bathroom, calculating how long of a walk it was and how much effort it would take to wash up, but as much as she wanted to feel clean, especially after everything that had happened, even the thought of it was exhausting.

Resigned to rest, she settled back into the pillow, snuggling down into the blankets, and closed her eyes. Someday, this would all be a bad dream. Until then, she would do her best to forget it.

THE HOSPITAL DISCHARGED Mia with a laundry list of dos and don'ts and a thin paper bag of medication. Nick volunteered to drive her home, as if there was any other option, and he gingerly helped her into the passenger seat of his car, even going so far as to reach over her and buckle the seat belt for her.

She looked at him with a raised brow. "I can do that, you know."

She rolled her eyes when he nodded and murmured in agreement, but he seemed not to actually have heard her at all. Or he just didn't care, which, knowing him, was probably more likely. He pushed the car door closed so gently it barely made a sound, slid into the driver's seat beside her, and carefully maneuvered the car out of the hospital parking lot.

Mia watched the late afternoon sunlight filter through the leaves on the trees as they passed, light and shadow dappling the windows of the car. She was grateful to be alive in a way she'd never expected to feel in her life. She took a deep breath and leaned her head back against the headrest.

"I think I should take you back to my place," Nick said.

"Why?" she asked, keeping her eyes closed.

"So I can keep an eye on you."

Mia opened one eye and looked over at him. His face was set in firm lines, his jaw muscle flexing, and she found his concern endearing. However sweet it was, though, she wanted to be home. Her home. She wanted the familiar, and there was something powerful about walking into her own home again, about taking a stand. Terrors both real and otherwordly had threatened her there, and she'd survived. There was comfort in that. "I need to be home, Nick."

"But how can I keep you—"

"Safe?"

Nick nodded stiffly, and Mia turned into a puddle right then and there. She reached out and laid a hand on his thigh. "I'll be fine, but if it makes you feel better, stay with me."

He looked at her quickly, his eyes saying more than words ever could, and he relented. Mia watched his internal struggle, but he nodded again.

"I'll go grab a bag once you're settled in," he relented.

When they arrived home, Nick pulled his car in beside hers in the driveway. He opened her door, and Mia stepped out of the car on unsteady legs, gripping the door frame for balance. She squinted against the overly bright sun, but she was grateful for it today. She tipped her head back to bask in the warmth of it, wobbling ever so slightly. Before she could so much as right herself, Nick was scooping her up and into his arms. She was caught off guard, but rather than fuss about it, she leaned her head onto his shoulder and sighed.

"I want to tell you I'm perfectly able to walk, but I really love this. I feel like a fairy-tale princess being carried over the threshold after the ball."

"You love this or you love me?" he asked, his mouth set in that lopsided grin she loved so much. He walked up the porch stairs and through the front door, shutting it behind him with the heel of his foot.

"Both," she said with a breathy exhale.

"Since I've known you my entire life, it's good that you've finally come to your senses." He laid her on the bed and let himself crawl over to her, kissing her as gently as his self control would allow.

"Good thing. I guess you'll have to marry me then," she said, brushing the hair off his forehead with her bandaged fingers.

"I guess so," he said. His gaze sharpened and ran down her body. "Does this mean I have to wait for the wedding night?"

"I hope not."

Nick needed no other encouragement, and when Mia welcomed him to her, his eyes sparkled with mischief and love in a way that felt so familiar and yet so unique. This time their loving was slow, every touch deliberate, as if no movement was to be wasted, and when they came together, Mia finally let herself believe they could have forever.

Afterwards, Nick propped himself on his elbow beside Mia, pulling her body to his and tucking the blankets in around her. He stroked her hair away from her temple and hummed the slow, deep tune of some old lullaby whose name he'd long forgotten. She closed her eyes, and her breathing deepened as she slipped into sleep, cuddled against him.

His throat clenched as he looked down at her, and his chest tightened. He thought of everything life had thrown at them so far, everything they'd lost, everything they'd gained, what could've happened.

He'd almost lost her, and he hadn't even known she was in trouble. There was no feeling more helpless. He did not know what he'd done to deserve a woman as strong and loving and determined as Mia, and if he spent every day for the rest of his life proving how much she meant to him, it wouldn't be long enough.

His eyes scanned the room, and he noticed a new arrangement of photos on the wall beside the bed. Each picture frame was a distinct design and color, an eclectic mix that reflected Mia's love of mixing styles, though it seemed at least from a color perspective she'd stuck with the greens and earth tones he knew she loved. Inside the frames were photos of Mia traveling with Ewan, their skydiving adventure, and one of Mia curled up on her favorite chair with a book. In the very center, there was a picture of the three of them. Ewan, Mia, and Nick.

They gathered close, their cheeks pressed together with mile wide smiles on their faces. Bright sunlight shone on them from above, and behind them was the forest and rocks and wilderness of the Appalachians, stretching for miles.

He remembered the day as if it was yesterday, but now he focused on Ewan's face, as familiar to him as his own. He thought about the years they spent together, their triumphs and their heartbreaks. Ewan was the closest thing to real family Nick had, and he hadn't realized until after his death how much he took that for granted. He imagined Ewan would be pleased with how things were turning out. He even imagined Ewan would choose him for Mia if given the opportunity. Perhaps that was a little fanciful, but he was feeling light and fanciful.

Reaching out to stroke Mia's hair, he looked from the photo to Mia and back again. Ewan smiled at him as if he was standing right there ready to pat his back and raise a toast to his happiness, and Nick's heart felt full to bursting.

"Thank you," Nick said to him. "Thank you for letting me love her, too."

AFTERWORD

When I wrote *Dream of Me*, I didn't realize how similar my life would be to my main character's. In 2023, two years after publishing the book, my husband unexpectedly passed away. We spent 14 years together, were married for 12, created a family with four beautiful children, and shared almost every adventure of my adult life up to that point.

I never imagined I'd be a widow or that I would come to understand Mia's story so well. It's painful and terrifying to be so young and know you'll spend the rest of your life missing the person you'd dreamed of walking through it with.

Knowing I'll only ever have the memories we already made makes me cherish them even more.

I often think of the mischievous glint he always had in his eyes or the way he'd give silly nicknames to everyday objects. I remember the way he'd turn on music at the end of a stressful day and dance with me in the kitchen, how he loved being a dad and going on adventures with our kids.

When I wrote *Dream of Me*, it felt important for Mia to have those kinds of memories, too. I think in a way I wrote her story knowing I'd probably live it one day. For reasons I'll keep private, death was often a topic of conversation between my husband and me when he was alive. Neither of us expected it to be a reality so soon, but we knew it could, and was maybe even likely, to happen.

I think part of me feared being a widow alone, feared the intensity of grief and facing it in isolation. I see Mia as a friend in this. As silly as it seems, she makes me feel less alone.

I'm thankful she is there to show us it's okay to continue living. To grieve our loved one and still seek happiness even if we have to continue on without them.

Most of all, I'm grateful that I could give her a happy ending that inspires us to hope for one of our own.

ACKNOWLEDGMENTS

Writing has always been my dream, but it was a dream I pushed to the side in favor of more practical career pursuits. I told myself I couldn't or didn't want to make a job out of it. Over the past few years, that dream became more and more attainable in large part because of the people I've found myself surrounded by, and I'd like to take a moment to thank them.

To my friends and family, thank you for listening to and supporting me. I know I'm often more like a magpie than a human, always collecting interesting things and ideas, and your support has allowed me to follow this path in my own meandering way. A quick request, though... please forget you actually know me if you read the spicy chapters.

To my husband especially, thank you for your unending love and for every single day I have with you. I hope you know how much of a gift those are.

To the online book community, the power of your support is unfathomable. I jumped into your circle with all the zeal of a fledgling bird, and you've helped me to fly. Thank you for following me, laughing at my awkward videos, and, above all, for being my friends. You humble and honor me.

To the influential authors and mentors who don't know me but made this book possible all the same, we may never meet, but you have impacted my life in more ways than you know. Thank you.

When I first wrote this book, I included the special thank you to my husband that you see above. Sadly, my husband passed away just two years after it was published. While this is the second edition, I couldn't bear to remove or change this little note to him, so I've left it intact just as I wrote it.

Matthew, I love you always.

ABOUT THE AUTHOR

Selena Collins is an author of contemporary romance who likes her characters strong and her happily ever afters spicy. Her work is often sprinkled with suspense, fantasy, and paranormal elements, making for sensual stories with a dash of "other."

Selena is a widow living outside of Atlanta, Georgia with her children and their zoo of pets.

In her spare time, she makes silly videos on the internet, shares behind the scenes and more on her website, finds new hobbies constantly, and is terrible at texting people back.

To learn more about Selena, read more books by her, or stalk her social media (in a non-creepy way, of course), visit selenacollins.com.

ALSO BY SELENA COLLINS

Read Book Two for Alexis and Sidney's story!

When the Snow Falls

Alexis Donnely is an independent young woman and a successful book editor turned author, but she hides a dark secret.

Alexis has visions—visions of horrific murders, kidnappings, and disappearances.

Hiding from the brutal images in her mind, Alexis refuses to consider they could be more than waking nightmares, but police detective Sidney Neal is determined to change her mind...

By any means necessary.

With a string of child murders eating at his conscience, Sidney will do anything to keep the families of his small town safe, including seducing a woman who may be the first real psychic he's ever met.

As Alexis comes to terms with the possibility that her visions are, in fact, very real, she is challenged to use her gift to solve these murders, but there is more at stake.

Her visions could help save countless lives, but they could also cost Alexis her own.

Read Alexis' story at selenacollins.com/snow